THE GUN TAMER

Also by Max Brand®
in Large Print:

Don Diablo
The Gold Trail
Gunman's Goal
The Happy Valley
The Masterman
Iron Trail
The Outlaw Redeemer
The Overland Kid
The Peril Trek
Red Devil of the Range
Stolen Gold
The Geraldi Trail
The Tyrant
The House of Gold
The Streak

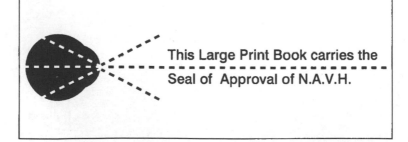

This Large Print Book carries the
Seal of Approval of N.A.V.H.

MAX BRAND®

THE GUN TAMER

Thorndike Press • Waterville, Maine

Published in 2004 by arrangement with
Golden West Literary Agency.

Thorndike Press® Large Print Western.

The tree indicium is a trademark of Thorndike Press.

The text of this Large Print edition is unabridged.
Other aspects of the book may vary from the original edition.

Set in 16 pt. Plantin by Minnie B. Raven.

Printed in the United States on permanent paper.

Library of Congress Cataloging-in-Publication Data

Brand, Max, 1892–1944.
    The gun tamer / Max Brand.
      p. cm.
    ISBN 0-7862-6214-1 (lg. print : hc : alk. paper)
    1. Ranch life — Fiction.   2. Sheriffs — Fiction.
  3. Outlaws — Fiction.   4. Large type books.   I. Title.
  PS3511.A87G79 2004
   813'.52—dc22   2003067194

THE GUN TAMER

As the Founder/CEO of NAVH, the only national health agency solely devoted to those who, although not totally blind, have an eye disease which could lead to serious visual impairment, I am pleased to recognize Thorndike Press★ as one of the leading publishers in the large print field.

Founded in 1954 in San Francisco to prepare large print textbooks for partially seeing children, NAVH became the pioneer and standard setting agency in the preparation of large type.

Today, those publishers who meet our standards carry the prestigious "Seal of Approval" indicating high quality large print. We are delighted that Thorndike Press is one of the publishers whose titles meet these standards. We are also pleased to recognize the significant contribution Thorndike Press is making in this important and growing field.

Lorraine H. Marchi, L.H.D.
Founder/CEO
NAVH

★ Thorndike Press encompasses the following imprints: Thorndike, Wheeler, Walker and Large Print Press.

CHAPTER 1

There was no harm in sending the colonel's daughter to the dance, as everyone in the household agreed.

She had been raised so delicately that nothing so rude and rough as a bandanna bedecked cow-puncher possibly could enter her inner horizon.

Besides, she was only seventeen, and, as the colonel said: "Only a child, much younger than her years. Of course, there's no place for men in her thoughts!"

So they got her ready for the dance.

The colonel had been begged to lend dignity to the affair by lending his presence, and, since the colonel had more dignity than he knew what to do with, he accepted the invitation almost in those terms.

His wife went, too.

Her name was Lydia and she was like her name — soft, that is to say, and clinging, and so very gentle and naïve that, before her hair turned gray, men watched her as they might have watched a star; but after the crow's-feet were printed at the corners of her eyes, and the luster was gone from her hair, she became no more than a shadow. Men hardly knew when she left or entered a room.

Her husband ceased noticing her at the same period. He had been a devoted lover until the honeymoon ended, and thereafter he remained devoted, in public, until the glory departed from Lydia. After that he was apt to talk through her or over her. He was gently restrained. In a way, this quiet creature was a foil to his brilliance; and the more gray her hair became, the younger appeared the colonel.

On this night she ventured a protest. The colonel was bringing his moustache to two neat points when he allowed her to enter.

"I shouldn't send Mary to a dance," said she.

"Ah?" said the colonel.

"Of course she's young," went on Mrs. Mackay. "But still, I don't think that she's young enough."

"Hum," said the colonel.

He leaned and regarded his work in the mirror.

"Dances are quite all right," went on Lydia Mackay, "for Mary and youngsters of her own — condition, you know — youngsters raised inside the conventions, my dear."

"Ah?" said the colonel.

"But these rough and ready cowpunchers," said she, "are quite a different matter, really! The moment that a girl begins to wear long dresses she is old enough for them to start flirting with her."

"Hum," said the colonel, twisting his moustaches a little tighter.

"Besides, Mary is growing into a lovely girl, and quite enough to turn the heads of boys — and boy-men!" she added with a little change of intonation.

The colonel at last turned around from the mirror. He rested one hand on his tailored hip. In the other hand he dandled a pair of spectacles. Spectacles were an ornament rather than a necessity with the colonel.

"Mary," he said, "is a child."

"She is seventeen," said Lydia, shrinking a little.

"Mary," repeated the colonel, "is a child."

"You know, of course," said Lydia, drifting further towards the door, so that her gentle voice barely reached her big husband, "you know, of course, that Juliet was only fourteen when Romeo —"

"Poets, really, are nothing but idiots," said the colonel. "I hope you're not going to draw your comparisons from a poet, my dear. This is real life."

He rarely put so many words together in one phrase, when he was talking with his wife. He never had, since their honeymoon. But still she hesitated in the doorway.

"You know, Winton, that I was seventeen when we first met —"

The colonel swelled. His color changed. And poor Lydia shrank almost out of sight.

"I hope," said Colonel Mackay, "that there is just a trace of difference between Winton Mackay and — these people!"

His gesture was meant, no doubt, to include all his neighbors, spotted here and there across the vast distances of the cattle range, pooled in a few small towns, or gathered in little clusters where there were mines in the mountains. His gesture was meant to sum up and brush away any actual significance in these rough men of the soil; but also, he seemed to be brushing Lydia from his presence, and she fled at once.

So they went to the dance.

The colonel strode here and there. Everyone noticed him. He was magnificent. He was so tall, his shoulders were so wide, and the coat fitted them so smoothly. Still, in civilian dress, he appeared uniformed, and one almost caught the glitter of gold lace, and saw the medals winking on his breast. He was cheerfully democratic. No one was too humble or insignificant to get a word or a moment of attention from Colonel Mackay. When he first came, he was observed speaking for a moment with the drummer of the orchestra, a little, withered old cripple.

Everyone noticed this and smiled and was pleased. The colonel had remained talking just long enough to be sure that everyone *must* be aware of what he was doing.

People began to say: "What a magnificent person our new neighbor is. An absolute gentleman. But very good natured and such a democrat! However, isn't it plain that blood tells?"

The ladies said these things, chiefly. The men were impressed, but they reserved judgment for a time, which is a habit and privilege, one may say, of Westerners.

The ladies also added: "*How* could the colonel have married such a little drab? Oh, yes, sweet enough — but just a shadow!"

They expected that the colonel's wife would talk about New York, Paris, London, and Rome. But she didn't.

In an entire evening the name of not a single prince, duke, earl, lord, baron, or knight fell from her pale lips. She did not say where she shopped in Paris. She referred to no London theatre, and to no modern painter.

In fact, one could not help feeling that her travels and her education had been wasted upon her!

Poor thing! One cannot pour a gallon into a pint measure.

Of course, that should be remembered!

As to Mary, she was quite another matter — very simple and quiet; but all the loveliness of her mother's youth had descended to her, and, besides, there was something imperishable about Mary, something of her father's perennial strength and charm. She had her mother's golden hair; she had her mother's blue eyes; but there was a touch of dignity and self-sufficiency in Mary even now that she was a mere wisp of a girl, as the saying goes.

Even so, she was three years older than poor Juliet.

And her mother, at just that age, had met the colonel.

So the dance began.

It was not quite so free-for-all as other dances in the schoolhouse. It hardly could be, with such distinguished guests present. And, strange to say, none of the young men showed the slightest disposition to approach Mary. They even seemed to vie with one another in staying away from her. That was simply shyness.

Henry Green, who was in a way the master of ceremonies, began to bring up the youngsters and introduce them to the beauty. She danced with them, as in duty bound. She did not talk. Dancing was enough, she felt. So she said yes and no, and when they brought her back to her chair she gave them each one faint smile.

Yes, it was enough.

A thread of fire seemed to have passed into the blood of the youth in that schoolhouse, and there was a slow and steady gathering of cow-punchers and miners and lumbermen in the direction of Mary, like a rising tide with its driftwood setting into a bay.

"They dance surprisingly well," said Mary to her mother.

"Of course they do," said Lydia Mackay.

"And they're extremely respectful," said Mary, the daughter of the colonel.

But suddenly all of those young men, in their Sunday clothes, became brown and drab and insignificant, for a glorious peacock had entered the room.

He was tall and slender. He was young. He was most, most good-looking. And he was dressed like a Mexican prince — except that there are no Mexican princes.

That is to say, he wore the short Mexican jacket, and around his hips he had knotted a magnificent scarf which once had been a beautiful altar cloth. Silver and gold overlaid him. He was like a jewel enclosed in a magnificent casket.

By the door he paused and surveyed the room, lazily, leisurely, with a little smile, and he held his head thrown back.

"Oh," said Mary, "what a —"

"Yes," said her mother, a little hurried to speak first, "*what* a silly young boy."

"Oh," said Mary again, in a quite different tone.

But when the stranger drifted across the room, her attention drifted after him.

"It is getting quite late," said Mrs. Mackay, "and I think that we'd better be getting back home."

"Why, mother, how can you say such a thing," said the girl, "when the evening is barely beginning!"

"It's eleven o'clock," said Mrs. Mackay, and looked at her watch.

She signaled sharply to her husband, who passed at that moment, but he was magnificently unaware of her. He had upon his arm the second loveliest woman in the room. She was transformed with the delight of having been chosen by the colonel. The colonel was charmed to have transformed her. For the colonel had a charitable heart

"Oh!" said Mary again, beneath her breath.

But her mother heard, and she saw that the peacock was coming daintily through the crowd, and straight towards them.

CHAPTER 2

"Who is that man?" asked the colonel's wife of a motherly ranch woman who was near by.

"You mean the Mexican dressed one? I never seen him before. And I know everybody around here. He's a stranger. Look at the buzz he's making among the girls! I tell you what, Mrs. Mackay, I got to say that when I was a girl, we had a little more sense! Why, he looks like a freak, dressed up like that!"

Mrs. Mackay regarded the stranger with a steady glance and then looked anxiously at her daughter. Mary was noticing the approach; there could be no doubt of that.

"What a silly looking fellow!" said Mrs. Mackay, as the peacock drew nearer.

For she guessed that ridicule usually is better than downright prohibition of friendships.

"Yes — isn't he," said Mary, but there was no heart in her agreement, and Mrs. Mackay saw the color of her daughter come and go as this Beau Brummell stepped closer.

He really was splendid. One expected, at the distance and in that place, that the fellow would be all tawdry color and flare and no actual substance. But, on the contrary, when he was near at hand, it could be seen that he was like a polished jewel, perfect in every facet. A small fortune seemed to be heaped upon his back. A square-faced ruby made a spot of crimson on one hand; and the pin which held his neck cloth was set off by the mysterious glimmerings of an emerald. And all the gold and silver work with which he was brocaded was masterly in workmanship. One wanted to put this dandy under a glass case and keep him there, in the midst of some graceful gesture, so that the world, from that time forward, would be able to behold the flower of Mexican civilization which had bloomed, it seemed, only to make this man splendid.

He came forward, then, in so straight a line that it appeared that he was aiming directly at Mary Mackay. And Mary quivered violently.

Instead, at the last moment he changed — or had that been his goal from the first? And now he was bowing in front of the daughter of the same ranch woman who had recently proclaimed the superi-

17

ority of the last generation.

She had a rather thin, angular daughter; and she bit her lip with anxiety, watching the contrast between the girl's plainness and this gay cavalier's splendor.

What was he saying?

At that moment, the trombone player was inspired to a wild flight, and all the anxious mother could hear was: "I beg your pardon. I do not much English spik. Do I not hear that you have the Spanish language?"

And Elizabeth Kane, better known by boys and girls as "Sandy," instantly burst forth in fluent Spanish, for she had lived on the border most of her days; the Kanes were recent comers in this vicinity.

Another moment, and off they stepped together.

"He *is* a silly fellow," said Mary Mackay to her mother. And straightway she went off in the dance with a happy-faced lumberman.

Mrs. Mackay and Mrs. Kane drew their chairs a little closer. Mrs. Kane had changed her opinion a little.

"He's really graceful, you see," she pointed out.

"Of course he is," said Mrs. Mackay, "and I wonder what else he is?"

"Oh, if he's a real Mexican — of course their standards of dress aren't like ours!"

"How could a real Mexican have fair hair?"

"Oh, but they could! There are lots of Castilians with fair hair. I dunno where they get it. But I've seen them in Mexico. Their descendants, I mean! Look!"

The last word called direct attention to her daughter and the stranger; and they were worth attention. Whether through the leading of the Mexican who did not "spik" much English, or through a mutual inspiration, the two had devised upon the spur of the moment a flowery little combination to insert in the plain one-step, and they tipped and swayed back and forth like two birds on the wing.

They became the center of interest in the dance. Other couples idled near the edge of the floor, and turned admiring and envious eyes towards them.

Mrs. Kane was delighted. The plainness of Sandy was a perpetual thorn in her side, and the tomboy frankness and carelessness which had made Sandy popular when she was a child now caused her to be totally neglected since she had become a woman.

Here, at a touch, she was transformed. Whether it was the dance itself, or the chance to talk the familiar Spanish, Sandy was transfigured and blossomed before all eyes as a veritable flower.

The very inmost heart of Mrs. Kane relaxed and melted in a moment. She wisely knew that girls cannot hold the center of a big stage even for a moment without becoming, to a degree, permanently eligible; and every man who had seen Sandy blossom in the arms of the strange cavalier would go the rest of his days expecting to see her blossom in his.

All dangers of old-maidship were instantly thrown into the discard.

In fact, it was a sensation, and Sandy came back to them radiant, and said adieu to her cavalier.

Behold! He bowed and kissed her hand, and two or three nearby cow-punchers sniggered not too secretly.

Mary Mackay, with rather a fixed smile, was again in her chair, and now Sandy overflowed with tidings.

His name was Felipe Christobal Hernandez Consalvo. Yes, he was from Mexico. He had lived all of his life there. He barely could speak English. But perfect Spanish. You see, he had been educated in Madrid. He had been presented to the Spanish king. Think of that!

Mrs. Mackay said "Ah?" in a queer little voice.

So did Mary, but her voice was not queer at all, and her eyes were saucers.

He had apologized for introducing himself, but here he was a stranger in a strange land, and when he knew that that dear Spanish was as native on her lips — but of course she had excused him, and explained that everything was very free and easy at such a dance as this. He had begged for another dance as soon as she would permit him to come for one. And when he came again, would Mary Mackay allow Sandy to present him to her?

"Thank you very much," said Mary, and she glanced at her mother.

"Why certainly, my dear," said Mrs. Mackay.

So that was settled.

The stranger did not dance in the interim. He had drifted out of the hall, leaving a whisper and a murmur behind him. Even the men did not laugh so much. Of course, if he really was a Mexican, and not some silly dude fixed up in a part — of course, that made a difference, as any man could see.

Then he came for his next dance, came eagerly, and before Sandy stepped away with him: "This is Señor Consalvo, mother and Mrs. Mackay and Mary Mackay, this is Señor Consalvo —"

He kissed their hands, bowing deeply; and then he was off with Sandy. If they had danced well before, they were fairly inspired now.

"Sandy took dancing lessons, and had a Spanish teacher," explained Mrs. Kane.

"She does very well," said mild Mrs. Mackay.

So the dance ended, and, afterwards, there suddenly formed a little pool of young men around Sandy. They had forgotten her existence at this and other affairs, but now, all at once, they remembered her. They all wanted dances.

Mrs. Kane sat back with joy moist and beaming in her eye. Sandy was "made," and she knew it; and she thanked the provident God who had sent this young man from Mexico to bring Sandy out into the light.

But who was chosen for the next dance with Sandy?

It was a handsome, elderly, dignified man, wearing his years with wonderful lightness. It was Colonel Mackay, himself, putting a crown upon Sandy's success of the evening. No wonder that the cup of the watchful mother was full!

The very orchestra seemed inspired, also. The trombone player lost some of his raucous violence. One actually could hear the singing of the fiddle, as the next dance began; and so Señor Don Felipe Christobal Hernandez Consalvo stepped out on the floor with Mary Mackay.

She seemed a little abashed and girlish, at first, with such a dazzling partner; but Señor Consalvo was so courteous, so gentle, and he spoke his bad English in such a beautiful voice, that before they had gone half of one round of the floor they were talking busily.

And if with Sandy he had managed to improvise a new step, with Mary Mackay he arranged a whole embroidery of graceful movements, through which Mary floated as if she had been practicing the business for hours every day.

She spoke some Spanish, too. Of course, when the colonel decided to buy the ranch in the West, he had advised Mary to study the Spanish language. You know, in New Mexico nearly everyone speaks that tongue. So Mary had had two years of drilling, and tonight she was glad of it.

One could see at a glance that, if he had nothing better to do in his life, this young man would make a most incredibly fine teacher. To say words after him was simply delightful. And his whole speech was flavored with a faint, soft lisp, from the Spanish "d," which of course is pronounced like "th" in English.

After that dance, they formed a little circle — Sandy and the colonel and Mary and Consalvo.

When the latter was introduced to Mackay — "Of course señor *el colonel* was to me pointed out when I first came. It is great honor, señor."

He bowed so low that it seemed as though he were about to kiss the colonel's hand, too!

But the colonel smiled graciously.

"Talk Spanish, Señor Consalvo," said he. "We all can manage a little in that language."

Don Felipe stood erect and pressed his hand upon his heart, his long, slender, graceful hand.

"Ah," said he in his native tongue, "it is as though I had stopped among a circle of friends!"

"My dear fellow," said the colonel, more kindly than ever, "perhaps you have!"

CHAPTER 3

In fact, the colonel was charmed by this graceful and gay young stranger, and, before the evening was over, he invited him to come out to the ranch house.

"If you don't mind roughing it, señor," said the colonel.

It was one of his ways of making a little joke. As though a Mackay ever lived roughly!

But the young Mexican took the matter seriously, and bowed. He always was bowing, on the slightest provocation, but he managed it so gracefully that in him it was no more than a gesture in another.

"I come from a country, señor *el colonel*," said he, "where one learns to live roughly. We have not, alas, the civilization of your great country!"

The colonel waved this suggestion aside. Like a majority of traveled Americans, he was fond of making light of the Great Republic.

"We have dollars and good plumbing, Consalvo," he said. "But there is something else to be found in a really important civilization! You come along and visit us. We'll expect you whenever you arrive!"

So it was that, three days later, Felipe Christobal Hernandez Consalvo came to the ranch house.

He came in odd style.

For himself, he was mounted upon a thoroughbred with limbs and eyes like a deer, a dark chestnut, with a white-stockinged foreleg and a blaze on the forehead that gleamed like a star. And the garb of Consalvo for the road was almost as gay and gold and silver splashed as his costume for the dance.

Behind this glimmering cavalier marched three strong mules, each carrying a large pack, and behind the mules, striding through the dust which they raised, was one of the ugliest creatures that ever walked the earth. He was a tattered Indian, his skin the true copper-brown, his face flattened as though by the kick of a horse, and given a high light in the form of a ghastly scar which ran from forehead to chin and puckered the flesh on that side of his countenance. His ugliness was given a point, so to speak, by the bulk of the man; for he had the shoulders and arms of a giant, and yet he was made so sinewy and muscular that it was apparent he was a member of one of those tribes of great runners who can do their hundred miles a day on foot, in case of need.

So the caravan came up to the house and found the colonel and his daughter about to ride out on a tour of their ranch. Of course the ride was postponed to welcome the visitor.

There was something knightly in his approach, and when he sprang off and bowed, hat in hand, it seemed as though the thoroughbred bowed its lovely head, also. The colonel was enchanted and personally guided his guest to a chamber.

It was a great house built in the Spanish style around a patio which in itself was of such dimensions that Mrs. Mackay had established a brilliant garden there; and here she was found, trowel in hand, when Consalvo went through. She welcomed the cavalier as in duty bound, and, if her welcome was a little less warm than that of her husband and daughter, it might be put down to her natural quietness of manner.

As for Consalvo, he was astonished and delighted with all that he saw. It was not a house, said he, but a royal palace, and he warmed the very cockles of the heart of the colonel by pausing again and again to admire the lofty, spacious apartments, and the old furniture which had been brought from Spain to keep the place in tone. His own guest suite was closed off by itself to give perfect privacy. There was a bedroom, a bathroom, a living room, and a little chamber for his servant, and, to crown all, there was a tiny little walled garden with a fountain in the center where the spray showered in cool profusion over a little bronze mermaid.

Here, said Consalvo, a prince might have felt at home.

"And this is your rough living!" said he, and shook his head in wonder and in admiration.

There was only one shadow.

"We too," said Consalvo softly, "once had a home where we could have received even —"

He paused; and the colonel delicately forbore pressing him for the unfinished portion of the sentence. He could guess at the cause of the passing darkness in the eyes of the young man.

To cheer him up, he invited him to accompany him and his daughter on their tour of the ranch; so Consalvo left his ugly Indian arranging the three great packs in their apartments and mounted his fine horse.

It was a splendid ride. The estate of the colonel was all that the heart of man could desire, and worth more than the huge price he had paid for it. For it was a little valley between hills that thrust out into the white and burning desert so that those who came upon it must ride through sun-scorched sands until they came suddenly upon this well-watered region of trees and green fields and ploughed lands. The wheat grew head-high, here, and along the creek the alfalfa gave five rich crops in a single year. On the uplands, on every side, were pastures for the best of thoroughbred cattle, and excellent saddle stock.

The admiration of Consalvo was something childlike and pathetic to behold, and at last, from an eminence, he halted his horse and threw out his arms.

"This is not a ranch. It is a kingdom!" said he. "And you, señor *el colonel*, are a king in the midst of it!"

The colonel cleared his throat and looked modestly upon the ground.

"After all," said he, "one hears the call of the soil, at last. A man must retire, eventually, and how retire better than to a quiet place like this?"

"Retire?" said Consalvo. "Retire to such

a place as this? No, it is the beginning of a real life!"

The colonel breathed deeply; his eyes shone; he could not help but respond to this heartfelt sympathy, and felt in the youth beside him a kindred spirit. In the old days, in the golden ages, a man of such possession might have been surrounded by just such youthful paladins, living under the shadow of his spear and shield, uniting their strength to his, surrounding his board with their wit, their grace, their homage.

The colonel hardly could speak, for some time, but when he did, he asked Consalvo about himself.

Don Felipe spoke with perfect openness, and a sort of courageous gaiety.

In other centuries, he said, men had ridden up out of Mexico upon the northern trail, crossed the Rio Grande, and gone exploring for treasure.

So it was with him in this later day!

He had ridden away from cracked walls and crumbling chambers. He had taken the northern trail, and perhaps — who could tell? — he might find the Seven Lost Cities for which so many had searched and searched in vain.

Patience, courage, and strength. They were required. They were all that he had to offer. They and some prospector's tools. So he had chosen from among his old family adherents the most trustworthy and devoted man — the tall Indian, who was named Pedro — and with him he had begun the voyage of discovery.

The colonel was more delighted than ever, as he listened to this tale.

"And if you find the Seven Cities," said the colonel, winking covertly at his daughter, who had been oddly silent during the entire ride, "what will you do with the spoils? Because I suppose that there *will* be some spoils?"

"Spoils, señor?" said Consalvo, staring in childlike wonder at his host. "Spoils, señor? Then you do not know about them?"

"I've only heard rumors — mention in a school history, or some such thing."

"Ha!" cried the Mexican. "Then you shall know! In those lost and buried cities, señor, there are halls plated with gold and lined with silver. There are jewels, too. And, in one, there is a temple to the sun where the very walls are solidly laid with bricks of silver and where the sun itself is represented as a great solid ball of gold!"

"Ah," said the colonel, again smiling covertly at his daughter. "And what makes you so sure that there are such places, Consalvo?"

"It is an old story in my family," said Consalvo. "For a blood cousin, Felipe Oñate, wandered here many centuries ago, and he heard the tales. He did not find them. He returned, and Christobal Oñate, his younger brother, rode out to see what he could find. It is said that he had a glimpse of the vast treasures in one of those cities, but he became sick; he fought with the jealous Indians, and came home only to die. Then a direct ancestor, Señor Don Hernandez Consalvo, rode here with a small army, but he was ambushed and killed by the treacherous Indians, and only one man came home to tell the tale of what might have been. For they actually had contested with Indians who wore necklaces of gold!"

"Felipe Oñate — Christobal — Hernandez — were you named for those three men?"

"I was," said the youth, "and therefore it seems that I was predestined to ride on the northern trail and try to accomplish what they failed to do."

There was a little silence, after that. It seemed that Fate had its shadowy hand in the life of this graceful young man.

"And when you have — found the Seven Cities," said the colonel, very gently, "what will you do then?"

"Then?" said Consalvo. "Ah, then I shall return to the house of my fathers, and the old walls shall rise again, and the great chambers shall be roofed, and the lands which have been lost shall be ours once more, and the old retainers shall return to us, and all shall be as it was in those lost ages. That is what I shall do, if I have fortune, now that I have ridden north under the Golden Moon!"

Talking in this vein, they came back again in sight of the wide-armed house of Mackay.

"I hope you have the best of good fortune," said Mary Mackay softly.

CHAPTER 4

Señor Consalvo did not leave at once. It was the colonel, chiefly, who prevented that, by pointing out that if his young guest were to begin a career as a prospector, among other things, he really should settle down for a time to a serious study of his art and his tools.

He had a foreman who had been a prospector in his younger days and who still, from time to time, drove a burro forth towards the higher mountains, and came back lean and tattered after some three months of exploring, but always with an unabsorbed fire in his eyes. The foreman spent much time with the Mexican, showing him how to break ground, and he pronounced Consalvo an eager and willing pupil.

Further to equip his dainty and delicate guest for the struggle with life in the wilderness, the colonel set aside the most formidable of his men, Marty Lucas, to teach Don Felipe the arts connected with guns.

Marty was a "bad one" who had gone

straight, and who spent the prime of his middle age, now, riding herd and doing all the other commonplace duties of a cowpuncher. It was said that he had come to a point where he knew the trail divided. Hereafter juries would not believe him when he declared that he had fired in self-defense because there had been a "hip-movement" on the part of his victim. And when Marty made that decision, he promptly began to play safe. For ten years he had shed no blood, and people almost had forgotten that once he was close to the desperado class.

So Marty was given the instruction of Don Felipe and worked out with him every day with revolvers and with repeating rifle, teaching him that the best position for a revolver, in case of instant need, is in a spring clip beneath the arm pit, with the owner wearing a loose coat, unbuttoned; and showing him that a rifle can be used with quite deadly accuracy even when it is carried loosely slung over the crook of the left arm.

There was little progress in the pupil, however, and Marty Lucas eventually shrugged his shoulders and declared to his pupil that he might become accurate enough to bring down a deer, now and again, but he advised him, in case of trouble with an armed man, to trust to his heels or the speed of his horse!

For nothing could be done to make him an expert.

Now, when Don Felipe heard these discouraging remarks, he accepted them with a sort of childlike and innocent opening of the eyes, so that the heart of Marty smote him, and he encouraged Don Felipe to continue. "In spite of hell," said Marty, "I'll teach you the art of self-defense!"

So, between marksmanship and gunnery, the days passed swiftly for Don Felipe, and every day he grew more and more earnest. And every evening he grew more and more light-hearted.

After he had been confined at these solemn tasks, during many hours of heat, he could not help putting on another self — or throwing off that unreal laborious one — and no sooner did he appear at the dinner table, than he was bubbling over with mirth.

He seemed to talk most freely, but he had an odd gift of beginning a theme himself and then transferring it to another person. He often had Mary chattering; he started the colonel upon long stories of his military days; and even mild Lydia Mackay from time to time was induced to talk, though she never held the stage very long, because it made her husband restless.

After dinner, however, Don Felipe stepped into his glory; for there was hardly a thing which he could not do to entertain, no matter how clumsy he might be reported with weapons. He could do complicated, fiery, Spanish dances. He could play on the guitar and sing old Spanish ballads which, so he said, had been passed down for many generations in his house. He could even do card tricks. And some times he would even venture on long tales of Mexico.

Those were serious moments. He preferred to talk in some shadowy corner of the patio, listening, and watching the central fountain shower and splash. Then, half lost in the dimness, his pleasant voice lowered, Don Felipe half closed his eyes and told tales of the wild Sierras, and adventures among strange peoples, and legends out of his family past, until one began to feel that there was behind him the storied romance of a fairy tale, peopled with giants and ogres, and with castles upon dizzy heights where lovely ladies dwelt.

"Upon the whole," said the colonel, in judicial mood, to his wife, one morning, "I never have had such a delightful guest in all my life. And, I dare say, neither have you!"

"Never," said Mrs. Mackay, "and of course there is an excellent reason."

"A dozen excellent reasons," said the colonel. "His modesty and his wit, his candor and his good humor, his well-educated mind and playful humor, his unfailing zest and love of life. I take it that all of these make excellent reasons!"

Lydia Mackay did not answer at once, and therefore the colonel, who kept a touch of the old military discipline throughout his domestic relations, said abruptly: "Or have you a better reason?"

"I think I have," said she.

"Oh, stuff!" said the colonel ungraciously. "But come along, then, and trot out the better reason."

"Everything that's dangerous is interesting," said she.

"Ha?" cried the colonel, and then waited for her to enlarge upon her theme.

But she did not enlarge. Instead, she turned away and began to fit on her heavy gardening gauntlets, drawing them over her soft and slender hands. In fact, Lydia Mackay rarely talked at any great length.

So the colonel expanded, for himself. He

always was prone to do that.

"Dangerous? Nonsense!" said he. "Dangerous in what way, if you please? Dangerous, I dare say you would answer, because one should not place such a dashing young Beau Brummell near a young and impressionable girl like Mary. Isn't that your idea?"

"You are so clever," said quiet Mrs. Mackay, "that you always see straight through all my ideas."

The colonel leaned back in his chair and turned his cigar comfortably in his mouth.

"Of course," he admitted, "there are differences between the mind of the man and the mind of the woman. The woman, Lydia," said he in exposition, "moves through a mist, lit by flashes of instinct, whereas the man disperses the mist by concentrating upon it the bright light of reason."

"Or wind?" suggested Mrs. Mackay.

"Wind?" considered the colonel. "Wind of reason? A very poor metaphor, I should say. However, if a man is able to go behind the words of a woman and find her hidden meanings, it is because he is superior in logic, you understand?"

"Oh, yes," said she.

"A woman," went on the colonel, devoting himself to his theme, "observes the surface and draws her conclusions at once, and without mental gain. Her mental life is almost physical. Her brain is like her eye or her ear. Either it perceives immediately or — or —"

"Or is deafened," suggested Mrs. Mackay gently, as her husband probed for a word.

"Deafened? I think not," said the colonel, who rarely had use for his wife's suggestions, no matter of what nature they might be. "But to come back to young Consalvo — of course at a glance I noted what now troubles you, but I looked deeper than a single glance could take you. Young, handsome, beautifully reared and mannered, gay and amusing, the very fellow, you would say, to break hearts. But observe how logic of fact falls down! Observe how suppositions lead us astray. Observe, my dear child!"

"What?" asked Mrs. Mackay, putting on her garden bonnet.

"Eh?" said the colonel, his long train of thought somewhat scattered by this brief word of question. "You must try to follow me, Lydia. You really must. It takes an effort, but it's worth while. I mean to say, at last, that in spite of these attributes of

Consalvo, as a matter of fact his nature is so clean, cheerful, open, and gay, that he never grows personal. I have noted him with our daughter. Good God, would I allow a stranger to step into the intimacy of our family circle without — Heavens, Lydia, what is your opinion of my discretion?"

She was tying the strings of her bonnet beneath her chin.

"I don't criticize you," said she. "But one has a thought from time to time, even if one is only a woman, my dear."

"Bring your ideas to me, child," said the colonel. "I am glad to have you bring them to me and examine them for you. Tush! It's my duty, isn't it? But about Consalvo. I've watched to see the calf-look in his eyes when he glanced at Mary. But it appears," concluded the colonel, "that he understands that there is a certain distance to be maintained between us and others; that there is, connected with a Mackay, a certain importance."

"Even when it is a woman?" asked the guileless wife.

"Good heavens," said the colonel, "does not my blood flow in the veins of Mary?"

"And yet, you know —" said the gentle lady, and paused.

41

"Well?" said the colonel briskly. "Well?"

"After all," said she, "Mary can only be half a Mackay."

"Nine tenths, at least," said the colonel cheerfully. "No, never doubt that the young Mexican will maintain the proper distance. In fact, his head is so filled by his absurd Seven Cities that he hardly notices our girl."

She lingered in the doorway.

He ended: "You look positively pretty this morning, my dear. Well, run along to your garden."

CHAPTER 5

Lydia Mackay went to the garden but she did not run, and indeed she went so slowly and softly that she was able to hear, in the distance, the faint strumming of a guitar, so delicately low that it made a vibration rather than a sound. She traced the murmur to its source, and so she came to an arched gate, overhung by the trailing vestments of a climbing vine with its little yellow, heavy-sweet blossoms; and through the opening, for the gate was not quite closed, she found herself looking into the guest's garden.

Mrs. Mackay was touched, hearing such delicately subdued sounds from the young Mexican, as though he were disturbed and in pain from the harsh environment which he found in this northern land, and, therefore, in the solitude of the little garden, he played some of the airs of his native land.

Played them, and sang them too. For now Mrs. Mackay was able to distinguish his voice. She had heard it before in the evening, many a time, a rich and ringing tenor that filled the big living room almost to overflowing, but now it was so reduced that it was like the music of a bird, half heard on the breeze. It floated on the air; it seemed to be born of no body. Only after listening intently for some moments was she able to distinguish the human sound which underlay the soft singing of the instrument.

She looked up, as one will do in moments of great pleasure, and she saw in the vast, pale blue of the sky a buzzard circling, an ignoble thing in noble flight.

Mrs. Mackay looked down again, and stepped a little nearer, in the hope that she might be able to distinguish the words of the song.

So doing she came in view of the musician, seated near the fountain under an umbrella tree, leaning back against its trunk, and keeping his eyes half closed, as though he, too, were listening to voices far away and dim.

It was not the sight of Don Felipe alone, however, which stirred Mrs. Mackay so much. But not far away she saw her daughter, her sole child, rapt in thoughtful attention, her head bent so that the mother could not see her face, but only the bright coil of the hair which, such a little time before, had been braided down her back.

Mrs. Mackay lingered only an instant, as a fox lingers, say, when it sees the wolf sniffing at the entrance to her lair. Then she went softly and discreetly back to the house and into her own apartment.

There she had a little Italian desk of yellow, painted with green leaves and with bright flowers.

Mrs. Mackay opened it, and in spite of her haste, she waited a moment until there rose to her the faintest scent of perfume, kept only here and consecrated to this spot. Then she sat down and took out a sheet of smooth linen paper, ivory colored, and translucent, every sheet. She picked up a slender pen, daintily chased with a half invisible design, but when she had dipped her pen in the inkwell and began to write, it was with a bold and open stroke, so freely and largely flowing that she put only a few words on each page; and then the sheets were tossed aside to dry; and sometimes one fell upon another and left ugly blurs, unregarded by the author in the haste or the emotion of her composition.

"Dear Sheriff Rankin," she wrote. "Do you remember the last time that the rustlers came down from the mountains and carried off the Herefords? You promised then that one day you would come back to visit us and look a little deeper into the matter. For just then certain odds and ends connected with a man-killing desperado from Montana called you away from us — and our cattle. And I remember that, as you said good-bye, you told me that you had spent some happy days with us, and that at some time you wanted to make a return to us.

"The time has come, Sheriff Rankin, not to fulfill a promise, but to do me a great kindness.

"I am in some trouble. Rather, I should say that I suspect some trouble is about to come over our sky like a sailing cloud, and I would like to have you here to be a weather prophet, so to speak. Or a strong shield in a time of danger, to speak my mind more frankly.

"But, unfortunately, this is a matter which I must keep to myself, at least for a time, and therefore may I ask you — if you find it possible to visit us very soon — to pretend that you have come merely to look into that forgotten business about the rustlers?

"I fear that I am making a little mystery of this affair, but I know that you are a tolerant man; and also, I know that you

46

would not postpone any really important public business in order to come and listen to the fancies of Mrs. Mackay.

"Nevertheless — forgive me! — I do expect you rather soon.

"LYDIA MACKAY."

She paused a moment, her pen making little undecipherable movements in the air, and then she added:

"And if you have two or three really expert fighting men, perhaps it would be wisest to bring them, also!"

Then she laid down her pen.

She did not re-read the letter, but gathered the sheets quickly, and gave them a little rustle in the air to dry some of the wet ink. After that, she packed them into an envelope, and then she went out and asked for a horse.

She did not go riding very often, though she was an expert horsewoman; so they gave her the tamest and gentlest of the fine animals who ate oats in the stable of the colonel, or danced or idled in his pastures. An old-fashioned sidesaddle was strapped on its back. By the time the horse was ready, she was in her rarely used riding costume, and ready for the stirrup.

Once she was put up into the saddle, she trotted her mount softly down the driveway, but, the instant that she had put a big double bend of the trees between her and the house, she cut straight across country; and it would have astonished even the dashing colonel to see his wife jump the fences that lay before her — not mere hedges, but stark, raking, barbed-wire affairs which are too dangerous for any but the wildest youths to attempt.

She saved herself five miles — going and coming — in this fashion, and so cantered gently into town, at the last, and left her letter for the sheriff at his office.

He was expected within a very few moments; but nevertheless she did not wait.

By word of mouth one never can say certain things as well as with the written word.

After that, she went home; and before the morning was over, the colonel strolled out from the house and found his wife in her apron and gardening gloves, with the old-fashioned bonnet laced beneath her chin. She was laboring, then, at a bed of pansies.

The colonel came near and allowed his shadow to fall upon her, at which she turned her head and looked over her shoulder at him. The colonel brightened.

"My dear child," said he, "even now, you have a certain something in your smile. Where do you keep it?"

"I only use a little at a time," said Lydia Mackay, "and so, you see, the supply never is quite finished."

"I don't quite understand that," said the colonel, tapping his boots with his walking stick.

"Don't you? How strange!" said his wife. "But you understand everything, dear!"

"Perhaps it seems so to you," said the colonel blandly. "You are such a trusting little soul, Lydia. But, as a matter of fact —"

Here he stuck.

And his wife murmured: "I can't make pansies do well in this soil, dear. I don't know what's wrong. I'm sure the earth was laid down with just the proper fertilizer. But there's something in this southern sun, perhaps. What is it?"

"Oh," said the colonel, "let the pansies go. They're a childish flower! But, to go back, I'm going to unbosom myself, Lydia!"

"Dear me!" said she, straightening on her knees and looking up to him with round eyes. "What could it be? What have you done?"

"Nothing to be jailed for, perhaps," answered the colonel. "But at the same time — well — in short — Lydia, I have a suspicion from time to time that you simply are laughing at me when you pretend to be so naïve!"

She merely stared.

"Making a mock and a scorn of me," went on the colonel with a gathering heat. "I have a suspicion that — that — confound it, Lydia, don't look as though I'd struck you, you know!"

"I don't know what you mean, dear," faltered Lydia.

"Stuff and nonsense," said the colonel. "Stuff and — I mean — forget about it. You really are quite charming — against that pansy bed, Lydia. You look — like an old-fashioned picture, really!"

"Do you think so?" said she.

And she looked down, and then she looked up again at him and smiled, a little hesitant, a little shy.

"Confound it! But really, Lydia," said the colonel.

"What have I done?" said she.

"Do you know," said the colonel, "that I often feel I never have married you?"

"What a shocking, dreadful thought," said she.

"All of you, I mean," said the colonel. "But something of that girl I met and carried away with me — why, something of her remained behind me in the place where I found her. Do you remember the place, Lydia?"

"Of course I do! At the mouth of the lane, wasn't it?"

"With the poplars running down behind you towards the old white house. And often, Lydia, it seems to me as though I took away into my world only a semblance of you; and the ghost — the other self — the real self, by heaven! — it turned and rode down the poplar shadows towards the white house."

"But oh, my dear," said she. "What an odd thought! And the old house has burned, you know, long ago."

"Of course it has!" said he with irritation. "But dreams are not made of stuff that flames can destroy. The more's the pity, sometimes I think. Ah, well, you never will understand me!"

And he strode hastily away through the double arches of the patio gate.

CHAPTER 6

The sheriff, as he gave his horse to one of the little Negro grooms at the Mackay barn, said to the boy: "Give that horse a rub-down, son. But don't rub his back legs, because he hates to be tickled. If he puts back his ears, it means that he's sleepy, so you might sing him a little lullaby. Y'understand?"

The groom looked at the lump-headed little mustang whose rough coat never had been graced by currycomb or brush, and then he grinned in broadest comprehension. Falling in the quarters, roached in the back, the pony looked like a small caricature of a camel, especially because of the shape of its head and its ewe-neck. But the sheriff affected mustangs and shrugged his shoulders at long-legged thoroughbreds; rather, he took naturally to the original stock of the country, and on the supple back of a hot-blooded mount he would have felt as out of place as though he were strolling down Fifth Avenue on Easter Sunday.

He was himself a son of the desert, and

in that gray and heat-drenched country it seemed as though he had been endowed with a protective coloration; for he was a gray man, hair and eyes and bleached skin; and the clothes he wore were faded to match. There was no more flesh on him than on a desert bird; and his clothes were so loose that it seemed he recently must have passed through a period of starvation.

He went slowly from the barn to the house, looking about him constantly, and when he came into the patio he paused and gazed as though he found food and drink in the showering green along the walls and dripping from the arches.

A slender and elegant youth in Mexican attire rose and came towards him, smiling.

"Do you want to see Colonel Mackay?" he asked.

"I do, sort of," said the other. "But don't you go botherin' yourself."

"Not at all! Not at all, señor," replied Consalvo.

"Well, then tell him that Tom Rankin has dropped out and would like to talk to him."

The colonel was brought; they sat, the two of them, on the shadowed side of the patio, with a gentle wind in their faces, puffing the fountain spray towards them in airy waves.

"I forgot that anybody ever could be cool in the daytime," observed the sheriff. "I clean forgot it. No, sir, I won't drink. There ain't much of me, Colonel Mackay, and so it don't take much alcohol to get me addled."

"My dear sheriff," said the colonel, "of course you are right — and you're keeping the law."

"The law?" said the sheriff. "I don't bother much about it, except when somebody starts me worrying. But one of these days I'm going to retire and set in the shade and smoke cigarettes till I dry up. Then I'm hopin' that a south wind'll come along and blow me like a dead leaf somewheres north, so's my ghost can be cooler than I've been!"

"But I thought you loved your country?" murmured the colonel.

"A parcel of sand and rocks," said the sheriff sadly, "and a parcel of sun and hellfire; who could love it? My eyes is all strained from looking across the distances."

"That," cried Colonel Mackay, "is just the glory of it — because the walls of the horizon are knocked down. And so it is with the mind. I think our thoughts are bigger and better here!"

"For you, maybe," answered Rankin, "because what you see you can send for and get it. But you take me, when I set out on my back porch and look across at Mount Locust, yonder, wagging his head in the sky, I say to myself I've been up its side five times, and pretty soon the sixth will come. They got their counties cut too big out here, Colonel Mackay. I tell you, sir, it's a doggone outrage. They ought to have a whole parcel of sheriffs, or get one that wears wings. I'm goin' to resign. I'm tired!"

This complaint was delivered in a slightly nasal drawling voice, while the sheriff made a cigarette with fingers that seemed uncertain and weak.

"Come, come!" replied the colonel cheerfully. "You wouldn't know what to do with yourself in any other place. And the county wouldn't know what to do without you. As for Mount Locust, I know that you love the place. It was up on the side of Mount Locust that you killed Red McGinnis, wasn't it?"

"I don't like to think about that day," sighed the sheriff. "Because just thinking about it makes the back of my head ache. I never seen it so hot. And the rocks was focusing the heat of that sun directly on me.

I was riding under a burning glass. I could smell the smoke curling up from my sombrero."

"Ah," said the colonel, "but you were strong enough to finish McGinnis!"

At this, a shadow descended across the eyes of the sheriff, so that his host became aware that the subject was not a welcome one.

"Everybody has his lucky and his unlucky days," declared Rankin, "and I found Red when his luck was out, just as somebody will find me, one of these days. But I wanted to talk to you a little about that rustling that happened up here when —"

"It's forgotten," said the colonel heartily. "Whoever did that job, sheriff, you trailed them so hot and hard that they never have forgotten; and they'll not return to take another chance. Besides," he added, "since then I've put Marty Lucas on my staff, and it will take a hardy lot of thieves to run their heads into a trap which he has manned."

The sheriff agreed. But he insisted that he wished to look the ground over and make a careful search of all the clues which, before, he had not had sufficient time to examine. He was made heartily welcome, and quarters were promised for the two or three men who would, the sheriff said, follow him out to the ranch within a day or two.

"We'll stay in the bunk house," said the sheriff. "We'd be better there, talking to the boys."

"What?" cried the colonel. "Sleep in the bunk house? Lydia, you've just come along in time. The sheriff is here for a few days, and he threatens to sleep with his men in the bunk house!"

"Has something gone wrong? Is there trouble, Sheriff Rankin?" she asked as soon as she came to them.

"The old rustling business," he assured her gravely. "And I'm bringing out a few of the boys to help me. Because my eyes are sort of old and failing me, Mrs. Mackay."

"Keep him here and persuade him," said the colonel hospitably. "I promised Consalvo to ride through the woods, today, and teach him about the birds. That lad has the making of an ornithologist, Lydia! And the book that I loaned him yesterday evening — by heavens, he appears to have read most of it already — and to have mastered it!"

So the colonel took himself off and left his wife in the patio, telling the sheriff about her troubles with the pansies — how hard she had worked on them! And would he have lemonade, perhaps? She knew the way to make it with the thinnest touch of egg —

"Ma'am," said the sheriff with a sudden smile, "I've rode on a good many trails, but I've never yet chased either a pansy or a lemonade; I don't even know their sign, and I reckon that I never will."

At this, Mrs. Mackay became silent, which she always was prepared to do, and with much grace.

"And I suppose," went on the sheriff, "that I should get to work on that old rustling gang —"

He paused, and she answered: "How long can you give yourself to us, Sheriff Rankin?"

"Ma'am," said the sheriff, "when I set here and look at the green, and watch that water — would you ask a poor damned soul how long he could give himself to heaven?"

"If you can stay a few days," said Mrs. Mackay, "and just look around — I don't want to be mysterious, sheriff!"

"Of course you don't," said the sheriff gravely. "I never knew any woman that ever did. Ain't you going to tell me, Mrs. Mackay, what made you want me out here?"

"If I were wrong," said she, "and nothing came of it —"

"You'd be pretty disappointed, of course," said the sheriff. "But just give me a hint."

"If you could simply look around," she suggested gently, "and with your practiced eye, of course you'd see more in five minutes than I would in five days! And — did you say you were bringing some more men?"

"When I got your letter," he said, "I looked over the boys. We have 'em rather hard-boiled in this neck of the woods. We have 'em tough as leather and mean as lye. I looked 'em over and I didn't go out and collect the first that I found, though most any would do. Instead, I took your advice, and I hand-picked three young gentlemen, Mrs. Mackay, who would ride to hell with a whoop if they thought that they could get a shot at the devil. I beg your pardon a lot!"

She was not offended and said so.

"I've come here, ma'am," went on the sheriff earnestly, "prepared for one of the worst jobs that I ever tackled in my life. One where I'd need help, and plenty of it."

"And I think," said she, "that you'll need all you've brought along."

The sheriff actually beamed, and he drew a long breath, as though he were drinking.

"Things was sort of going to pot," he explained, "and I was aiming to change counties, it was so quiet around here. Now maybe you'll give me a little lead? Who are they?"

"I don't know that I should say there is more than one," said Mrs. Mackay.

The sheriff leaned back in his chair.

"Only one!" he echoed.

"And if you'll simply live here for a few days — and look matters over — I hope you won't mind. I don't want to wrong anyone. But —"

"All right," nodded the sheriff. "I'll start cutting for sign. Only — might I ask if you're fearing poison, or murder by night, or something like that?"

"Murder?" said Mrs. Mackay in her quiet voice. "Oh, no, sheriff. It's something a great deal worse than that."

CHAPTER 7

The sheriff went over the place, as the saying goes, with a fine-toothed comb, but all that he could bring forth from his work was a dapper, slender young man — Señor Consalvo.

He broached the subject to the Colonel. He broached it delicately, not hoping that he really had come upon the cause of Mrs. Mackay's profound trouble, but in the spirit of one who leaves no stone unturned. One soul was troubling that lady. A woman or a man — no doubt a man — was upsetting all her tranquillity. And though the sheriff saw nothing in the young Mexican to warrant taking him as the cause of the disturbance, still he could not help taking every possible lead.

The colonel waxed eloquent in reality. Señor Consalvo was a gentleman, he declared, and an exceptional one. About him there floated, said the colonel, the tang, the flavor, the incomprehensible something, of an ancient nobility. The colonel had had many guests but, he declared, no guest had been so delightful, so sympathetic, in both the English and the French meanings of the word, as Don Felipe. He was glad, in short, that the sheriff had noticed that young man. Because, he said, he had not thought that the sheriff would cast his eyes upon such a person.

"And why not cast my eyes?" said the sheriff bluntly.

"Why, sir," said the good-natured colonel, "you are a blunt and rather matter-of-fact fellow, Rankin. You haven't the time, naturally, to observe these delicate creatures — such as this Mexican gentleman, you know!"

"I've known a lot of Mexicans," said the sheriff in combative humor, "but the only thing delicate about them that I ever seen was the way that they slipped a knife between your ribs. Maybe this one is a faker," went on Rankin.

The colonel merely smiled.

"What makes you so sure?"

"No faker," answered the colonel with infinite decision, "ever rode such a beautiful horse."

"Many a horse," said the sheriff, "is a picture, and got nothing but pretty lines."

"I don't mean to say," said the colonel, "that this picture horse has the qualities of one of my proved and registered thorough-breds."

"Well," said the sheriff, "why not make a match race with a good one of yours? Why not see what the young man really is ridin'?"

"An excellent idea!" answered the colonel, for he was fond of sport and regretted his distance not from Manhattan but from the bookmakers. "But why," he added, "do you seem to have such a poor opinion of my friend Consalvo?"

"Me?" said the sheriff. "I got no opinion of him at all, never having laid my eyes on him, but I know that young Budge Lakin has an opinion."

"Who is Budge Lakin," asked the colonel, smiling, "and what might his opinion be?"

"Budge," said the sheriff enthusiastically, "is the straightest-shooting and quickest-drawing young fellow that hasn't had his neck stretched up to this time. I been waiting for him on a murder charge for a few years, but he always contrives to make it self-defense."

"But how does he manage that?"

"By letting the other fellow go for his gun first. He waits just long enough for the other man to be seen by the spectators, and then Budge simply kills him, you see!"

"But I don't see," exclaimed the colonel, "how any man can afford to give a handicap in gun-drawing in these regions where everyone knows how to draw fast and shoot straight."

"If you was born with a talent," answered the sheriff, "and spent about four hours a day cultivatin' it, you'd understand how it is with Budge."

"Ah," said the colonel, "I understand! A real professional, then?"

"He is."

"But what has made him hate Consalvo?"

"Oh, for nothin' more than a girl. Take a man under forty, and when he's got a good hate on you'll usually find a girl at the bottom of it. For that matter, take a man *over* forty and you'll usually find the same thing. But Budge feels that the greaser has stole his girl."

The colonel writhed a little under the impact of these impolite terms, but then he murmured: "What girl, sheriff?"

"By name of Sandy Kane," said the sheriff, "and a straight shootin' little thing I'd call her! It seems that she ain't had much use for Budge since a dance, a while back!"

The colonel remembered the dance, the girl, and the Mexican in one breath. He flushed a little, and nodded.

"Jealousy usually is blind," said the colonel, and twisted his moustaches a trifle.

"That night," said the sheriff, "she seen something or someone that made her hand Budge a frosty eye. He says it's the Mexican, and if you want that young feller to live to a ripe old age, I say that you'd better get him a life guard!"

The colonel was indignantly interested. How anyone in the world could be hostile to such a delightful person as Señor Consalvo was beyond his understanding. But he would, by all means, mention the danger to Don Felipe.

"Lemme know how he takes it," said the sheriff. "And by the way, you might ask him about the race, too!"

The colonel saw no harm in combining the budget of news. He first put the question about the race in the most tactful possible form, asking young Consalvo the blood of his mount; whereat he was told that it traced its ancestry back to one of those magnificent barbs such as the conquistadores rode when they conquered Mexico in the very old days.

When he asked about quality and tests,

the Mexican smiled.

"They are not great sprinters," said he, "but in a five mile race over natural country, uphill and down dale, then I would back Conquistador."

"Is that his name?"

"Yes."

"My friend," said the colonel, his sporting blood rising fast, "I have a mind to take you up on that. I have a stallion in my stables —"

"You mean the bay?"

"Yes. Jerome Second is his name."

"I know him very well."

"Have you seen him gallop?"

"I have seen him exercised over your private track."

"Now tell me, honestly, do you think that your horse, beautiful as he is, would have a chance against the long legs and the breeding of Jerome Second?"

The Mexican made a characteristic gesture with both hands.

"The feet of a horse," said he, "are all that can tell what is in him. Do you suggest a race, señor?"

He asked it rather anxiously, and the colonel remarked:

"It would not be fair. I know what is in Jerome Second."

"And I," said Consalvo, drawing himself up a little, "I, señor, know what is in Conquistador!"

"Confound it, man," said the colonel, "what would five miles be to the long legs and the true heart of my stallion?"

"Almost as little, I hope, as they would be to my horse. Though an all-day race would be more to my taste, sir!"

The colonel flinched.

"All day! I've never heard of such a contest. But for five miles. Are you sure that you want it?"

"Sure, señor, and certain."

"Well, let us go, then. And I'll bet you — I beg your pardon, Consalvo, since you're out hunting your fortune, no doubt you're not in a betting frame of mind!"

The colonel had put it as delicately as he was able, on the spur of the moment, but not delicately enough to prevent a deep flush from stealing over the face of Consalvo, who said with a touch of heat: "I have only this ring to venture, señor. I have been told that it is worth ten thousand pesos. Let me stake it for half that amount."

The size of this wager fairly took the colonel's breath.

"My dear fellow!" he exclaimed, aghast.

"It is too much," said Consalvo, in

apology. "Let us make it less — let us make it half of the sum — let us say, merely a hundred dollars for the sport!"

But the colonel answered, his pride stung:

"A hundred dollars? A hundred devils, Consalvo. You mustn't talk down to me like that."

"I talk down? Señor, you smile as you say it!"

"I'll accept your ring for the ten thousand; ten thousand dollars against it. By heavens, Consalvo, we'll have a real match out of this. But, first of all, you're sure of yourself?"

"As to weights, however?"

"I have a stable boy who will weigh about like you, if I slip a few pounds of lead into his saddle."

"You mean, señor, the professional Negro jockey?"

"He outgrew his work. We can't call him that, any longer. That was the fellow I had in mind, though. Or did you expect," added the colonel, looking down at his embonpoint, "that I'd do the riding against a sliver of a fellow like you?"

"Ah, no," replied the other. "Let us make a race of it, by all means. Tomorrow, if you please!"

So they agreed, and settled a few details, such as the moment for the starting of the race, and the course to be covered, which they judged should be straight up the valley on the western road, and curving around on a cross lane to the eastern road, and so down the valley again, finishing at the ranch house.

When all of this was settled, and only then, the colonel said discreetly: "And by the way, Consalvo, I've heard that there's a fellow who bears a grudge against you for the sake of a girl."

"A girl?" said Consalvo, changing color a little.

"Elizabeth Kane."

"Ah," sighed the Mexican, relieved, as it would seem. "I hardly know her!"

"I thought so. But it was my duty to mention it. He's a young man-killer, by the name of Budge Lakin, as I've heard."

"But to me!" cried the Mexican, extending his graceful arms. "What have I done? What have I said? By heavens, señor, in a time like this one should appeal to the sheriff, and I thank God that he is here with us, under your roof. I shall ask for his protection!"

And, straightway, he did!

CHAPTER 8

The argument of the sheriff was simple and clear.

By the things which cleave to man, and to which he in turn cleaves, he may be judged. And if the horse the Mexican rode turned out, indeed, to be a grand one, then it might appear that Consalvo was something more than a graceful parlor decoration.

On the other hand, by the manner in which the youth bore himself in the danger of Budge Lakin, he might be judged again. And in fact, in the second matter young Consalvo acted with such excitement that even the lip of pretty Mary Mackay curled a little and her blue eyes turned cold.

For Consalvo openly proclaimed even at the dinner table that he was no warrior, no fighting man, and that he demanded the protection of the law against Lakin. The sheriff smiled a little and assured him that he would do what he could.

Mrs. Mackay, on the other hand, seemed much pleased, and in her quiet way she said: "I admire you, Señor Consalvo, for this attitude. We have had enough of the wild young Westerners who go about carrying guns and shooting men as though they were rabbits. I see, indeed, that you follow a higher morality!"

And she smiled gently on the youth.

Mary Mackay, however, scowled at her plate, and writhed in concealed anguish which was not, however, lost on her mother, who smiled genially upon her and commended to her another portion of steak. Mary Mackay seemed not to hear.

Then at the next moment, the talk turned upon the horse-race which had been proposed; and the Mexican showed more signs of life, for the conversation became quite heated as the merits of Jerome Second were brought forward.

He had shaped handsomely as a yearling, trained well, and won his first two-year-old start in magnificent fashion, coming up hard on the bit at the end of the six furlongs, and pulling sweetly away from the rest of a big field, even so. So handsome did his win appear that the colonel, observing, bought the animal on the spot and shipped him West to head his stud on his new ranch.

"And," said the colonel, "you have to

know, Consalvo, in all fairness, that among the colts he beat that day was the three-year-old champion of that season. At least, he had an equal claim on the championship. I mean Ormuzd; you've seen the name!"

At this, Consalvo studied the table and shook his head.

"Ah, well," sighed he at last, "Conquistador never has failed me, and I should be failing him if I scratched him from the race."

"Indeed," said Mary Mackay, "you should!"

She spoke it so meaningly that all heads turned towards her for an embarrassing moment — all save the head of her mother, who appeared not to notice, and who now carried the talk gaily into other channels.

However, the race was set for the next morning, and it was run.

A sort of semi-holiday was declared; all work fell through for the day, and the whole force of cow-punchers, except a vitally necessary few, together with the farmers from the lowlands of the valley, and the lumbermen from the upper reaches of that land, and the sheep herders, and the store-keepers, and all the others on the long, long pay-list of the colonel, foregathered at the appointed time and place to watch the running.

They could have a good view of it, for they could stand on a little hill which looked up and down the ravine floor over which the course was laid out. There the road looped loosely and turned back towards the hill, around whose foot it curved. So that those who stood on the crest could watch every stride of the contest, and, by shifting a little to the side, they could be at the very finish.

All were there, and among the rest the gigantic and sullen Indian, Pedro, stalking slowly from place to place, and turning his night-dark eye upon Conquistador on the one hand, and upon Jerome Second on the other.

They were far different types. To make Jerome Second a picture horse, one would have wished to clip a few inches from his legs — there was such an excessive deal of daylight under him; but otherwise, he was an ideal creature.

Conquistador was manifestly shorter in the legs, but his shoulders had a magnificent slope and the length of his rein promised to make up, somewhat, for the deficiency of stride that showed in his legs.

He bore himself quietly and proudly;

73

whereas Jerome Second, as if he scented the race in the air and hungered for it, danced up and down, and threw his lofty head, and glared fire from his eyes like any dragon.

The Negro on his back, for all that he had been a professional jockey and lived in the saddle ever since weight kept him from the races on the flat, was worried and hard put to it to keep his mount in some order or prevent him from bolting down the road.

The Mexican was full of admiration for the tall thoroughbred. It seemed that he could not help exclaiming as he examined the beautiful creature, and he congratulated the colonel on having such an animal in his stables.

"For," said Don Felipe, "one touch of that fire will last through ten generations!"

"He's leaving his race at the post," exclaimed the colonel. "Confound it, if everyone is here, let's begin the thing. Richards, get out there and drop your handkerchief for the start, and try to do it without scaring Jerome to death. Are you ready, Don Felipe? Are you ready, sir?"

"Ready," smiled the Mexican.

And again, looking askance at Jerome Second, he shook his head deprecatingly.

"He is beaten," said Mary Mackay, in a tone between contempt and disgust, "before the race starts! What a way to go into a contest!"

And she actually turned her head and looked at a cloud blowing out of the tree-angle on the north and then sailing through the blue above the valley.

At this moment the sheriff approached Mrs. Mackay.

"How's your bet on the race, ma'am?" he asked.

"Is there any betting?" she replied. "Oh, I know that my husband got a bet from poor Don Felipe. But I'm going to persuade him not to collect it. Of course the little horse hasn't a chance!"

"Little?" said the sheriff. "He stands within an inch of sixteen hands, I take it! And I've finished betting a couple of hundred myself, on him!"

"Who in the world would take your bets?" asked Mrs. Mackay.

"Your cow-punchers think that Jerome Second is the wind," grinned the sheriff, "and they're offering four and five to one. So I just stepped down and took a chance. You never can tell. Besides, that Señor Consalvo sits the saddle pretty well."

"You have some sort of inside information," declared Mrs. Mackay, with much interest. "Now, what can it be?"

The sheriff hesitated, and then with a still broader grin he pointed at the tall Indian.

"He's got three or four hundred dollars out of his wallet and bet it on his master's horse," said he, "and where the money of the stable goes there's sure to be a bet worth something! They're off!"

At that moment, the handkerchief dropped, and the two horses bounded forward on the road.

Jerome Second, his head high and his ears flattened, floundered for a moment and fell well to the rear, but coming into his stride, presently, he caught the other with what seemed a ridiculous ease, and then flaunted into the lead.

"There you are!" said Mrs. Mackay. "The race is as good as over!"

"Is it?" grinned the sheriff. "I tell you, ma'am, that pony of yours thinks that he's still running two-year-old sprints, and he may kill himself off before they reach the turn. This here is five miles, you got to remember!"

The Negro rider, at least, knew the length of the running, and he was fairly leaning back with the strength of his pull.

Even so, Jerome Second continued to put distance between him and Conquistador until the far turn was reached, and, far in the lead, he turned towards the finish.

"Blood!" said the colonel, striking his hands together. "Blood will tell! The blood of the English race horse will tell, and all this nonsense about the Arab — why, sir, the Arab is two centuries out of date, at the present moment!"

The sheriff merely replied — for he had been addressed: "Look at that!"

And he pointed again to the Indian.

Pedro, muffled in a blanket in spite of the heat, wore a faint smile as he watched the progress of the contest. Certainly there seemed little reason for that smile, for if Conquistador was not losing any more ground, at least it was sure that he was not regaining any of his disadvantage.

His master sat erect in the saddle, seeming to have little knowledge of how a horse is jockeyed to a high speed by throwing the weight towards the withers, or swaying the body in rhythm with the stride.

So they came within a half mile of the finish, towards which the spectators now streamed hastily down the hill.

"Look!" cried the sheriff. "Now comes the tug of war!"

Suddenly Don Felipe had leaned forward, and the stallion beneath him seemed to gather strength and speed; he flung forward, cutting down the distance between him and the leader with every stride.

It was the rider, however, and not the horse, upon whom the sheriff focused his glass at this moment.

"Cool as a cucumber," he murmured to himself. And then, turning directly away from the race, he glanced towards his hostess.

He saw that her hands were clenched, and her face had grown a little pale. She seemed to pay no attention to the race, but, instead, her attention was fixed upon her daughter.

Towards her, in turn, the sheriff looked, and he saw that Mary Mackay had clasped her hands at her breast, her lips parted with the wildest excitement, and with faint nods of her head she kept time with the labor of the runners.

"By God!" whispered the sheriff, to some all hearing ear, "have I got the clue at last?"

He turned to watch the finish.

The voice of the colonel now dominated the scene. He was yelling to his jockey instructions which the Negro could not possibly hear.

"The whip, the whip, you fool! Give him his head! Stop that pull! You're killing him! Now favor him through that soft bit! The whip! The whip!"

It seemed, actually, as though the Negro had heard the voice calling, for with the finish a furlong away, and Conquistador a pair of lengths in the rear, he went to the whip and cut Jerome Second severely.

Nobly, nobly the stallion responded. In his blood lines there appeared the name of no faint-hearted stallion, no weak-souled mare, and he went forward under the whip with a fresh burst of speed.

No whip, on the other hand, flashed above Conquistador. No whip was needed. Straightened like a string from the tip of his nose to the end of his wind-blown tail, he darted arrowlike for the finish. If his stride was shorter than the thoroughbred's, it was more rapid, more smooth with the smoothness of bounding water down a cataract. He gained. He reached the hip, the girth, the head, of Jerome Second.

And suddenly the taller stallion seemed to stagger as though struck; Conquistador, that instant, pricked his ears, and he shot to win by an open length.

CHAPTER 9

When the colonel could speak it was to say: "He sulked, the brute! I'll sell him. No, I'll give him away! Sulked, by heaven!"

As for the Negro jockey, tears were streaming down his face.

"I done what I could, sir," said he. "But that other had the devil in him. He went by, and Jerome, he jus' seemed like he was sick. There was no more running in him! The Indian drugged him, sir. Look at him now!"

Trembling in every limb, head down, blackened with sweat and streaked white with foam, Jerome was the very picture of an exhausted horse.

"And look at that!" said the colonel.

He pointed to Conquistador, nuzzling at his dismounted rider, and with pricking ears stealing, as it were, the sugar lumps from his hand.

"Remember," said Mrs. Mackay gently, "that the winner always seems to be comfortable!"

"Ay," said the wise sheriff, "it's easy to

win after you're once across the finish line. But before that — however, I guessed that there was something in the Mexican's horse. And I guessed" — he said this looking Mrs. Mackay full in the eye — "that there was something in the Mexican!"

Mrs. Mackay said not a word in answer. Her anxious eye was tracing her daughter through the little crowd, and taking note of the fashion in which she greeted Don Felipe, and then rubbed the wet muzzle of Conquistador.

She came back radiant.

She said: "Felipe says that Conquistador has taken a fancy to me. He's not usually so gentle with strangers. But what a *lamb* he is, mother! And how beautifully Felipe rode him!"

Mrs. Mackay answered: "Mexicans are almost born in the saddle, my dear. Of course he rode his horse well. And you know," she added softly, "that the race was worth winning!"

"Money?" said the startled girl. "Oh, Felipe is quite above any thought of that!"

"One knows a man very well before one knows that," said Mrs. Mackay, and her eye wandered a little, and fell upon the face of the sheriff, a keen and intent listener to this little dialogue.

But how did the Mexican take his victory?

He was the height of smiling good humor, and he could be serious, too, for he said gravely to the colonel: "Of course Jerome Second was too anxious. You know, a race horse has to be worked regularly. But coming in fresh and soft from the pasture, so to speak, his nerves were all on edge, and he killed himself off in the first mile. I could see the change. I gave up hope when he darted past me. As though he were thrown out of a sling! What a horse! But then I saw that, as you feared, he'd left his race at the post. Of course, it really wasn't a contest, at all!"

The colonel listened, and he seemed to take some small comfort from this thing.

And so they came back to the house.

In the patio they had tea, and the colonel was fortifying his spirits with whisky and soda, when the sheriff touched his shoulder and leaned above him.

"Colonel Mackay," he said, "I dunno but there may be trouble out there in the barn."

"In the barn?" murmured the colonel. "And why, if you please? There ought to be trouble, though, and there will be trouble, if I have the courage of my convictions and discharge the whole lot of them for a troop of lazy inefficients! What condition was Jerome in? He was soft! The scoundrels have been writing down oats in the bills and feeding my horses hay alone! I'll have an eye to this, by heaven!"

"I mean trouble of a slightly different kind," said the sheriff. "I mean — Señor Consalvo is out there, ain't he?"

"Yes. He's with his horse. He said that he'd come in to tea later. More glory to Conquistador — but I wouldn't own a horse with legs like those!"

"Not about horses, either," insisted the sheriff, "but just now I seen Budge Lakin ride past the patio gate with a cloud of dust around him and a mighty businesslike look about him!"

"Lakin? The fellow who's been threatening Don Felipe's life?" cried the colonel. "In the name of heaven, man, are you going to sit here and wait for a murder —"

At that moment, there was a sound of a double explosion of guns, muffled only slightly by the distance between the house and the barn.

The colonel sprang to his feet; there was a sharp clattering of glasses and dishes; and the hiss of many indrawn breaths.

"Rankin," exclaimed the colonel, "if there's a tragedy in this — I'll hold you personally responsible for gross slackness in the execution of your manifest duty and —"

He was cut short by the scream, sharp and terrible, of Mary Mackay, who ran hurriedly through the patio entrance.

The sheriff alone seemed undisturbed — he and Mrs. Mackay.

"If there's a tragedy," said he, "I got a little idea that 'twon't be the blood of Mr. Consalvo! You wait, my friends, and see. And as for Budge Lakin, he's had trouble comin' to him these many months!"

Then he went with the others slowly towards the noise.

Other sounds had followed the noises of the explosions. There had been great shouts and many voices calling, and as they started from the patio, a white-faced man rushed up to them: "Get a doctor! Who's a doctor here?" he shouted. "He's dying!"

"Who's dying?" asked the colonel, grasping his cow-puncher by both shoulders. "Consalvo has been murdered!"

"Him? It's Budge Lakin that's been shot down, and dyin' he is, if I ever seen a man!"

But Budge was not dying.

Kind providence had made the bullet glance along his ribs, causing him to shed much blood, and think bitter thoughts of death and a life of judgment to come; but, after all, he had not more than a surface ploughing of the flesh to complain of.

Budge was carried to the house on a plank and he lay in a guest room, cursing softly.

"How did it happen?" asked the colonel.

"I come out here to throw a scare into the Mexican," confessed Budge, "and I sure succeeded. I fired a shot over his head and told him to quit the country, and he begged for his life. And then I juggled my gun, and tried to do something fancy, but the damn thing went off, and I plugged myself!"

"You're lyin', ain't you?" said the dry sheriff.

"How d'you know?" exclaimed Budge, amazed. And then he added sullenly: "Ask him, if it ain't so!"

They found the Mexican sitting on a box in a corner of the barn, his face buried in his hands.

"It was the hand of God!" said Don Felipe devoutly. "He struck down the bully! Let Him be praised! This day I vow to the blessed San Guadalupe —"

The sheriff left the colonel and Mary Mackay with Don Felipe, the colonel half amused and half contemptuous, and the girl half contemptuous and half sad and frightened.

He went back to the house and took up the guns of the would-be man destroyer, Budge Lakin, and examined them with care.

"A neat, nice balanced pair, Budge," said he. "And I hear that you got hopes of bein' a regular two-gun man!"

"Humph!" snorted Budge. "I got no ambitions at all. I'm gunna get a job and settle down. This here — it was only a game, today."

The sheriff smiled slowly.

"I've always sort of understood," he said, "that when a gent flashed two guns, he did the missing with the one of 'em and the hitting with the other. But still, it's a strange thing —"

"What?" said Budge.

"Nothin'," said the sheriff, and left the room abruptly.

Outside, however, he sat down and pondered over that same mystery.

It was very odd, thought the sheriff, for in all his long life, he never had heard of a revolver making two loud reports while firing only one bullet.

And certainly there was only one empty chamber in the revolver of Budge Lakin!

CHAPTER 10

Lakin was not the only invalid in the house of the colonel.

The other was the young Mexican, Señor Don Felipe Christobal Hernandez Consalvo. He went to bed also, and gave as a reason the shock which his system had received from the close call he had had with death.

Some of the people who heard of this illness were amused; only Mary Mackay was openly indignant and disgusted; and then the sheriff looked up Mrs. Mackay and found her at a sunny window with her knitting.

"My husband wants to buy Conquistador," said Mrs. Mackay.

"I'd say," said the sheriff, "that he'll never get him."

"And why?"

"Because Don Felipe ain't a fool."

"That isn't the reason he gives."

"What does he say, then?"

"That after his encounter with Budge Lakin, he's so terribly upset and frightened that he is sure that he must have at hand the fastest horse in the world to snatch him away from the teeth of danger — which he feels closing about him — and his destiny —"

"Aw, I know all that Mexican lingo," sighed the sheriff. "I been south of the border and I've heard a lot of it. Fate and destiny and death and life all hashed up together and poured out in one fine sausage. But I dunno, Mrs. Mackay. D'you think that that was the real reason? The one he gave, I mean?"

Mrs. Mackay went on with her knitting, tilting her head gracefully and thoughtfully to the side.

"And what do you think?" she asked rather abruptly, looking up at the sheriff.

"I think," said the sheriff, "that two heads are a lot better than one, ma'am!"

"Of course they are — sometimes. But what has that to do with this matter? Ouch!"

She cried out as a great wasp darted through the open window and flashed its wings in her face.

"Heavens, sheriff," said Mrs. Mackay, "can you be expected to uphold the law when you can't keep a poor woman from being stung to death?"

"Where was you stung?" asked the sheriff.

"I wasn't stung, but I might have been."

The sheriff rolled a cigarette and lighted it before he trusted himself to continue the conversation, and then he said with some remnant of emotion: "When my wife was livin', that was just the sort of a remark that she would of made. Well, ma'am, suppose that we get out of the dark and into the daylight?"

"What dark, sheriff?" asked Mrs. Mackay brightly.

"The dark of foolin' around and pretendin' not to notice the other fellow's ideas," said the sheriff with a touch of heat.

"Really," said Mrs. Mackay, "I don't know what you mean!"

"Don't you?" said the sheriff. "Don't you, ma'am!"

And he sat back in his chair and swung a foot excitedly back and forth — a wonderfully meagre foot and leg to support the reputation of such a man as Rankin.

Then he tried again, and declared bluntly: "I know what your trouble is, I think."

"Oh, do you!" said she, and clasped her hands with a sort of girlish brightness.

"Doggone it, Mrs. Mackay," remarked

the frowning sheriff, "sometimes you can be sort of tryin', can't you?"

"I hope not!" said she, trustfully.

"When I looked things over," said the sheriff, "I seen that there was no possible chance, unless it was among the servants, of anything being wrong in this house. Nothing possible except the greaser — I mean, Don Felipe. Excuse me, ma'am!"

"It's quite all right," said she, and resumed her knitting.

"I looked at him and I said that sure he was a safe man, all right. And yet, there's nothing like trying. I started to try him out. Like horse like master! Same as with dogs. I worked up the race. And it seemed to me, ma'am, that Don Felipe, he rode like a man, and his horse ran like a horse!"

"I suppose it did," answered she.

"Ma'am," said the sheriff, "would you mind doin' me a first-rate favor?"

"Certainly not!"

"Then lay down them doggone knitting needles and look me in the eye while I'm talkin'!"

Mrs. Mackay laid the needles aside obediently and then sat up straight, and folded her small hands, and looked at the sheriff out of mild, large blue eyes.

The sheriff blinked.

"All right," said he. "You're gunna make me work it all out for you, and then, if you agree, you'll say yes at the end. But the second thing that happened today was something more!"

"Oh, you mean the terrible accident?"

"Accident, ma'am?" said the sheriff.

"But what else would you call it?"

"Well, I'm gunna tell you just what happened, so far as anybody knows. Budge Lakin comes pilin' out to the barn and throws himself off of his horse. 'Where's the Mexican?' he hollers, and one of the stable boys points out where Mr. Consalvo is. Budge disappears in search of him. There's a couple of reports. And the boys run in — after a minute allowed to get over the shivers — and they find Mr. Consalvo on his knees beside Budge, who's bleeding bad, and holding Budge by both shoulders, and talking to him hard and fast."

"Yes," said she.

"Now, after that, Mr. Consalvo got a terrible case of nerves, and he pretty near threw a fit, and he said that God had saved him from bein' killed, and what not."

"But certainly it seemed that way!"

"Hold on, ma'am! When that race was bein' run, did you ever see a man ride cooler or steadier, or with more nerve?"

"I know very little about such things."

"I doubt it!" said the blunt sheriff. "I've seen you ride, yourself. And I've watched. But wasn't it sort of queer that Don Felipe should of gone so much to pieces right after the shooting that he had to go to bed and take sal volatile, and what not?"

"I never thought of that."

"I think that you have, though," declared the grim sheriff. "Only you wouldn't help me along by admitting nothing. But now I'm gunna speak up loud and bold, ma'am!"

"Of course you may speak as loudly as you please, sheriff," said she. "Shall I close the window?"

The sheriff, instead of shouting as he had threatened, leaned forward and whispered: "During that race, I watched Miss Mary!"

At this, Mrs. Mackay started ever so slightly and reached automatically for her knitting, but the sheriff snatched it away.

"No, no!" said he. "Look me in the eye and tell me if I'm a fool or a wise man. The thing that bothered you more than the danger of poison or murder was that this here smooth talking, grinning greaser — that he'd up and marry your girl. Ain't that right?"

Mrs. Mackay did not speak. She merely stared.

"He's got the colonel hypnotized," went on the sheriff in the same insidious whisper. "And your daughter, she couldn't keep her eyes off of him!"

"Until the shooting accident! Then, of course, she began to despise him!"

"Do you really think that she did?"

"Haven't you heard what she said about the poor fellow? Of course he can't help his nerves when they get the better of him."

"Nerves?" said the sheriff, rising to his feet. "I tell you that there's more nerves in the hard hoof of Conquistador than there is in the whole make-up of that same young gent!"

Mrs. Mackay rose also. She seemed horrified.

"Oh," she cried, "do you mean to insinuate that he — that he's playing a part?"

"I don't mean to insinuate nothing else," said the sheriff firmly, "and you don't mean nothing else, either! We understand each other perfect!"

"I'm sure that I don't know what you mean!"

"You do, though, but I'll tell you a little more exact what happened when Budge

Lakin walked into that barn. No, I don't *know;* but I just the same as know. Well, ma'am, when Budge come in, he seen the Mexican, and he got ready for a slaughter. There ain't a thing that Budge likes so well as a gun-fight. I mean there ain't a thing up to today. But I miss my guess if he ever pulls a gun again so long as he lives! He's got a changed look in his eyes, I tell you, and it ain't the loss of blood that's changed him!"

Mrs. Mackay seemed frozen with interest.

"Mind you," went on the sheriff, "it sure looks like a slaughter. For here's the slender Mexican, all dolled up like a joke, almost. And about as sensitive as a girl, you'd say! And on the other hand, here's Mr. Lakin cool as they come, working out with his guns hours every day, practicing his draw, and thinking of nothin' but blood and death, as they say in the books.

"But what happens?

"Why, Mr. Lakin, he outs with a couple of double-jointed insults and swears a little, and announces what he's gunna do. And then he goes for his gun to do it. He's never failed and he's been there before. He knows he's about the fastest man in the world, pretty near. But what he knows doesn't pan out. He gets out his gun as fast as ever. But the Mexican beats him to it and puts a bullet right through him — or what should have been right through him, except for the luck of the devil that played on Lakin's side, just then. And Lakin's gun goes off and drills a hole in the roof, or punches through the floor, I dunno which! That, ma'am, is what really happened out there in the barn!"

CHAPTER 11

When Mrs. Mackay had heard this startling re-statement of the event, her eyes grew a little larger and her mouth became an O.

"But," she said, "but —"

"But," interrupted the sheriff, "how come it that he would play the coward afterwards? Well, after he'd dropped young Lakin, he leaned over him and grabbed him by the shoulders and says to him: 'Look here, Lakin, there's still a spark of life in you, but I'll put it out now unless you talk turkey. This is the yarn you'll spin — that you fired both the shots, and that the second one hit you by accident, when you were doing the double-roll. And if you welsh on that story, Lakin, or if you ever let a soul in the world guess that I shot you, I'll find you, Lakin, and by the love of' — excuse me, ma'am — 'I'll fill you fuller of lead than any herring ever was filled with salt!' That's what he said to Lakin, and Lakin believed him. And that was why there was the queer look about Budge's eyes when I talked to him. He seemed sort of in a dream, and believe me when I say that dream was a nightmare!"

"I've never heard any supposition so extraordinary!" said the lady.

"Ain't you?" grinned the sheriff. "You didn't guess out something like this yourself, I suppose? No, maybe not. Because you figure that he wouldn't of purposely made a fool of himself before your girl. But you forgot something else. Maybe he was worse scared of being known to be a man-killer than he was afraid of losing the favor of Miss Mary."

Mrs. Mackay said at last, "I've never had anyone talk to me so frankly. But it's made me know that I'm right. My husband took Don Felipe for an extraordinarily charming and helpless young Mexican. But I didn't! There was only one thing he said that I believed!"

"And what was that?"

"He admitted that he'd left his country to try to find treasure. I believed that! Yes, but I don't think that he'll ever blister his hands working for it! Only — no — I didn't imagine that he was such a desperate character as you suggest. And yet — there's something about him that fits in with what you say. He has a cold look in his eyes, now and then!"

The sheriff shuddered.

"There ain't any need to describe that look," he said. "I've felt it, a couple of times, when my back was turned, and it sent the chills through me!"

Mrs. Mackay frowned.

"But he couldn't suspect you of being here to — to — well, to investigate him!"

"If he's what I pretty well know that he is," said the sheriff, "there ain't much that he wouldn't suspect a sheriff of doing. He hates me like poison. His smile turns to wood when I come near him. And maybe I'm gunna have a chance to make him realize that all he guesses about me is true! Only — whatever I do, I got to do it quick!"

He began, at this, to walk nervously up and down the room.

"Because," said the sheriff, "if I leave, there may be trouble while I'm gone. And if I stay, there's *more* than sure to be trouble. Oh, I tell you that he has his eye on me! He knows that I could finish his trick!"

"You could?" exclaimed Mrs. Mackay. "How could you finish it, Mr. Rankin?"

"There's never a crook as polished and smooth as he is," said the sheriff, "without there being a record behind him. And there's never a record that can't be looked up somewhere. And if the police on this side of the border ain't got it, the police on the other side have. And inside of a couple of days of work, I got an idea that I can work up all the details. He'll be known; and his horse'll be known too. Unless I'm reaching in the fog, that horse has saved him more than money, before to-day!"

"What else do you mean?"

"His hide," said the sheriff roughly.

"You mustn't stay here another minute!" said Mrs. Mackay. "I asked you out here to help me through a great problem. You've guessed what my problem is. Now I can see yours. But your men will be here before long!"

"Sure they will," said the sheriff, "but what good would they be in a polite and careful game like this? They can understand if you show them a target to shoot at. But what else are they good for? They'd call the Mexican a sissy, ma'am!"

"I suppose they would," she nodded. "Then you must leave at once. Suppose that he *should* suspect! Suppose that he *should* feel that you must be — must be —"

"Shot?" filled in the sheriff briskly.

"B-r-r!" shivered the lady. "Of course I'm not really afraid of that, because I know what a famous lot of things you've —"

"Humph," said Sheriff Rankin. "Famous bunk and fiddlesticks! If you ain't scared for me, I'm scared for myself. I'd rather be dropped into a den of rattlers at midnight than dropped in the way of that fancy-shooting young devil. I never fought for fun in my life, ma'am; and I never felt less like getting into trouble than I do now. And at the same time —"

As he spoke the last words, he raised his voice even louder than before, and side stepped rapidly towards the window. Out of this he suddenly leaned, and barked in a sharp tone: "Get out of there, Pedro! You're spoilin' the garden!"

Mrs. Mackay ran to look.

There was a private patch of her garden spotted underneath that window, to be sure, and the bare feet of Pedro were standing in the garden sod, while he looked up with sullen respect to the sheriff.

"What are you doing there?" repeated the lady of the house, adding to the sheriff, "Of course, he doesn't understand a word of English!"

But she had made her question in Spanish, and the Indian slowly brought his hand from behind his back and exposed in its fingers a small bunch of little red roses, such as blossomed at that season on the climbing rose vine.

Mrs. Mackay was touched.

"The poor thing!" said she. "There's the Latin love of beauty for you! Now, what one among our cow-punchers would have wasted any time in stealing flowers or even in begging them? You may have all that you want, Pedro!" she said, leaning farther out the window and smiling beautifully down on the great creature. "Just be careful that you don't crush things with your feet, won't you?"

At this appeal, the face of the great fellow lightened a little, and a strange, twisted smile of happiness appeared on his lips. Something he muttered in a husky voice, and bowed, almost with worship, to the lady of the house. Then he withdrew, and he went off with his usual soft, long strides.

"How silently he goes!" said Mrs. Mackay, still leaning to watch him. "Even when the cat runs on that gravel I can hear it; but not a sound from that man. However, size doesn't always count. They say that the elephant can go through the jungle without noise."

"And the moose," said the sheriff hastily. "I been nearly smashed from behind by one that I was looking for ahead of me. Now, what d'you make of that Indian?"

"I don't know," said Mrs. Mackay thoughtfully. "I've thought that perhaps if he were approached tactfully, you know, and with a little persuasion, he might be induced to tell something about his handsome young master!"

She turned to Rankin as she spoke, and he answered with a mocking nod.

"If all those flowers was gold pieces," said he, "and all the leaves on those vines was silver, and you could collect 'em all and pour down all that money at the feet of that Indian and then beg him to tell us one doggone syllable of the truth about his boss, d'you know what he'd do?"

"Do you think he loves his master as much as that?"

"Love him? I don't know," replied Rankin. "But I do know that he's mortal scared of him."

She studied this new phase carefully.

"I suppose you're right," she said at last, "and this man Consalvo —"

"Or whatever his name is," said the sheriff.

"Whatever his name is," she accepted the emendation, "is really a formidable person. But don't you think —"

"Hum," said the sheriff.

"Are you thinking of something, sheriff?"

"I am."

"And what, please. Because we're complete partners now, aren't we?"

"I'm thinkin' of Pedro," said the sheriff, "and the blank look of him when I yelled from the window."

"He didn't start," said she.

"He should of," said the sheriff.

"But he doesn't know English."

"Neither does a mule," said the sheriff, "but a mule jumps out of his skin when I yell at him the way I yelled at that Indian."

He continued moodily:

"When I yelled, a sort of a wriggle went up and down his back. But he waited a minute before he straightened up."

"What on earth do you mean by that?"

"Wouldn't you guess, now? A smart woman like you?"

"I'm not. I'm very silly and vague, and my brain is simply spinning with this whole affair."

"It meant, ma'am, by my way of thinking, that the scoundrel was out there spying on us."

"But not knowing the language —"

"Ma'am, any poker face can hide more knowledge than that!"

"Heavens!" cried Mrs. Mackay. "If he understood what we were talking about!"

"Ay," said the gloomy sheriff, "if he did! And by the wriggle that went down his back I judge that he did. His nerves was all fixed and set against the shock. He waited — so's I wouldn't think that he knew what I was saying. But he waited too long. When you slap a wolf in the face, it doesn't stop to ask what language you're doin' it in!"

CHAPTER 12

Lydia Mackay, like one exhausted, leaned back in her chair and pressed her hand across her eyes.

"The moment your men come, you could trump up some excuse and arrest him!"

"Trumped up excuses don't go in this country. What could I arrest him for? Winning a race? Not getting himself shot?"

"We can go to my husband and tell him what we think!"

"The colonel would only smile. He knows men pretty well. He's had a lot of experience, I mean. Would he listen to us? Mrs. Mackay, stay here and run this end of the game as well as you can. I'm going to head for town and look for the records of a handsome young gent that rides a fine horse and speaks Spanish like a native. That ought to lead to something!"

He went straight to the door and there Mrs. Mackay overtook him and took one of his bony hands in both of her soft ones.

"Whatever you do, be careful of yourself, Mr. Rankin," she said. "People have told me that this county never could be run, if it weren't for you. Now I understand why. You've looked through this whole mysterious tangle as if it were a bit of crystal. Everything that you suspect, I feel also. My poor dear Mary is only a child. But she doesn't know it. She thinks that she has a mind to make up for herself. And heaven knows what may come of it. If there's anything to be done — anything to make away with this danger — oh, Sheriff Rankin, do it quickly!"

The sheriff nodded, compressed his lips a little, and left the house.

He passed Mary Mackay in the patio and thought that her expression was particularly black.

"How's the invalid?" he asked.

"He? Consalvo? Oh, he's up again, I think!"

What utter contempt!

"A narrow squeak for him," said the sheriff.

The girl said nothing, but looked back to her book; yet it did not escape the sheriff that the leaf she was holding trembled though there was no wind, and her head was bent unnecessarily low.

He almost hesitated and spoke again, before he realized that this was the very time for silence; after that he went slowly on towards the barn, much disturbed, for he was enough of a practical psychologist to understand that the very violence of the girl's disgust and contempt must have meant a feeling of quite another sort beforehand.

And what she once had felt she might feel again.

If she were to guess, for instance, what he guessed, that the young Mexican was just the opposite of the cowardly part he was playing, what would her reaction be? Not suspicion or chagrin, he felt sure!

So, at the barn, he saddled his mustang and climbed on its back, and so headed it across the hills. He was just going for a little slant towards the mountains, he said.

Once well out of sight of the whole establishment of Mackay, he turned sharply to the right and began to angle towards the town.

The mustang was suited excellently for this sort of business, for though it might not be able to muster any great speed, yet it could gallop all day long and buck the saddle off at the end of the trip, and its wise feet hardly cared whether they went over rough or smooth. Many a speedy running horse carrying some violator of the law had learned to his cost that the little mustang and his withered little fly-weight rider would not be denied — if only the race were long enough!

So the sheriff made excellent progress across the roughest sort of going, and he was more than half way towards the town, where the telegraph and telephone and his own records would put him in touch with the criminal knowledge of the southwest, when something glanced up behind him, and, casting a look over his shoulder, he was aware of Don Felipe on Conquistador.

The sheriff halted, and faced about; and, without thinking what he was doing, his hand went down to his cased rifle. No, rifle-work would be too slow, if this youth were what the sheriff thought.

Up came Conquistador, running with a marvellous lightness and ease.

"You'd never think he was in a race yesterday," admired the sheriff.

"Would you not?" said the youth. "I saw you ahead, señor," he went on, taking off his hat and making his usual low bow of greeting, "and therefore I came after you. I suppose that you are riding to town?"

"Me? Nope. I'm just wandering around getting a little exercise."

"Ah, yes," said Consalvo. "I understand!

To sit all day in a great house and listen to talk — it makes some people very weary."

"But not you, Señor Consalvo?"

"I? Alas, señor, I am as one of those butterflies that pass idly from flower to flower — sun myself on a green leaf — and fly on again. There is no pleasure to me except in aimlessness, and no joy except in every moment for itself. You see, señor, that I am not one of the burden-bearers of the world. I realize my faults and weaknesses. They are almost feminine, perhaps! But I admit the greatness and the nobility of other and stronger men. However, señor, we are as God made us, are we not? I have prayed to the blessed and powerful saints to intercede for me, for I have managed nothing, as yet. And when even prayer will not accomplish a thing, why should man with his puny power attempt to do it?"

In this manner Don Felipe babbled aimlessly on, making gestures with both his graceful hands, and guiding his stallion merely by the touch of his knees.

The sheriff observed and admired this singular youth. Either Don Felipe was a great fool, or a great actor. Still the sheriff could not decide which, and he determined to bring the matter to a head instantly. Delay he did not mind, in ordinary matters, and he was as willing as any man to use the patience of the snake or the hunting cat.

Now, however, too much depended upon a swift solution of the problems which were before him, and he determined to strike without warning. After all, the highest moral right was on his side, in thus breaking the law of fighting men, no matter of what nation.

"Consalvo!" he said suddenly and sharply.

"Señor?"

"I want your real name!"

And so saying, the sheriff whipped out his revolver.

He found himself covering blank nothingness where recently a man had been seated on the back of the stallion and the same instant a revolver exploded under the neck of Conquistador.

It was the old Indian trick of dropping down the side of one's horse and shooting whether arrow or bullet under the neck of the animal; but the sheriff, though he had seen the trick a thousand times before, never had dreamed that it could be managed with such a neat facility.

He had no time to wonder or ponder. While his gun hung in the air, for that fifth

111

part of a second, the weapon of Consalvo exploded and a well-aimed bullet sped for the forehead of the sheriff.

Good fortune saved the sheriff then. By all tokens, he should have died on the spot, but the gun whose shot had been delayed was now poised high before him, and the slug encountered it, tore it from the hand of the sheriff, and dashed the Colt into his face, so that he reeled and toppled headlong from the saddle.

By the time his spinning wits had recovered their equilibrium, and his eyes cleared, he saw that Don Felipe was sitting on a rock beside him, and with a clean white handkerchief, the Mexican was binding a cut in the sheriff's forehead.

"I thought I was dead," said Rankin soberly, "and that you was the first devil I met in hell. But you turn out different, Consalvo!"

"Alas, señor," said Consalvo, making an appealing gesture with both hands, "you frightened me almost to death! Was it only a joke that you were playing?"

The sheriff, seeing that both hands were engaged, made a swift movement to snatch out his second revolver, for he intended to die fighting, on this occasion of his first defeat.

The gun already had been taken, and Rankin saw that he was helpless.

He pushed himself into a sitting posture; the bandaging was completed that moment.

"You'll have a bad headache for a minute or two," commented Don Felipe. "But after that, nothing will be wrong. There is no fracture. Everything is well with you! The skin is hardly broken. There will be a little black and blue place, however, in the center of the forehead. And that is all. It is where Señor the Sheriff accidentally struck his head against a low branch, while riding through the woods —"

The sheriff had fallen into a deep trance, so it seemed. He stared before him, and he saw no created thing, but only his own thoughts.

"And I didn't get in a single shot!" said he.

"Señor, your gun hung in the holster. I myself saw it!" said the Mexican, in the most conciliatory manner. "It was the shock of fear that enabled me to strike back; and it was luck that made me succeed. How otherwise could I ever have succeeded in — in answering the question of Señor Rankin, that famous man?"

Rankin, curiously looking into the face

113

of the youth, saw that he was not speaking with a sneering smile, but rather with the most open-eyed innocence.

"By God," said the sheriff, "you remind me a terrible lot of somebody!"

"Do I?" said the other, and seemed delighted at this notice. "Señor, señor, who could it be?"

The sheriff grunted.

"Oh, damnation, Consalvo, or whatever your right name is," said he, "won't you stop this damn fooling and talk straight to me? Lead me to the place where you're gunna dump a bullet through my head, because I'm pretty tired of this damn play-acting, and I'd just as soon have the thing finished."

CHAPTER 13

The sheriff said this with an air of real annoyance and impatience, but Don Felipe threw both his hands out in a wide gesture, and then drew up his shoulders in such deprecation as was worth much to see.

He closed his eyes; he leaned back a little and raised his eyes to the dusky sky of the early evening.

"Murder, Sheriff Rankin!" said he. "Murder! Good heavens! To connect me with such a thing! Murder! Would you have me kill you in cold blood?"

At this, the downright sheriff could contain his feelings no longer, and he burst out, with bitterness: "Look here, Consalvo, there ain't any audience. There ain't any use. Be yourself. Be nacheral. By which I mean, what good does it do you to go on acting your little part?"

"Ah, Señor Rankin," said the other, "it hurts me very much to hear you say this! I have been looking up to you as to a great man, a colossal figure" — he magnified the diminutive form of the sheriff with a great sweep of his eloquent hands — "a hero of the frontier, and now you descend to such speech —"

"Son," said the sheriff, "my Spanish has pretty near given out, and I'll have to start cussing you in plain English before long!"

"I would endure it," said Don Felipe with a patient air, "because when I was even a child, señor, the good father priest, who taught me, made me learn the value of forbearance!"

"Friend," answered the sheriff, "shall I tell you where you learned patience?"

"Tell me, then."

"From seein' the way that a cat sits by a mousehole!"

The sheriff grinned a twisted smile as he made his observation. But the Mexican replied gravely: "To him who wears smoked glasses, all the world is dark. Believe me, señor, when I say to you with all my heart that I am not an evil man in all the ways you think."

"You are not," answered Rankin with much sourness. "You're a lamb, Consalvo. A damn lamb, and the point is that you'll never be shorn till somebody sinks a bullet in you."

"Let us forget all talk about guns," said the Mexican with earnestness.

"You hate 'em, don't you?" said the sheriff. "You hate 'em like poison. But you've practiced enough with 'em to be able to make a quicker draw than Budge Lakin or me!"

"As for Señor Lakin," said the Mexican, "of course the terrible accident that happened to him was a great shock to me and —"

"Quit it!" barked the sheriff.

Don Felipe was silent, and rolled a cigarette.

"You fair choke me," explained the sheriff. "I seen that only one shot was fired out of the kid's guns. Where did the other one come from, then? Because there was two shots fired! Why, hell, Consalvo, it's as plain as day. And even if you'd shown nothing against him, the trick that you've turned on me was as pretty and smooth as I ever seen in my life."

"As for Señor Lakin," said the Mexican seriously, "it well may be that he loaded another shell into his gun to take the place of the second —"

"Well, and how did you happen to do the old Indian trick and nail me, Consalvo?"

"I was terrified when you spoke so sharply and moved for your gun. Naturally I dropped for protection. And then it happened that I acted instinctively. In my youth I was much with the wild Indians on my father's estate. They had taught me many of their tricks, and that was one of them. I hung by one hand in the mane and the heel of one foot. But what should I do? Hang there forever? No, no! So, filled with fear, I snatched out a gun and fired blindly —"

"It's smooth," said the sheriff. "It's mighty smooth and pretty neat, altogether. But it won't half do, old son. It simply won't begin to do, I got to admit to you. No, Consalvo, you're an old hand and a rare one. And if God ever made me look a killer in the eyes, I'm lookin' at one right now!"

Don Felipe sighed, and answered nothing at all.

"The remaining question is," said the sheriff, "what and when, so far as I'm concerned?"

"Why, I help you back on your horse, señor, and hope that soon you will recover from the ugly bump you received when riding so unluckily close beneath the tree —"

The sheriff stared, and then he swore softly and fluently for a moment. After that, he shook his head.

"Oh, God, Consalvo," said he, "you are

a deep one! I thought so before. Now I see just how slick you are! I'm square, and you know it. I see through you, and you know it. You don't want to have a murder on your hands, right now when you're playin' your game with the little lady in the big house, yonder. So you'll do a cleverer thing. You'll turn me loose, because then I can't squeal on you! Is that it?"

"What a way to put such an action!" exclaimed Don Felipe.

"Ugly, ain't it? But now, Consalvo, I'll tell you where I stand. I ain't clever, and I ain't smooth. But I'm honest. And being honest, I got to do my job the way that I swore I'd do it when I took my office. You know what that means. To uphold the law and capture its breakers. If I was loose, my friend, I'd have you behind the bars in two days, if I could catch you. And if guns were needed to bring you down, I'd use guns, and a posse to shoot 'em! That, Consalvo, is where you stand with me. I've spoke my piece. Now you can play the rest of your own game. The cards are all in your hands, right up to the aces."

The sheriff then cleared his throat, and, sitting back in turn against the rock at his back, he rolled a cigarette with perfect calm and lighted it, then, blowing out the inhalations with a deliberate enjoyment, he watched them rise and dissolve in the air far above his head.

So, for some moments, Don Felipe watched him, and the sheriff watched the smoke. Silence lived between them. They could hear in the nearby trees the noises of birds returning to their nests and settling down with many little musical family squabbles.

"Alas! Alas!" sighed Don Felipe. "O Dio mio!"

The sheriff turned his head and regarded his conqueror with a sort of dissociated interest.

"It is as I feared," continued Don Felipe. "How much better if the bullet had flown straight and true to the mark, and taken away your life, señor! How much better for me, and perhaps for you, also!"

He waited, but the sheriff made no remark, and Don Felipe entered into a soft-voiced soliloquy.

"Observe how part of our life is used, and the rest wasted! When we are children, we are burdens to our parents. They love us because they begot us and because we come to endure their caresses. We grow older and enter our young manhood. We must be taught, and still we are a drain.

And after we have been taught, we are cast out into the world, or led gently by the hand into it. It hardly matters! In both cases, soon the friction of real life begins. On some of us it raises callouses. From others it simply removes the skin, and leaves them naked spirits in a hard world — naked and sensitive souls like mine, señor."

"Hell!" commented the sheriff briefly.

The younger man flowed charmingly on, carried away by his own thoughts, picking his words with some care, delighted with the music and the rhythm of speech.

"And after all these periods, at last a man enters upon his age of usefulness. It is a short age. Soon his little store of original ideas is consumed. Though he goes through the gestures and though he uses many words, he is saying nothing except what he has said before. Upon part of the world these empty gestures make an impression; to the very end of his doddering old age a portion among mankind will believe in him as he sinks into the grave, mumbling nothingness. But to a few it is given to see that there is no great virtue except wisdom, and that there is no great vice except folly. And to those of us who have such a perception, it appears that we are walking among men who either are green and useless, or withered and fit to fall. And perhaps so it is with you, señor! Perhaps so it is with you."

He made another pause.

But the sheriff merely yawned, and then said: "It's getting sort of cold here on the ground, Consalvo. Are you about done?"

Consalvo sighed once more.

"You have done many things," said he. "You have made yourself a great name. You are one of those figures who, when they are seen from the future, will appear great, and cast a broad shadow which will swallow the names and the fames of ten million lesser creatures. But now I fear that you have reached the crest and that you must begin to fall! You must descend at last! How much better, then, if you had died in battle against a foeman worthy of yourself even when you were in your first and earliest prime! But, no! Fate chose to divert the bullet!"

"Son," said the sheriff, a little stirred, "the way that I was ten years ago, I would of shot the whites out of your eyes before you had time to blink twice!"

"Self-confidence is a noble thing," said the Mexican gently. "How I love to see it. Pride, pride is the greatest of virtues! All that is good and great must spring from it. And yet, señor, never in your life have you been as I am, whether with horse or dog, with gun or with woman —"

He paused and dusted a speck from his sleeve.

"Never, señor," he said with a soft finality.

The sheriff broke in: "If you've talked yourself out, my young friend, I wish that you'd cut it short and finish with me. Because I'm beginning to hate the look of you!"

"I should," said the Mexican gravely, "I should take you at your word and finish you. But a foolish scruple holds me back. Never have I drawn a weapon on a helpless man!"

"If that holds you back, hand me my gun, will you?"

"It would be more proper. It would be better. But still it would be useless. To me God has entrusted an ineffable and terrible power. In the old tales, the great knights tilted and lesser men fell before them as by witchcraft. A touch of the spear of Lancelot, and a dozen common warriors fell softly to the dust. A wave of his sword, and a score of giants shrank blinded into their castles. And so to me, also, a power had been given —"

He leaned, picked up a stone, and tossed it high into the air.

"— to conquer with ease. A gift, and not a labor to me, my dear Señor Rankin."

A gun exploded from his hand. How it came into his fingers the sheriff could not tell. And the stone, dropping swiftly towards the earth, was snuffed out. Only a shower of dust descended lightly.

"I cannot pistol you in cold blood. In the heat of action, as you led on your posse — ah, that would be another matter. But as the matter stands — no, you must live."

"Son, I've explained the danger to you!"

"Live, but not at large," said the other. "You place a great burden upon us. Already our hands were filled. Mrs. Mackay is almost as dangerous as you. Or shall I say: She is far more dangerous? Yes, I shall. Oh, wonderful, graceful, delicate, and terrible creature! If she were younger, nothing could keep me from her. If she were a beggar in the street, I should have taken her and raised her, till she could have raised me. Beautiful and noble Lydia Mackay — weighted down and tied to an ass, who does not even see the danger in her mild eyes! Be sure, señor, that the duel I fight with her sends me to bed at night with a weight on my brain and exhaustion in my soul. To endure for five minutes the calm question of her eyes is a torment worse than all the pains of hell. I have endured, not once but many times. I see her, as it were, raise a lantern above her head and throw the long shaft of the light far, far within the shadowy depths of my secret soul. Already she has seen too much. She has seen the glint of the steel, and the hidden weapons. And now, while I combat with her, I must divide my forces and keep you a prisoner, also. So you understand, Señor Rankin, why it is that I am sad?"

"My lad," replied the sheriff, "what I see is enough to make me sort of sad that you ain't an honest man. If you could use your gift of gab, say, like an honest man, what a hell-cracking politician you'd make! Why, they'd change the laws so's you could be president before you was thirty! You're gunna jail me, are you?"

"I am. I must. Unless — for the last time — you will give me your parole? Unless you will swear —"

"I love cussing," said the sheriff, "but I hate swearing."

"Simply pass me your ordinary word that you will know nothing about me —"

"And give up all chance of squaring things with you?"

"No. Only for two weeks."

"Two years of hell, you might as well say!"

"Give me a week, then. Give me only five days, and you go as free as ever you were in your life. And at the end of the five days, you can take my trail! Agree, sheriff!"

"Consalvo," said the sheriff, "in five days you'd finish your job."

"Perhaps and perhaps not," argued the other. "I have Mrs. Mackay against me. She is a terrible force. Even with an extra pair of ears serving me, she almost circumvented me."

"The Indian understands English, then?"

"As well as you do, señor."

"Well, I thought that! You're going to steal the girl, Consalvo?"

"Steal her?" said he. "Good heavens, señor, am I a fool?"

"What will you do, then?"

"I, simply, will be forced, persuaded, dragged into a marriage against which I protest from the first. I shall be dragged, not by my overwhelming love for her, but by her own persuasions!"

Consalvo paused and smiled genially.

"Man," said the sheriff, considering, "I dunno but what you're plain and plumb nutty! D'you think that anything could make a fine, high-strung, well-bred, delicate girl like that, proud as the devil, already ashamed of you for the way you treated yourself after the affair with Budge Lakin — d'you think for a minute that she'd ever urge you to marry her?"

"It is difficult," agreed Don Felipe. "Oh, it is extremely dangerous and difficult work, and a single misstep will ruin me. The idiot Lakin already nearly has destroyed all my work. I must walk over quicksands. And yet, señor, I would not have it otherwise. What is the victory, unless it is dearly won? What is the glory, unless there is peril with it?"

"Glory? Glory?" said the sheriff in a rising voice.

"We have come," said the other, "to a point where we are separated by a difference in definitions. But now, señor, the time is not far off when I must go home to dinner, and ride past the cow-punchers, who will scowl at the weak and cowardly Mexican. Will you come with me, at once?"

CHAPTER 14

They waited dinner for the sheriff.

Felipe Christobal Hernandez Consalvo was much concerned and offered to ride out to explore the country.

"It would hardly be safe, Don Felipe," said Mrs. Mackay gently. "You know, there are apt to be rough men abroad, at this hour. I hardly would vouch for the safety of the roads. Would you, Mary dear?"

And she leaned a little towards her daughter in anxious inquiry.

Mary, playing a softly fingered tune at the piano, struck a loud and sudden discord.

"I don't know!" she said fiercely, and began to play with a noisy abandon.

"We'll have to sit down before long," said the colonel. "Odd that Rankin didn't leave word that he would be away for a while."

"But, my dear, something may have come up — he has a thousand things to think of, you know!"

A moment later a cow-puncher rode in

with the evening mail. And among the rest was a ragged scrap of paper, of just the size of that which fitted into the sheriff's notebook. On it was written: "Mighty sorry. Met with business while I was riding, and I'll have to be away for a few days. Will you please just send my boys to town? Will explain when I get back."

This note was signed with the sheriff's name, and the eyes of Mrs. Mackay brightened as she read.

"The poor dear sheriff," said she. "What a dreadful life for a man to lead!"

"Every man's business looks pretty mysterious to those who are not in it," declared the colonel conclusively. "I suppose that he wouldn't take up other work if he could! And then, he's a single man, of course."

"Of course," said Lydia Mackay, "and no doubt that makes him braver. Shall we go in to dinner, then?"

They went in, except Mary, who had to be called twice before she left the piano.

"I'm not hungry," said Mary gloomily. "I — I'm going up to lie down. Where's Tag? Has anybody seen Tag?"

"You must eat your meals, child," said the colonel.

"I had too much for lunch."

"You hardly touched your food at noon," answered the father severely.

"I want Tag," said Mary. "Who's seen him?"

"I think he was out playing with the men," said Don Felipe. "They were having him climb the rope ladder to the top of the bunk house, you know. May I get him for you? Please let me!"

"No," said Mary. "NO! I'll get him myself!"

And she swirled out of the house.

Dinner for the "hands" being a good deal earlier than that in the big house, she found the cow-punchers taking their ease in the cool of the evening.

"Where's Tag?" she asked.

"He's taken a fancy to the top of the house, ma'am," said someone.

And, at that moment, there was a shrill barking from the top of the bunk house.

"I want him down at once," said she. "You haven't any right to take him up to such a dangerous place. Where's the ladder?"

There was a narrow rope ladder that sometimes was thrown up from the upper end window of the bunk house so that it hooked over the edge, and up that ladder Tag loved to climb when he was in the slightest degree encouraged.

He was a little Irish terrier, with a wise beard and a pair of sparkling eyes, and he loved battle with a consuming devotion.

"Somebody took the ladder away to see what Tag would do," was the answer. "But Tag don't seem to mind it. Hey, Charlie, where's the rope ladder?"

"I dunno. I didn't have it," answered Charlie, from within.

"I don't care how you get Tag, but I want him in the house — in five minutes!" said the girl.

And she turned and stamped away.

Silence fell over the group she left behind her, and darkness unillumined even by the gleam of a cigarette or the dull glow of a pipe.

"She's plumb wild," said someone softly, at last.

"I never heard her talk like that before."

"You take any woman," said Zeke, the oracle, "and they're all like that. Every once in a while, they go bad. Like a mustang. Got to buck a little and kick the man they love the most in the face. The best way is just to forget what they say. A woman, she always says more than she means!"

"Does she?" said someone drily. "Well, I

131

say that hell will be popping soon, if we don't get that fool of a pup down! Who took the ladder, I say?"

"Jerry done it."

"Hey, Jerry!"

"He's inside the bunk house, sleeping, I suppose."

"I never seen such a fool for sleeping. Jerry!"

"I'll go wake him up and ask him what he done with the ladder. He's got to get the pup down and take him in and explain to the girl. *I* won't do it!"

The speaker strode into the bunk house, and there he saw Jerry, not asleep, but stretched on his bunk, trying to light his pipe and at the same time remain buried in the magazine story which he was reading.

"Jerry, come here!" bellowed the voice of justice. "Get the ladder and snake the pup down off of the roof, will you? And do it pronto, you bonehead. Miss Mary is around raising hell about her dog!"

With that, he turned his back, and Jerry, with a groan, swung his legs off the bunk.

"I dunno where the ladder is," he mumbled.

He was a heavy man; ideas came to him slowly.

"I say I dunno where the ladder is," he

repeated, but the other had left the bunk house and there was a noise of voices on the outside.

"I better go tell them," said Jerry. "Ouch!"

For here the match flame touched the tip of his finger. He dropped it, and, rising with a great groan, he strode towards the door, and then out into the darkness where the others waited.

In the meantime, the glowing end of the match fell to the floor. In nine cases out of ten, such a fall would have put out the last flicker of fire that clung to the bit of wood, but in this case a tiny head of flame remained. Even so, it should have caused no damage, but Jerry was a careless man, and his mattress was so loosely tied that some of the straw had dribbled out of it and fallen to the floor, and the match struck squarely in that long-dried tinder.

It seemed to go out. Then a thin twisting streak of smoke arose, wavered, and was followed by a bright red eye of fire, looking upwards, and growing instantly wider and wider.

CHAPTER 15

Outside the bunk house, discussion increased, helped on or almost inspired by the
yelping of Tag from the roof. He had heard
the voice of his mistress, and he wanted to
go to her. It was high time that he had his
dinner, to be duly followed by the chewing
of a bone or the ceremonial burial thereof in
the back yard. What treasure of those bones
had been stowed away, Tag alone could tell,
and he, like one of riches beyond counting,
was himself a trifle uncertain. Except that
now and then, as he wandered about, up
from the earth came a reassuring fragrance
which was not all of the soil. Now and again,
a stray dog would venture to unearth a bone;
and Tag invariably fell upon the intruder
with a fury that made him a giant. He was a
valiant dog, was Tag, with a soul so great
that often it seemed to be bursting from his
body. Yet even great souls sometimes descend to lesser matters of the day, and Tag
knew that having chewed and then buried
his bone, he could scratch on the back door
until he was admitted, after which he might

wander upstairs and go to the room of his mistress and there curl up on the little bed specially appointed for his use. Or indeed, on cold winter nights, he would be welcome if he sprang onto her bed, and lay at her feet.

Such thoughts as these now disturbed the warlike soul of Tag, and therefore he yelped higher and louder with every moment.

"Well, we gotta get him down," said Zeke, the sage.

"Go on, Jerry, don't be no quitter. Get the ladder and snake him down, will you?"

The voice of Jerry rose at last to a fury.

"Why, damn all your hearts!" said he. "I tell you that I unhooked the ladder, but I didn't take it. It was Booze Hammond that took it, I think."

"That's a lie," said Booze, who was stretched in comfort on his back. "I never touched no ladder."

"Quit your yapping, Jerry, and fetch the dog down."

"I'll be damned if I do."

"You'll be damned if you don't. The old colonel'll fire the lot of us if the girl gets sore. And where'll you get a softer lie than this job, Jerry?"

"You'll beat us all out of our jobs, Jerry, unless you try to be a white man, for once!"

135

"I tell you," screamed the badgered Jerry, "I didn't have the ladder. I roped it to the ground. Somebody else can get it. I'll be damned if I won't *fight* before I touch it!"

After this, a bit of a silence followed. Not that there were not many men there quite willing to fight with Jerry about smaller matters than this, but his passion amused them in part, and in part it awed them, to see so big a man frantic with the sting of so small a gad-fly.

"Well," said old Zeke, "some way we gotta get the dog. That seems clear."

"Get him yourself, then!"

"All right," said Zeke. "I ain't as young and spry as some of you, but I don't mind doing an extra turn for the sake of the rest of you lazy loafers — and, God!" gasped Zeke, as he rose to his feet.

Attention had been focused on big Jerry, up to this point, but now, turning towards the bunk house, they saw through the open door, and far in the interior of the long lower room, a standing ghost of fire, a red, wavering figure.

Horror kept them still for an instant, then they pitched to their feet and broke for the entrance in a wave so solid that it caught and jammed in the doorway.

It was fortunate for some of them that they stuck there a vital instant, for the low-hanging lantern, by the light of which Jerry had been reading, had been bathed in an increasing tide of fire all these moments, and now it burst with a loud crash and hurled burning oil over the entire hall.

Instantly a thousand bits of fire were weltering on the floor, on the ceiling, on the walls, and on the bedding; curls and then clouds of smoke sprang up. The whole place was seething with white mist, made choking by the oil fumes.

Those who had bunks near the door made an instant and valiant effort and dragged their belongings to the outdoors, where they were busily engaged in beating out the sparks and the fumes.

In the meantime, two or three ran to the big house for help, others rushed to get water, and not a soul thought of the dog.

He had fallen silent on the roof.

It was well enough to yowl and yelp because he happened to realize that his supper time had come, or because he began to dream about the soft bed which was waiting for him in the room of his mistress. But it was another matter when an important mystery began to unfold, literally, beneath his nose.

There are only two sorts of fires worth considering, Tag knew. Those which sweep across stubble fields in the autumn, and those which are connected with the smell of cooking food. But this fire, which was rising in the house beneath him and sending up choking mists of smoke, had nothing to do with either of the above categories. It was something very special and different.

Therefore, it would be distinctly unmanly to make noises which might be interpreted as fear.

Tag was never afraid!

He sat down at the end of the roof peak and watched the confusion and the bustle of the men until his tail began to twitch from side to side and he yearned mightily to be down among them, leaping at their heels in this odd game of theirs. He had not been named for nothing!

In the meantime, that fire was increasing with bewildering speed, and great, thick waves of heat rolled trembling up through the air and clung about him, until he sneezed and coughed and shook his head.

He went to the other end of the roof and sat down there.

Here was less smoke and certainly far less heat, so that Tag could sit in reasonable peace and observe the commotion beneath him. In the distance, of course, there were growing sounds of men shouting sharply and wildly, just as they shouted at round-up, except that there was a different note in their voices. There was, in short, no fun in the sounds they made. When he heard men talk like this, Tag always got out of the way discreetly and lay down in a dark corner. It always was wiser. The most thoughtful boots in the world sometimes were capable of trampling upon one in a brutal haste.

There was another noise, however, which was far more exciting than even the calls of his human friends. That was a dull roaring sound which, after it began, increased with great rapidity. Underlying it, at first, was a slight crackling, but this element grew with speed until it began to lead; it turned into a series of explosions; and now and again, there was a rapid booming of guns.

The fire had reached loaded weapons, which were scattered here and there through the shack.

And now the roof was growing so extremely hot that Tag, like a cat walking on wet ground, began to pick up one foot after the other, hastily, for fear lest they might blister.

Now, too, he saw that he was standing in a terrible peril, and with all his soul he wanted to cry out for help. And as his dog-mind cleared in this emergency, his memory stretched straight back to puppyhood, when his wail had been sufficient to bring his dear young mistress running at any moment of the day or the night.

If he were to send up one cry like this, she would of course appear before him and stretch out her arms, and he would leap down into them. How happy he would be!

However, a time comes when a boy no longer cries, even in an agony, and on that day he is a man. And a time comes when a good dog no longer whimpers; on that day he has come to his own.

So the old cry formed a dozen times in the back of Tag's throat, but it would not break forth. He set his teeth over it, and grinned, as it were, at his own terror.

Now other voices had approached from the house, deeply familiar, and running into the very heart of Tag. Above all the rest was the shrill and trembling note of his mistress, calling his name.

He turned to rush closer to her, but all that farther end of the roof was now a wall of fumes which drove him back, and as he

140

shrank to the verge of the roof, again, a tall arm of crimson ripped through the shingles, and towered high into the air — instantly withdrawn — but thrust forth again with double brilliance, with double might!

"Tag!" screamed Mary Mackay from the ground. "Tag — darling —"

CHAPTER 16

That voice brought the light of hope to Tag; it was, in truth, the rift in the storm; and for the first time he definitely felt that those rising fires dared not eat him. Not while Mary Mackay was trying to get at him.

And trying she was, beyond doubt.

Tag, on the roof-crest, saw her standing with both arms thrown up to him, with the flames that shot from the windows and the fire-worn gaps in the first story billowing almost in her face. She looked to Tag like a glorious divinity. So, as a matter of fact, she always had appeared to him, not only for beauty but also for power; for, cowering in her lap, even in his puppyhood, he had found her a shelter and a harbor and haven of refuge against the very wrath of the colonel himself.

Now, at her cry, men came swirling around her. And the consuming inwards of the house were forgotten. All was forgotten except that a little Irish terrier stood upon the roof above the fire and looked bravely down at them, and wagged his stubby tail as a sign that he knew all was a game, and that, when it pleased these magnificent but just creatures, having put him upon that roof, they would, of course, take him down before peril devoured him.

"I want Tag!" cried Mary Mackay. "And if he's lost — you're murderers! You're murderers!"

Mrs. Mackay and the colonel were hurrying up. The colonel gasped and struck his hands together.

"Who has done this thing?" cried the colonel, like loud Macbeth in the third act.

"It doesn't really matter who has done it," said Mrs. Mackay. "But how can it be undone?"

The colonel could think of one way only.

"Get ladders, instantly," said the colonel, "and let some of you climb to the roof and bring the dog down!"

It was explained that the long ladders from the barn had been sent for, but that the roof was apt to crash before they arrived.

The colonel stamped.

He raised one arm in a Roman attitude and shouted: "A thousand dollars to the man who brings down that dog!"

But it did not seem that the offer increased the efforts or the intelligence of anyone. The flames were mounting, and tearing momently a wider hole in the roof; so that poor Tag was set off in a crimson flood.

Nearby, two excited men were holding ladders, rearing up their heads as though to measure them against the hopeless height of the roof.

Mrs. Mackay caught them and drew them together.

"Tie those ladders together!" she urged.

They shouted with joy, and instantly the lashing was under way.

"Good!" shouted the colonel. "Five hundred dollars for the rescue of Tag. Come, boys! Show yourselves to be what you are. For the sake of my daughter and for me! Four hundred dollars," went on the colonel, seeing that the two ladders, since they were united, promised actually to span the height. "Three hundred dollars to the man who brings down Tag!"

He paused.

The ladder was reared, wobbling just a little in mid-air, and then its head was set down close to the rim where Tag stood.

Instantly, up ran one of the cowpunchers, and no doubt, all would have been well had not old Zeke, the wise man urged on by the frantic cheers, doubtless wishing in some way to thrust himself forward into some prominence in this work, now run up the ladder behind his mate, and the result was that as the latter came to the point of junction, suddenly the hastily laid wrappings began to give way, the ladders sagged at the joint, and then collapsed.

The pair tumbled to the ground, unhurt by a happy chance. And immediately afterwards the entire forward portion of the roof sagged and then pitched downwards with a mighty crashing. Up boiled myriads of sparks, and small fragments of flaming wood, on the rebound, and whirled aloft in the conflagration, and scattered widely in their fall.

"Look to the barns!" shouted the colonel. "Look to the sheds! Look to the house! Never mind the dog. He's lost!"

Lost, indeed, he seemed to be, for all the end of the house on which poor Tag stood was sagging inwards and shuddering. But as the riot of sparks died out of the sky and only the mighty red arm of the flames soared upwards, there was Tag still, now driven from the roof rim onto the stout pole which projected outwards a little, the main beam-end of the roof.

Perched there, precariously, once or

twice he turned his head and glanced behind him at the roar of the fire, but these were only temporary weaknesses, and the rest of the time he continued to look down to the crowd, still with head canted on one side and his tail wagging in ceaseless good humor, as much as to say that he understood it was still a game — a grand and great game, but nevertheless one which he would try to comprehend. Only — they really would be kind if they snatched him away from this danger with the magic of their hands!

"The house!" shouted the colonel, seeing a wave of sparks wafted in that direction. But neither wife nor daughter nor hired man stirred, but held their looks upwards, stricken still, except Mary Mackay who had fallen on her knees and buried her face against her mother, weeping.

Then old Zeke, recovered from his fall, lurched out of the crowd, blubbering foolishly, and moving with clumsily useless hands here and there.

Mrs. Mackay, her face a little pinched, but her eyes cold and steady, fondled the golden head with both her hands and neither stirred nor spoke, as one who knows that hope is gone.

All this while Don Felipe had fluttered,

so to speak, hither and thither upon the rearwards rim of the crowd, offering soft-voiced suggestions which were lost in the roar of the fire or, if they were heard, were received and paid for with deep-throated curses. And heavy arms knocked him out of the way.

But when he saw Mary fall on her knees, in tears, he ceased his butterfly actions and cast one stern glance at the dog on the roof beam.

Then he picked up one of those buckets of water which had been hurried towards the fire and left standing when it was seen that they were of no use. This he raised in both hands, and, with a little shudder of distaste, poured it deliberately over his head, so that it soaked him and all his finery. After that, he caught up a lariat from the pile of salvaged material from the house, and ran swiftly forward, skirting the edge of the watchers.

Just beneath the roof beam and the dog he went, shaking out the noose of the lariat as he ran — shaking it out with gracefully expert hands. Then he whirled it over his head, and hurled it up. Straight and true it sped, faltered at the top of its rise, and then settled on the beam. One jerk made it fast.

And then what a shout rose from the spectators.

A sharp cry from her mother — and Mary started to her feet, to watch also.

And yet there was surely no hope, for now that end of the building was mightily warped inward, and Tag stood aslant upon the rooftree. All across the blackening side of the wall, tongues of flame were eating through, and now and again the structure shuddered, with a groan of creaking timbers.

Moreover, to climb a rope hand over hand to such a height was a trick which even a powerful sailor would hardly have cared to attempt. And there were no sailors present!

Don Felipe, however, seemed to have no doubt about the matter, but giving the rope one loose twist around his leg, to secure himself in case of his hands breaking loose, he raised himself rapidly, reaching upwards with his long arms and sweeping himself along without a pause.

He was almost to the goal when the whole wall sagged and staggered, and a long tongue of fire shot out directly at the rescuer, bathing his entire body below the arms. It was as though a personal malice had directed that shaft of crimson. But while a groan of apprehension burst from the little crowd, Don Felipe swiftly worked his way upwards and through the flames until, with one hand, he clutched the beam.

It was a part of the game which Tag recognized instantly. He hesitated just long enough to kiss the brow of his deliverer, and then he leaped lightly and fearlessly upon the shoulders of the man.

The descent was made in one swift drop, the rope curling with a hiss around the leg of Don Felipe. And now he stood upon the ground, and watched the wall sway slowly inwards, as though it had maintained itself for a merciful purpose just this long, and now willingly gave way to ruin. It fell. The sparks leaped in a hurried throng for the last time. And now they looked across a small, low hcap of ruins, covered with welterings of fire.

As for Tag, he jumped to the ground and made with arrowy speed for his mistress. Into her arms he sprang, one convulsive wriggle of delight. For he knew that he had played the game, and he was tremendously proud of himself. Moreover, he knew that it was her voice, her cry, that had directed the help towards him.

For, of course, there was no one else in

this universe so wise, so just, so merciful, so all-powerful!

Don Felipe, among the cow-punchers, had been "The Mex" or "the greaser," up to this moment, but now old Zeke was heard asking: "Where's Señor Consalvo! I want to tell him he's dead game!"

Señor Consalvo was not to be found. He had slipped skilfully away into the darkness and was gone.

CHAPTER 17

When they searched for Don Felipe, they had to extract him from his room, and then he confronted the inner circle of the Mackay family.

The colonel, of course, made a speech.

He held the hand of Don Felipe and said:

"My dear Consalvo, when you first came among us" — it was very like the dictation of a letter — "we knew that we were fortunate to have you. And during your stay you have — ahem! — become a very pleasant — er — may I say member of our family? I must say it, Felipe! And — in fact —"

The colonel paused a little, dragging his words till a new thought came to him. But then the dog furnished him with a theme, and he concluded: "As I see Tag run to you, my dear fellow, I want you to know that he's only expressing our entire affection for you, Felipe!"

He released Consalvo with a final warm pressure of the hand, only adding: "Though where you found the strength to do such a Herculean thing — well, I can't tell!"

"Of course," said Don Felipe modestly, "any of the vaqueros would have done it, if they had happened to think. It was nothing. My great pleasure to take Tag down from that fire. Be my very good friends, and forget all about it!"

He leaned to pat Tag, said good-night, and extricated himself without haste, and very gracefully, only aware, as he retired, of Mary Mackay watching him with eyes like two stars.

In his room, Don Felipe saw that Pedro was hard at work, seated cross-legged with a board across his knees, and on the board was one of his master's richest jackets. It was covered as by a jeweler's craft with gold and silver thread, curiously applied, and Pedro leaned above it with an ardent attention. He had by him spools of silver and of gold thread of the costliest nature, and there was an assortment of needles which, from time to time he threaded with a sparkling filament and repaired some frayed spot on the jacket. That work required the hand of a fairy and a genius for minute attention, but the gross-handed Indian seemed to possess both.

Or, advancing in his careful examination,

he found a tiny spot which had to be eradicated, a button to be affixed more firmly, or another which needed polishing, and every portion of the work was done with the same meticulous honesty of labor.

Don Felipe stood by the door, smoking at leisure, and watching with infinite interest the handiwork of his servant, and the great, ugly shadow which squatted on the floor in front of Felipe.

He began to undress. Pedro, abandoning his other work, stood up and took the articles which his master threw to him one by one, folded them, put them away.

He brought forth pajamas, slippers, silken dressing-gown; at length Don Felipe sat by the window, lighting another cigarette from the end of the first; Pedro went back to his work and for some time he continued in this fashion, bending closely to his task with a loving exactness, but now and again raising his great, ugly head, and looking at his master, and then past him at the night-sky, and the faint glimmer of the stars beyond. There was an odd combination of awe, wonder, fear, respect, and amusement in this look of Pedro's. The head of Don Felipe constantly was turned away from him, and yet he was not surprised when the voice of his master said:

"Why do you stare, Pedro?"

The Indian no longer spoke Spanish, but lapsed into his harsh, natural tongue.

"The lizard on the stone, and the eagle in the air — they both have eyes and see with them," replied he.

Don Felipe puffed, blew smoke forth, and spoke again.

"Sometimes I understand you, Pedro," said he. "Sometimes what you say goes by me like an arrow and misses my mind. For you continually are talking around a corner."

He had answered in the Indian's own tongue, and the sound of it made Pedro bend his ear, as though he listened to the most delicate and delicious music.

"Father," said he, "I hear you, but I do not understand you. Unless it is that I speak as my fathers taught me to speak."

"Every man's way may be a good way," said his master, "but when you speak Spanish, I understand you more clearly. That is all."

"In Spanish," said the Indian, "I can ask for bread and meat. In Spanish I can tell a horse to go on, or a dog to stop. In Spanish I can ask for my money or I can pay a bill. But I cannot speak!"

Don Felipe considered, and then he nodded.

"Speak to me in your father's tongue then, Pedro. There is something that you wish to say. You have been staring at me. What is it?"

"I?" said the Indian, and then he added: "It is true. As I sat here at my work — if a pleasure like this can be called work, spinning pleasant things like a spider making a web — then I said to myself that Pedro labors with his hands. But his father sits with his head against the stars, and he is working, also, although his hands are still."

The white man turned his head, a sign that his full attention had been caught.

"When a cat," said he, "wishes to catch a mouse, first it pretends to sleep; and then it comes softly on the mouse. Now, Pedro, you have something more to say to me."

"I?" said the Indian.

"Yes."

"What could I have to say?"

"Today and yesterday," said the master, "I have seen you putting away things in the pack."

"That is the part of a wise man," said the Indian. "For he constantly prepares for the march when he is sitting still."

"I have told you," said the master, "that this is apt to be a summer's camp."

"That is true," said the Indian. "But the

155

wolf starts on a long trail and changes with the wind at midnight."

"I am not a wolf," said the master sharply.

Pedro was silent.

"I am not a wolf," said Don Felipe sharply.

"No, señor," said the servant submissively, and in Spanish.

"Speak your own tongue! Speak your own tongue and your own thoughts," commanded Don Felipe sharply.

Again Pedro was silent.

At last, Consalvo took a more conciliatory line and added very gently: "For, Pedro, without your thoughts spoken freely I should be half blind, and all that came before me would be seen dimly; but with you, I see with two eyes. What has your eye seen, Pedro?"

The Indian paused for a moment, inhaling this compliment with an expanding chest and a brightened eye.

At last he said: "Is it true that my father has need of his son?"

"By night," answered Don Felipe, "and by day, I have need of you, Pedro! I should not sleep, except that I know you are watching."

Pedro breathed again, and then he raised his head a little.

"There are some among my nation," said he, "who have two sights."

"I have heard that."

"One sight is outward; and one is inward."

"It is true."

"Does my father believe in such things?"

"In a way, yes. There never was a thought that did not have some reason behind it. Go on, Pedro."

"My grandfather was possessed of both sights, the outward and the inner."

"I have heard you talk about the old man. And I saw him, as you may remember."

"I remember," said Pedro, his voice touched with emotion, "and I remember that he said a strong prayer for you to the sun-father in the sky, who is the parent of all living things. You will not remember, for then you did not know our tongue."

"He was a kind old man," said Felipe Consalvo. "I remember his face, at least, perfectly well."

"And I too, father, inherited from him a little of his gift. I also see with the outward and with the inward eye, but never so clearly as he could see; for he discerned the actual forms of things, and all that appears to me is a shadow or a brightness."

"That is possible, and that I could understand."

"Ah, señor, then if you believe me, let me make the pack up tonight. I shall saddle the three mules. Long before dawn we shall have reached the mountains, and lose our trail behind us!"

"There is danger, then, before us, Pedro?"

"There is danger, señor! I felt it here when we first came in sight of the place. It was as clear to me as the shadow that slept beside the house!"

"So? Tell me, then, what sort of danger it will be?"

"That I cannot say. But I know from my heart that before we leave we are in danger of a great trouble, either to me and my life, or to the life of the man who is more to me than my dead father when he lived."

And his eyes, for a moment, softened and lighted as he looked at Felipe.

The latter returned no answer for a time, though finally he said: "Have you seen or heard anything here to make you feel that your dream is true?"

"Nothing, señor."

Again Consalvo was silent, but finally he said:

"I shall sleep, Pedro."

The Indian stood up with a sigh.

"You will not listen, my father?"

There was silence for an answer.

"Then," said Pedro gently, "I pray that the danger shall fall on my own head! I shall pray to the sun and make a sacrifice."

Here again he had no reply, and he went to the door which opened into his own small chamber. There he paused, as though wrestling with a great idea that struggled to break from his lips; but as though the words failed him, or his mind changed, suddenly he passed on.

CHAPTER 18

Pedro was in bed, in darkness when his door opened.

He knew it not by the noise but by a softly whispering draft that passed over his face, and clutching a gun beneath his pillow, he turned himself as if to face a danger.

For what comes upon us with such softness that is not dangerous?

Then, though there had been no sound of an approach, he heard a voice speaking softly and distinctly just above him. He shuddered. He who owned that voice could have reached out and stabbed him as he lay in his bed, for all his wakefulness, and it made small difference that the voice came from his own dear master.

"Pedro, you are not sleeping yet?"

"No, father."

"All that comes and goes in my mind, you should be free to hear. There is no distrust in me for you, Pedro. But as if you were my son and I were your father, as you call me, I have a perfect faith in you."

"It is the will of the sky-people," said the Indian, "that you should be served by me and accept my service. That has been revealed to me; it cannot be false!"

"I have wished to say this much to you, Pedro. That now in this house we are opening the door of danger, and, on the other side of that door, we may find riches and happiness forever."

"The rich man cannot be unhappy unless he has children," said the wise Pedro.

"That should be true," resumed the master. "However, it is, as I said, the door of danger. Tell me, then, where the danger may lie?"

"In the large señor?"

Don Felipe chuckled softly.

"Not in him, but in his squaw!"

"In a woman?" echoed the Indian with wonder.

"In a woman, Pedro. In that woman there is all the wisdom of a wolf and all the secrecy of a serpent. No man is wiser than she, and no cat is more secret. All that I do she has guessed at before I have done it. In all my life, though I have known many people, never have I known people like her. She is the greatest of all. She is to them like a moon among the stars, and she puts them out with her brightness."

161

The Indian murmured: "I hear you, father, and I believe you."

"Believe me entirely," said Consalvo. "This is what I have come to say to you: Day and night, when you are awake, think of her, stay close to her. Listen to her words."

"She speaks little Spanish except to you," said the Indian.

"You yourself understand English, a little," said the master. "Never forget what little you know, and use it when you are near to her. Wear a strong mask on your face, but let your ears be like the ears of a fox."

"I shall!" said the Indian.

"That is all. Sleep well. In the morning, begin to watch. She is often in her garden. Remember!"

"I shall not forget!"

There was no sound, but presently the draft ceased to cross Pedro's face, and he knew the door had been closed. And he knew that his master once more sat at his window watching the stars, and, with folded hands, minute by minute, hour by hour, watching the sky and sinking deeper and deeper into his own reflections, where success and failure and all their causes would be weighed in a scale far nicer than the most delicate balance that a chemist uses for weights unthinkable.

However, there was in the house another person as wakeful as "my lord." And that was Mrs. Mackay.

She had been in the room of her daughter and sat on the edge of her bed. Tag, clasped in the arm of his mistress, his nose on her bare shoulder, was fast asleep, and giving way in his dreams to the weakness which he would not show when in danger; for now and again he whimpered and shrugged his singed coat. Then a whisper and touch would make him wag his stubby tail, and he slept soundly again.

In the meantime, the hushed voice of his mistress flowed on. She was full of the great event of that evening. Her voice trembled, and her mother could feel the girl's body tremble, also, as she spoke.

Never, never, in all this world of men, had there been a deed so matchless, so heroic, so unthinkably swift and manly! And she had scorned this hero as a coward! She had scorned and slighted him! She had spoken to him roughly. How, indeed, could she face him again? How could she make her peace with him? How could she tell him of the splendor that she saw in him?

Mrs. Mackay held her daughter's hand.

And all that she said from time to time was: "Dear child! Dear Mary!"

And then, at length, the girl murmured: "But you make everything seem so small, so unimportant! One would think that this whole world were hardly a pinpoint, mother!"

"In a way, it's hardly that," said Mrs. Mackay.

"And in a way, it's a vast thing!" cried the girl passionately. "And even Tag — even Tag's a vast thing. A tremendous thing, mother. Poor darling puppy! Do you remember? How he waggled his tail and looked down at us. He — he thought — he thought it was only a game — the blessed — hush, Tag! Sweet puppy! You're safe now. I'll never let him out of my sight again so long as I live. The scoundrels! I hope father discharges every one. I won't rest till he does!"

"Would you send poor old Zeke away?"

"Not Zeke, of course. Where would he go? Nobody else would have the slow old thing."

"And Charlie, then?"

"Charlie's exceptional, of course. And it wasn't his fault."

"We'll let Jerry go, at least," said the mother. "He caused the fire, you know!"

"Poor Jerry! How frightfully he took it! One would have thought that he had put a human being in danger of burning! Oh, no, we couldn't discharge Jerry! You wouldn't think of that! Did you ever see anything so strong?"

"As Jerry?"

"Mother, silly! As Felipe, climbing the rope, I mean!"

"It was very strong, of course."

"It makes my shoulders ache, just to think of it."

"He may have been a sailor, and learned at sea, you know."

"Felipe? Señor Consalvo? Mother!"

"Why not?"

"Think of him as a common sailor?"

"But, my dear, why not?"

"It couldn't be possible!"

"He's a — what shall I say? a prospector, now?"

"A prospector! What an idea! Imagine Felipe finding gold!"

"Well, he must have some occupation."

"I don't see why."

"Most men have a business, haven't they?"

"He's different."

"He's a very brave young man. And very polite."

"Mother, you reduce things so!"

"But, dear, he's flesh and blood. Like us. Like old Zeke, even!"

"Like Zeke!"

"In a word, he's human, Mary."

"He's like himself, and no one else."

"But even that self of his must have bread and butter. And how will he earn it?"

"I don't like even to think of that."

"Is it a disgrace to work?"

"I suppose not."

"You see, dear, we don't know a great deal about Felipe, as you call him."

"Do you mean that I shouldn't call him that?"

"You are a bit hostile, Mary. Of course you have a right to call him what you please. Only — we haven't known him very long."

"But you see, he's different, isn't he?"

"Different, dear?"

"Of course! You must feel that. He's not like others. To talk to Felipe — it's opening a new book — a sort you've never read before!"

"At least, it must be either prose or verse."

"Oh —" began Mary, and then she was silent.

Her mother waited for the completion of that sentence, and finally she laid her hand on the brow of her girl, and she found it hot.

Still there was no new word, and Mrs. Mackay stood up.

"Good-night, Mary."

"Good-night, mother."

So Mrs. Mackay stole from the room and went to her own chamber.

"Lydia!" called her husband.

She went into her husband's room.

"I want you to hear this. It's about Newton. He's marrying again, old ass! Listen!"

She listened, her eyes on the floor. Her husband, finishing, roared with laughter.

"Gad, Lydia, you really have no sense of humor."

"My head is aching a little, tonight."

"Ah, well — run along, then."

She went back to her room, and passed the mirror like a ghost, in the dim light. On her balcony she drew up her chair near the railing and sat down with hands folded in her lap and watched the stars, minute by minute and hour by hour, never moving.

And as she watched them, she was weighing the chances of success and of failure in scales so nice that, compared with them, how gross were the scales of the chemist, balancing imponderable matter!

So the night wore away over Mackay House, and in all the place only two people were wakeful.

CHAPTER 19

"It's an ill wind," said the colonel, "that blows nobody good, and as for the wind that took the bunk house up in smoke, it will blow good to the ranch in several ways. The old building was an eyesore. It stood up like a sore thumb near Mackay House" — he was fond of referring to his residence in this formal fashion — "and now we have a chance to rebuild in a proper way. Now, Lydia, what would you suggest?"

"Something over the hill in the hollow, where we won't hear them quite so plainly."

"Wrong!" said the colonel triumphantly. "You've missed, my dear!" he continued, as though he had been asking a riddle, and not merely for advice. "The thing to do is to have the new bunk house a decorative feature and a member of the whole group of buildings. Something quietly beautiful — Spanish type — patio — garden — a touch of color — a red roof, I should say. What do you think of that, Mary?"

"Nice," said Mary. "But what would the

boys do with anything nice?"

"I don't understand you," said the colonel.

"Well," explained Mary, "they want a house where they can carve their initials on the walls. 'Sunshine Bill, Oklahoma,' 'Mississippi Slim, bound north,' and things like that. What fun would they have in a neat house?"

The colonel cleared his throat.

"In all men," he announced, "there are elements which respond to the stimulus of a higher life. Whether it be in mental food, or physical food; whether it be in pleasures of the spirit or pleasures of the senses. I shall have better and finer cow-punchers if I give them better quarters. The ruffians will be out of place. The more intelligent, sensitive souls will remain, and find their home here."

"I never saw a cow-puncher so sensitive," said Mary, "that he wouldn't want to dump his saddle on the floor rather than hang it on a peg. I never saw one that didn't want to shy his boots into a corner and scratch a match on the wall and drop it on the floor. I tell you, dad, you won't get a crowd of young poets and such to ride herd for you. And you've got to give a cowman what a cowman wants! I'd do what mother says. Build them another shack just like the old one, over the hill where we hear them whooping it up so often on Saturday nights. And I'd build them their own lane to the main road, so's when they wanted to go into town after pay day, they could go sober and come back drunk and not bother us."

"By heavens!" said the colonel, much moved. "This from you, Mary! Is it my own daughter who makes such speeches as this? Is it possible? Mary, Mary, are you hardening as young as this?"

"Well," said Mary, "there's a bit of a difference between hardness and common sense."

"To crowd our hired men into a detestable shack and —"

"I'm not trying to save money," said Mary. "I'm just trying to make them happy. You want to give them truffles. But I know that they'd rather have ham and eggs. Believe me, they would. And if you want to make them happier, give them *more* ham and eggs, and then some more of the same. You want to feed them wine; they'd prefer whisky. You're right for yourself, but they're right for themselves."

The colonel threw up his hands.

"This is," he said, "the Twentieth Century. God help it! This is the type of our best young womanhood! Consider such ideas, Felipe," he went on, turning to the other. "And from a girl — a child! Where are the higher and tenderer sentiments to find a shelter and place to take root if they are excluded from the minds of our women? By heavens, Felipe, I tell you that the world is rapidly traveling down hill!"

"I should think," said Felipe, "that the easiest solution would be to ask the men what they'd prefer to have."

"Ha!" cried the colonel, turning pink. "Ask them? Let them once step into the saddle — let them once feel that their opinions count, and there'd be no holding them. No, Felipe, a stern hand, and arm's length away. That's the only system, I assure you!"

Felipe lighted a cigarette and said nothing, and the colonel straightway settled down to the drawing of plans for the new bunk house along his own ideas, with a delightful garden in front, and a patio framed with arches. Neatly and lightly the colonel drew it. He might have made a living by his pencil, had he chosen.

Mary Mackay went off with Tag, and Tag barked at the feet of Don Felipe.

"Tag wants you to come along, too," said

Mary. "I'm going to walk up the ridge, if that interests you."

So Don Felipe went along, and Mrs. Mackay followed them with her eyes. She glanced at her husband. He was absorbed in his work, and Mrs. Mackay went slowly into the house.

In her room, she took a strong pair of field glasses, and with it she climbed into the tower; from that post of vantage, shamelessly she scanned the ridge, until she made out the two strolling up it, from one patch of trees and brush to another, and crossing the intervening meadows.

Once or twice they paused, and each time Mrs. Mackay fixed the glasses closer to her eyes, with a little shudder of apprehension. But first it was only that they had halted to watch Tag dig at a gopher hole. And again it was to watch a low-circling hawk. They walked on again.

And, as they walked, they talked idly of any idle things, until Mary stopped short and thrust her walking stick firmly into the ground.

"Felipe!" she said.

Felipe straightened a little and his eyes widened.

"Good heavens!" said Mary Mackay. "You act as if you're afraid of me!"

"I suppose that I am," said he.

At this, she bent her brows upon him, after a fashion which she had inherited from her father when he was in an imperious humor.

"Something is going to happen," said Mary.

Don Felipe retreated a little farther — a withdrawal hardly to be measured even in inches.

"I'm going to be rude!" said Mary.

"Señorita!" murmured Don Felipe.

"But why?" cried Mary. "Last night — oh, I thought that last night you could — and now you're — I don't know what to make of you, Felipe Consalvo! *Fire* didn't bother you!"

"But what is fire?" said he gently. "It is something that can be known. But every human being is a mystery. Their joy is beautiful, and their anger is terrible. And yours above all."

"Mine?" said Mary Mackay.

He was silent for a moment, his eyes on the ground, and then he said quietly: "Yes — to me!"

That was all, and how much remained unsaid she might guess at, if she chose; but she felt that she never could draw the words from him.

Yet she felt that he had given her a clue to the weakness which she felt she had seen in him. Men he could fear, but not other dangers, and therefore he had been willing, with the frankness of a child, to admit his terror of such men as the young gun-fighter who now lay wounded in the house. There was not a cow-puncher on the place, she firmly believed, who would have declared such weakness as this; but on the other hand, what one of them had dared to venture himself for the life of poor Tag?

She looked down at the terrier, and found that he had lain down for a rest — and chosen as a pillow for his head one of the feet of Don Felipe. And then, raising her eyes, she looked into the face of the Mexican and found that he was smiling faintly.

"Felipe!" she said.

"Señorita!"

"There's a lot about you that I don't understand; and there must be a lot about me that you don't understand; but I want to like you; I do like you; let's promise to be good friends!"

With that, she held out her hand, but instead of shaking it to clinch this amiable agreement, Don Felipe bowed above it and touched it to his lips.

It was very odd to Mary, and the grave and gentle reverence of Don Felipe touched her to the heart. There would have been more confirmation, she felt, in a handshake, but after all the ingrown ways of a man could not be changed, even if she wished.

She was rather bewildered, too, because, after all these advances she had made, she remained, in some odd manner, as distant from him as ever. If she had been half so free with any youngster of the range, she knew that he would have felt almost the last barrier was cast down; but Don Felipe continued to regard her, so it seemed, as though there were something inherently queenly in her nature, so that no action could lower her beneath herself.

They walked slowly through the woods, and across the pasture lands; and when she fell thoughtfully silent, Don Felipe made conversation about little things around them — about a blackbird that flashed across a thicket, and a red squirrel that ran up a tree trunk. He seemed to know all about the wilderness and its people; and yet she listened to him with only half her attention.

She decided, at last, that she must go back, and as they turned they saw the low, square tower of the house far off above the tree tops.

"I have made you unhappy," said Don Felipe anxiously. "I have seen that I make you ashamed because I am not a man who loves battle as your people love it; still it makes you unhappy to be with me!"

He stood a little behind her, but with an alert eye he watched every stir of head and shoulder and throat, reading her swiftly and skilfully.

She spoke towards the distant house, rather than to the man so close to her.

"You see, Felipe, I've wanted to open my heart and talk, sort of. I never have a chance to do that. Mother is so quiet and so different. Father never understands. But you —"

Don Felipe sighed.

"I remember," said he, "when I was little, and my father was even then quite poor, that I stood in front of a jeweler's window in Mexico City and looked at the treasures, green and red and crystal. One blow would break the glass and one grasp of the hand would make me rich forever and make my father rich also. But although I was not very old at that time, still I was old enough to understand that there would be terrible things to follow, if I did what I wished. And now, you see, I am again near a treasure. There is not even a pane of glass between me and what I wish to say, but I know that I dare not!"

"I don't understand you," said Mary in such an unsteady voice that it was plain she understood perfectly well. "I don't know what you mean, Felipe."

"If I should speak to you, carelessly and freely, and use your name as you use mine, do you think that I could check myself so easily? No, but a wild torrent would break out, and I should fall on my knees and tell you, Mary, that I love you, that I adore you — and I dare not do it. For even if your kindness should listen to me, I should know that I am a fool to speak in that manner, and a coward to take such an advantage of your gentleness!"

To this Mary said not a word, but she began to tremble violently. She was frightened, too, but she cast not a single glance over her shoulder at Don Felipe, so she could not see the flash of triumph that gleamed in his eye and was gone again.

"Tag!" she whispered.

And Tag, willing to help if he knew how, stood up and put a forepaw on her knee, and so stared up towards her face to ask what he could do.

CHAPTER 20

The length of this walk had not overtried the patience of Mrs. Mackay. On the contrary, the glasses never left her eyes, and she strained them willingly, except that now and then a slight tremor disturbed the focus and made her hunt again, rather wildly, until she found the pair.

And every time they passed through the shade of a grove she lowered the glasses and leaned like a very weary woman against the side of the window, and every time they appeared she studied them with an anxious patience again until, at last, she saw them turn back, and come to that stand.

The excitement of Mrs. Mackay grew so intense that, in spite of herself, the glasses wobbled this way and that, and picked out a hawk, hanging high in the pale blue heaven, and then made a distant tree top jump up to her so close that she could see in the boughs the bird which had taken refuge there from the hawk which towered above.

Then, freezing her glasses upon the mark at last, she saw Don Felipe make one stride closer, and saw his arms surround Mary, and saw the head of Mary fall back upon his shoulder.

Mrs. Mackay dropped the glasses. It was a priceless Zeiss with the finest lenses that could be ground, and these lenses now crashed with an ugly tinkling sound.

She heeded it not, but hurrying down from the tower, she ran into her husband's study, crying: "My dear, my dear!"

The colonel looked up from a large sketch which he was completing.

"I have it!" said he. "I have the grand idea at last! We'll put the new bunk house on the top of the hill south of the house, and in the center of it a little blunt tower, like one of those old Norman remains, with perhaps a telescope mounted on top — you understand? — a little touch — something aspiring — to lead the thoughts of our men —"

"Yes," said Mrs. Mackay.

"But I haven't explained —"

"I thought I left my needlepoint bag in here," said Mrs. Mackay. "Have you seen it?"

"Needlepoint! Needlepoint indeed!" cried the colonel. "And when I'm working out such a thought as this — good heavens, Lydia, how can you have the soul to think of such a thing? No, I haven't seen the confounded needlepoint!"

Mrs. Mackay retired softly to her own chamber, but there she turned confusedly from one thing to another — picked up a book and set it down again, and moved a chair, and leaned an instant at the window with an unseeing eye.

At length she hurried down and out to the stable, where she had a horse saddled and once more rode straight across country for the town.

There was white lather on the shoulders of her mount when she came to the office of Sheriff Rankin. Tilted back in a chair on the little veranda of that small office she found the sheriff's old retainer who acted as messenger boy and random deputy.

"Where can I find Sheriff Rankin?" she asked.

"Where can you find the sheriff?" repeated the old fellow in a daze, and pushed his hat far back on his bald head. "Where? Why, ma'am, I would of said that you can find him on your own ranch!"

"But," she said impatiently, "he left the ranch the other day, you know! He must have come here."

"Not a sight or a sound of him, ma'am."

"He's been to his office and you haven't seen him," she insisted.

"I sleep in the back room," replied the other, "and if a mouse could come through the front door without me hearin', I'm a liar!"

Mrs. Mackay, overcome, stared helplessly at him; and he stared back, equally in a riddle, but foolishly anxious to help.

"Tell me," she went on at length. "He carries a great deal of criminal information in his office, doesn't he?"

"In the big desk," said the other with a smile of pleasure to be able to say something definite. "Stacks and stacks, ma'am. Photographs, and writing on the backs of 'em, and letters and papers of all kinds, till you wouldn't think that that many bad men ever was in the world!"

Mrs. Mackay felt her brain reeling.

For, with this whole reference library ready at hand to consult, where else would the sheriff have gone to work up what leading clues he might have concerning the identity of Don Felipe?

And yet he had not come home!

She turned her horse and journeyed more slowly back to the ranch, turning and re-turning the problem in her mind. Something had to be done! Something had to be done! It rang in her brain like a bell; but what could she accomplish by herself?

Of course, she could tell the colonel what she had seen, but she knew perfectly well what that would lead to — a scene between her husband and the Mexican — a violent outburst, in which the colonel with military precision confronted the girl with her lover — the frank admission of Mary — the furious denunciation of the colonel — the polite coolness of Don Felipe — his retirement from the house — the flight of Mary to her room —

And after that, the kind God who sometimes has mercy upon mortals come to her help in this mystery and maze of woe, for beyond a doubt Mary could not be kept from a man she had chosen for a husband, and least of all from such a husband as Señor Consalvo.

She thought, then, of striving in some way to make Mary see that the man had been living a lie — that he was as desperate a warrior as ever rode out of Mexico, in paint and feathers or in civilized garb. But she knew that the joy of Mary in such a relation would far pass her suspicion and her bewilderment. For if the girl had loved such a man, believing him a coward in the face of his fellow men, what could break his hold upon her?

In short, there was only one possible way to answer, and that was by placing Señor Consalvo securely behind prison bars where Mary might vow eternal fidelity, of course, but Mrs. Mackay was wisely willing to trust to this Twentieth Century of the colonel's detestation, and the swiftness with which it dissolved all ties.

So she reached the ranch.

To find the sheriff — that was the grand purpose, of course; and first of all to solve the mystery of his disappearance. For though it was possible that he might have gone straightway towards the state capital, say, to consult the criminal archives deposited there with the head of the police, yet it was a strange thing that he had not, first, touched at the home town and all the information which he had pooled there for just such emergencies as this.

Feeling as she did, it was only natural that Mrs. Mackay should pick up the sheriff at the last step she knew of him — namely, the scrawled note which had been dropped in the mail box and had come to her.

Going to her room she took it up now, resolved and critical, and studied it with the most minute care, trying to read some extra meanings into the words; but it struck her as a perfectly straightforward note, sent back to cover his departure so that he might appear excused in the eyes of the colonel while, secretly, he went forward with his mission.

Yet there was something about it that was not quite like the sheriff, something in the phraseology, perhaps. So she picked out from the same desk a note which he had written long ago, in the days of the cattle rustling affair. She laid that note beside the second; and, the instant that she did so, her heart leaped with fear and excitement.

She felt, at first, that it was merely a dizzy optical illusion, and therefore she resolutely covered her eyes with one hand and counted twenty before she looked again.

Now, however, clear-eyed and clear-minded, there could be no doubt at all. For, indeed, long ago she had had a passing fancy for the study of the gentle art of deciphering character by handwriting, so that she was quite intimately familiar with such matter.

And she knew, with a positive knowledge, that the scrawl on the rough sheet of note paper varied not only because it might have been done in haste, but because it was a manifest though rather skillful forgery of the sheriff's handwriting!

CHAPTER 21

Never had there been an evening so wretched or so strained for Mrs. Mackay. For she had to be what her rôle demanded, the child-wife of the colonel; and on the other hand, she had to watch Don Felipe and Mary.

They had decided, doubtless at the importunity of the Mexican, not to speak of their grand event for the time being, at least. Don Felipe carried off his part of the deception with the most consummate skill, but Mary was very excited. Even the colonel, absorbing all conversation with his plans for the new bunk house, had to exclaim, at last: "Good God, Mary, what makes you so jumpy? Can't you be still? And if you're going to play the piano, at least finish the piece you start. What's the matter with you?"

"You never could guess," said Mary, and laughed with such a swelling note of joy in her throat, that the heart of the mother ached.

A single quiet glance from Don Felipe

sufficed to draw Mary part way down from her seventh heaven and place her again in touch with the facts of life.

But still she played her part badly, and she could not help referring constantly to the wishes of Don Felipe. What music did he wish to hear? Did he think it was too cool for them all to go out into the patio? And so she ran on, and Don Felipe's name was in almost every sentence.

Two things were instantly apparent to Mrs. Mackay. One was that Don Felipe knew she suspected something. The other was that this knowledge worried him greatly. So much so, indeed, that he fell into sparkling conversation and strove to carry the talk back to Mexico, and the wild, gay days among the mountains, where his father's rancheria had stood.

For her own part, Mrs. Mackay would have preferred to let her knowledge remain unsuspected, but since it was well guessed at, to say the least, she decided that it was better to talk with apparent frankness to Consalvo. For, if she kept her peace, certainly he would begin to suspect her.

With all her might she desired some sage brain on which she could depend for counsel. But there was no one. The colonel early retired to his study to complete his plans; and then Mary, after many nervous glances at her mother and the eternal needlepoint, said good-night.

Don Felipe rose immediately after; it was plain that he did not wish to be alone with his hostess, but she called him back, and motioned him to a seat facing hers. She was in a corner nook, much shadowed, and the light which struck over her needlepoint illumined nothing else but the yellow of her dress and the gilded toe of her shoe. It left her face in such a shadow that one had to peer really to see her; and the gray of her hair seemed, now, a faint shimmer of solid silver. But Don Felipe, taking his place opposite her, was in the full tide of the light, which glittered back from the silver and gold work of his tight jacket.

"There's something which I think we ought to talk over," said Mrs. Mackay.

"Whatever you will, dear señora," said he.

And he smiled, and sat forward attentively polite, in his chair. Nevertheless she felt that this was not the sort of attention which even so well-trained and courteous a youth as Don Felipe would ordinarily pay to such a woman as herself, old to the point of grayness of hair, no matter how young her face might be. There was a keen awareness in Don Felipe, a restrained watchfulness like that of a fencer; so that she knew she had lost her first trick before the game began; this was a man who did not undervalue her, and therefore he would give nothing away.

She cast about for the best means of beginning, for there were many things which she might attempt. To play her usual *ingénue* part, she felt, would be a bit foolish against such a fellow as this, if he were half what she suspected. So she decided to try the effect of shock tactics and said instantly, but quietly: "I want to know about you and Mary."

She had a fierce but subdued pleasure in seeing his color change and his smile freeze; certainly she had shocked him to the quick. But almost instantly he was rising to the part. "Ah," said Don Felipe, "of course you see and notice everything! Of course you understand!"

And he made a little gesture of surrender, so to speak, still faintly smiling as though in apology, or in despair; but at the same time he shot a glance which, she knew, found her face in spite of the shadow and read every feature. It was as though he had the power to cast a strong ray that revealed her very soul; and she was deeply thankful that there was not the light of day around them.

He had given her an answer, however, which might be taken as revealing everything, though as a matter of fact he had been adroitly unspecific. No doubt he wondered just what she knew, and what she merely suspected.

She replied in kind: "One couldn't watch the pair of you tonight without understanding that there's something between you. You could have done very well, Don Felipe. But not Mary. She wears her heart on her sleeve, poor dear child!"

Don Felipe might have been tempted to say many things. Instead, he merely sighed and looked down to the floor.

But Mrs. Mackay had no intention of helping him over clumsy places, and with a beating heart she allowed the silence to endure until the pressure of it forced him to speak.

"I don't know what to say," said Don Felipe, lifting saddened eyes towards her. "I don't know where to begin!"

Of course there was an excellent bid for some sort of talk from her, but Mrs. Mackay cruelly saw her advantage and took it. She said not a word, but laying down her needlepoint for the moment, she raised her head and waited, as one who expects some confession of importance.

She could see that the test was trying Don Felipe terribly, for even his professional calm, as she felt it to be, was giving way a little. His eyes, his smile, his posture remained perfect, but one hand, which perhaps he thought she could not see, was knotted into a hard fist!

"Well," said he at last, "I have done a terrible thing. I have done the most terrible thing. I have done the thing for which you never will forgive me!"

She said, then: "I won't believe that, Don Felipe."

"God knows," said Don Felipe, with an apparent passion, "that I've tried to keep it back. But — I should have left long ago. I should have escaped and fled away. I could feel this rising in me like an irresistible tide, señora, and I thought, like a fool, that I could keep the words from breaking through. But I could not!"

He paused and bowed his head a little, breathing audibly.

"Poor Don Felipe!" said she, making her tone as gentle as the rage in her heart permitted.

"For every day," he went on, as though carried away, "I told myself that I am a poor wanderer, an outcast of fortune, little better than a beggar —"

He paused, as though choked by emotion, and she was forced to say in the interlude: "You must not speak in this way of a Consalvo!"

"But then I would see her," said he, raising his head and looking far past the shadowy face which watched him. "And she was — like the beauty of the morning — to one who has wandered all through the dark of the night, señora!"

"She's a pretty child," said Mrs. Mackay. "Of course, she's not grown up."

Don Felipe bit his lip. This placing of Mary, as it were, in the cradle, took half the sting from the remarks which he was about to make; but, having committed himself to this strain, he was forced to go on.

"And so, at last," said he, "I could not keep the barrier up. I had a dreadful sense of guilt and impertinence. I felt that I would be stared at and then laughed at. But this morning — I told your daughter that I loved her!"

There was, of course, a pause.

Then Mrs. Mackay made her voice cheerful and answered: "And Mary, of course, was a very happy girl! After the affair of Tag, the other night, she hardly could be anything else."

It was a cruel thrust, but she was not in a humor for mercy.

Don Felipe murmured: "I did not think that a dog, señora, would influence your daughter in such a thing as this."

Then he waited. It had been a hard passage at arms, but now it was the turn for Mrs. Mackay to speak, and she knew beforehand what she must say. Opposition, such as swelled and stormed in her throat, was of no use.

For if she resisted, she felt she knew exactly the mode of procedure which Consalvo would follow. And what could be easier than to persuade a romantic girl like Mary to elope? Somehow this marriage might be prevented. The colonel would be of no use. The whole burden lay upon her slender shoulders, and she knew that she must have time — time and someone like the wise sheriff to help her.

And as she paused, watching the composed face of Consalvo, she wondered if that delicate young man had had something to do with the disappearance of Rankin, so extraordinarily opportune for him!

But, in the meantime, how was she to

gain a safe margin of time?

She had thought out the way, and she said gravely: "Of course it's a shock to think of one's girl marrying — so very young as our Mary is! But, after all, I was her age when I married Colonel Mackay. And there's no use making a disturbance. Besides, you know, we all like you very well — Felipe!"

The name burned her lips!

"The colonel may be difficult. But I'll try to handle him. And then, of course — the thing to do is to have a little party and let your engagement be announced."

Engagement?

Ah, of course that was a matter which did not enter into Don Felipe's plans at all. Engagements? They might last six months, a year, two years! And a whole eternity of events might take place in the meantime.

But what could he do? Only what he did, which was to spring from his chair, and bow before her, and press her pale, cold hand to his lips.

CHAPTER 22

The next point was to secure the colonel.

For, of course, if he put down his foot and resisted, it would be even more fatal than resistance on her own part; the Mexican simply would take Mary from under their eyes and steal her away forever.

The securing of the colonel on the safe side — that is to say, on the side of the marriage — promised to be a difficult matter, and long and deeply Mrs. Mackay pondered the subject that night, and awakened again and again from a brief drowse.

Persuasion might be tried, but the colonel preferred to persuade rather than to be persuaded. Won over he must be, or the elopement would follow the fiercely insulting speech which he would make to Don Felipe. So she delved in her mind and searched for inspiration, and found none!

But in the morning, cold water dashed in her face, and a resolute plunge in a cold bath, brought a new thought.

She put on a soft negligee; she rubbed her eyes until they were red; she rubbed her cheeks until they were redder; she sprinkled water liberally on her face; and then she went to her husband.

He was in slippers and a bath robe, finishing his coffee and sketching a gate for the patio of the bunk house. He did not even look up, but when she had entered and he heard the rustle of her robe, he said: "What for the gate of the bunk house patio, my dear?"

He did not wait, but answered himself: "There have to be trail breakers and pathfinders. And I have it! A delicate wrought-iron tracery, against the green of the garden inside, a rare and arabesqued design facing the west. The men will sit in the patio and see the sunset with this beautiful design patterned against it! That will be something, my dear! That will touch them! Beauty cannot be wasted," he went on, adding a touch to his drawing. "Like the mechanical law that force cannot be wasted and that matter is indestructible. Plant beauty in human soil, and the plant must grow! I'm going to write out that idea. It ought to have a page in *Arts and Decoration*. Page with flower design around the margin. I'm going to let the world have some of my thoughts, Lydia. Confound it, why should a man keep what's best in him to himself?"

Mrs. Mackay threw herself on a couch and buried her face in the silken pillows. She began to weep, hysterically, wonderfully.

"Hello!" said the colonel. "What's up?"

He waited, then he laid aside his drawing with a sigh.

"What's wrong, Lydia?"

A few stammered, obscured words. More sobbing.

The colonel finished his coffee and rose. He knotted the cord around his waist and then, approaching his wife, he leaned above her.

"My poor child," said he, "what's wrong?"

"Oh, terrible!" moaned Mrs. Mackay in her choked voice.

"Of course," said the genial colonel. "It's a terrible world. Now tell me what's wrong? What's upset you, my dear? Tell me all about it?"

"It's ruin!" gasped Mrs. Mackay.

"The devil it is," chuckled the colonel. "Let me see what's in your silly little head. Not one chance in a hundred that it's terrible at all!"

"How — how — how —"

"How what?" said the colonel.

"How can you say such a thing?"

"Because I can guess. Now, what's up?"

"Mary!"

"Eh? What about Mary?"

"Don Felipe!"

"What about the two of 'em, eh?"

"Oh!"

Tremendous sobbings resulted. The colonel yawned and patted her shoulder.

"They're going to be married!" choked Mrs. Mackay into the pillow.

The colonel caught her by the shoulder and raised her until he could look at the swollen, red, wet face.

"Good God!" said he.

Mrs. Mackay sat up, her handkerchief to her face. Above the rim of the lace she could watch him.

"I knew you'd see it was terrible! Oh, oh, what's to be done? *What* can we do!"

The colonel was pale and staggered.

"An ignorant, low Mexican!" cried Mrs. Mackay.

"Ignorant?" said the colonel, instinctively arguing. "On the contrary, a well-informed young fellow. But if the puppy dares to think that he —"

"A lowbred creature!" sobbed Mrs. Mackay.

"Lowbred? The Consalvos are an excellent family, I have every reason to believe. But what the devil! Does he dream that he is on a par with us so as to —"

"You, you!" cried Mrs. Mackay.

"I what?" cried the colonel, growing more angry. "Stop blubbering, Lydia, and talk sense, will you?"

"*You* brought him into our house!"

"By heavens," said the colonel, "are you going to throw the blame on me?"

"Mary's future is ruined! *You* did it!"

"Lydia, you talk like an absolute idiot! Why not invite him? What's wrong with him? Did we ever have a more pleasant guest!"

"— a — *greaser!*" sobbed Mrs. Mackay.

"Lydia, what under heaven are you talking about?" exclaimed her husband. "Greaser? A highbred gentleman of pure Castilian blood —"

"*He* says so!" she wept.

"Do you think that I can't use my eyes? Do you know the world better than I do? I tell you — a gentleman from old stock and flawless descent!"

"He's stolen her under your eyes!" sobbed the wife.

"Under my eyes?" shouted the colonel, defending himself desperately. "Confound it — I — I — I've seen it all along!"

"No!" cried Mrs. Mackay. "You don't approve! Oh, oh, oh, what shall I do!"

"Lydia, you're letting yourself go. Pick yourself up and take yourself in hand. Is Consalvo poison? I introduced him into this household. That ought to be sufficient for you. Besides — Mary has to marry some time!"

"She's only a baby — my poor little darling Mary!"

"She's taller than you are — and a great deal stronger. How old were you when you married?"

"A penniless wretch!" cried Mrs. Mackay.

"I have, thank God, enough money for two."

"Not even a title!" sobbed she.

"Lydia," cried her infuriated spouse, "do you think that I'd let my girl go title-hunting through Europe? No, I thank God that the name of Mackay doesn't need a title! Title? I'd see a title damned! What nonsense you have in your precious brain!"

"It will kill me!" wept Mrs. Mackay.

She fell back on the couch.

"Who told you about this?"

"He — he — had the effrontery to ask my — permission — to — to — speak to you —"

"Exactly as he should have done," said the colonel, wiping his brow. "What else would a gentleman do? I — I'm not surprised. In fact — I'm glad — that Mary has showed such good taste! I prefer Felipe to one of the bridge-playing, cocktail-drinking young puppies who idle around Manhattan!"

"My heart is broken!" sobbed Mrs. Mackay.

"A little time will heal it," said the colonel heartlessly. "But if you're going to keep on crying like this — I'll leave the room, Lydia. I can't stand it!"

And he left the room.

No sooner was he gone than Mrs. Mackay rose and went quietly to her own chamber. There she reclined in an easy chair and began to comb her hair, for there was nothing that soothed her so much as to brush the long and silken masses and watch the light go shivering across it.

After that, she made her toilette by careful degrees, and when she was dressed she looked at herself in the mirror. "Oh, Lydia," she said, "what a golden chance you missed in life!"

Then Mary came bursting in.

She was wild with excitement. She was as foolish and frantic as Tag, who danced around her.

She embraced her mother. She danced from one end of the room to the other and danced back again.

"Dear mother, mother darling," cried Mary. "And you both approve! And you see what a wonderful man Felipe is! And you don't care if he's poor! And — I never heard of two such wonderful people as you and dad. So that Felipe and I can be happy to the end of the world! And I'm going to burst. I want to hug everyone!"

"There's Felipe now," said Mrs. Mackay. "I think he may be waiting for you!"

Felipe, indeed, sat the saddle on Conquistador, dressed in his gayest, and the most splendid of saddles on the stallion, and the bridle and the reins a tangle of gleaming rays of silver light.

Mary shrank back against her mother.

"I'm afraid to go down," she said. "Suppose that it was all a sort of joke — or a dream! And — and how could such a wonderful man even look *twice* at me, mother dear!"

"Men are very strange creatures, Mary," said the mother. "I long ago gave up trying to explain them; and you'd better stop, too! Run along, dear. Felipe will be frightfully impatient!"

And Mary flew and left Mrs. Mackay

standing deep in the shadows of the room and staring out with narrowed eyes at that glorious and flashing horseman.

CHAPTER 23

In some natures mental excitement drives people into social intercourse. In others it sends them into the wilderness, and Mrs. Mackay was of the second order. She went hurriedly down to the stable and there found her husband, talking over the merits of a newly broken three-year-old which was wandering around the small pasture near the corral. The colonel took her aside.

"I see that you've taken a better view of things, my dear," said he. "Mary tells me that you've let yourself be persuaded to be sensible. I've had a long talk with both of 'em. The attitude of Felipe is ideal. He seems to have a great respect for me — for us, I mean. And he appreciates what it means to ally himself to the Mackays. There will be no foolishness. I put my foot down at once and let him see, for future reference, so to speak, that there is to be only one head to this house. He has the delightful attitude of the well-bred Mexican. The oldest man in the family carries the undisputed authority. He at once asked my advice. Should he take out citizenship papers? Would his faulty knowledge of English permit that? Of course I told him it was the one thing to do. Everything is to be arranged. Everything! The affair is going to be perfectly handled!"

She could not help saying: "What a romantic adventure it is, after all! He started out to find his golden treasure, and even if he hasn't located the Seven Lost Cities, he's found his pot of gold, hasn't he!"

"In a manner of speaking, yes," said the colonel. "And when I consider the youth and the good looks and the grace of Felipe, my dear, I imagine that he's just the sort of a Prince Charming who might have stepped out of the fairy tale. And —"

Here he stopped short, stabbed by an uncomfortable suspicion.

"Lydia, was there something ugly in that remark of yours?"

"In mine, dear?" echoed Lydia naïvely. "Why, how should there be?"

The colonel sighed, with suspicion still in the corner of his eye; but, after all, he was much interested in the colt which was under examination, and he turned reluctantly from his wife. But there was a shadow upon his brow.

Mrs. Mackay continued the affable smile

which made her beloved on the ranch until she had mounted a horse and ridden out of view among the trees. After that, sternly she set the head of her mount into the wind and galloped hard across country, jumping fence and ditch, until she had turned up the valley into the ravine in which it ended.

And all the time that that ride was in progress, she was turning her thoughts swiftly in her mind, trying to find a starting point, a sort of purchase from which she could exert lifting power in the direction which she wanted.

The best thing that occurred to her was to make some sort of a search into the actual past of Don Felipe — locate the lost rancheria of the Consalvos, and determine what had been the actual position of Felipe in regard to his family.

That, however, would take time. But, after all, if she could keep Consalvo from being suspicious, it might be that she could keep him safely on the ranch until her investigations were completed — and if those investigations did not return a most rich yield, then both she and the wise sheriff had been oddly mistaken in their judgment of this youth.

She turned her pony — her mind quite

darkened by these reflections — up the side of the ravine, and climbed a dangerous and twisting course to the higher land above. It was a narrow and lofty ridge which commanded a good prospect in every direction except to the north, where the higher mountains rose. All to the south and west and east extended a wilderness, a region of brush traversed by many cañons which ran water only for a few weeks when the snow was melting fast in the higher valleys.

Over that gloomy region she looked, feeling that it was much in tune with her state of mind, where so many cross and devious intentions were springing up every moment, and where there was such a dark thicket of doubt.

And then, as she watched, she saw a tall and ragged figure break out of the jungle and head swiftly across an open stretch, disappearing at once in another small thicket.

Mrs. Mackay stiffened in the saddle, for the man was Pedro; and the body servant of Don Felipe ran with such steadiness and rhythm to his stride that she could not doubt he was bent on some mission of a definite nature. No one entered such badlands as these for the mere pleasure of a jaunt across country, and certainly no one would perform such a journey on foot and at the run unless there were an important need.

She rode higher up the ridge, and now she had a view of the runner again, pressing on steadily, and weaving through the underbrush with an amazing skill.

Nothing suggested itself as an explanation of his goal, but she felt that, somehow, it must have to do with Don Felipe's affairs, and therefore it was her business, distinctly.

Again he disappeared, and again she rode higher up the slope; but this time he was definitely lost. She rode still farther, but there was no further view of him, and at last she turned down from the ridge, entered the cañon, and went back towards the house.

It was late in the morning when she arrived. But Mary was not back; she would not be there with Felipe until lunch time, she had left word.

And Mrs. Mackay went to her room and walked nervously up and down, up and down.

She had the desperate sense of obligation pressing upon her, and yet she knew not what to do immediately. Even how to start the investigation of the Consalvos seemed a puzzle to her. There was no detective agency in the town. She knew of the address of none in a more distant place; and if she asked for funds from the colonel to fee the investigators, he was sure to ask embarrassing questions.

Once he had committed himself to the whole affair, of course he would take it as the grossest insult to his intelligence if she showed such suspicions of Mary's husband-to-be!

And then she made her first decision — such a thing as, ordinarily, would have been beyond her wildest dream. She left her room, went down to the patio garden, and tried the gate into Don Felipe's little private ground.

The gate was open, and passing through when she had made sure that no eye watched her, she crossed the little winding paths of the inner garden and pressed against the door.

It was locked!

But there was a window yawning wide. She was no expert climber, but she managed to drag herself up to the sill. There a rending sound stopped her. She had torn her dress squarely across the knee!

Well, it was a small tragedy, but it made

her heart thunder, for she felt that even so small a detail as this might serve as a clue against her.

From the window she stared hungrily around the room.

There was not the least detail that could serve to excite any suspicion. Some one had lain on the bed since it was made up in the morning, and on the little bedside table was an ash tray containing a few butts of cigarettes.

She lowered herself to the floor, cautiously, watching where her feet fell, for she felt sure that the eye of a lynx would fall on that room before it was many hours older.

There was nothing worthy of observation. A little paper-bound book lay crumpled on the center table. She picked it up and glanced. It was Froissart, and in the Old French — a battered and much thumbed volume. And Mrs. Mackay opened her eyes very wide. It was such a book as one might imagine the young cavalier delighted in, but after all — in French — in the original French of that ancient century!

Decidedly there was much to this youth that would bear careful and patient study.

She was trembling with a greater fear than ever when she went on. In a closet, she found the wardrobe of Don Felipe, but not such a bulging one as one would have suspected from the contents of the three great mule-packs which had been driven into the yard of Mackay House and unloaded there.

She opened the second closet, which lady guests were apt to use as a dressing-room, because of its dimensions and the little window that lighted it. There she found two packs, apparently intact since their arrival.

She prodded them with a tentative foot, and encountered something hard and unyielding as metal.

But what could be in it?

She tried the other, and found, as nearly as she could judge, nothing but cloth under the point where she pressed.

Then, yielding to an impulse that made her crimson with shame, she undid the knot and opened the pack with shaking hands.

Inside, there was nothing at all!

Nothing, at least, of any value. Some ragged blankets of age were wrapped on the outside, and inside there were bricks, wood, cotton waste, and other junk, made up so as to serve for the dimensions and the weight of an ordinary pack.

And Mrs. Mackay looked slowly up, with a fierce and satisfied gleam in her eye. Certainly this excursion had not been for naught!

She folded back the covers of the pack as swiftly and as carefully as she could, and then drew up the cords. As for the making of the knot, she must be sure that it was correctly done, so first she studied the knot of the remaining great bundle, and when she was certain of the way, she made the knot.

After that, she stood up and surveyed the room carefully, to make sure that she had left no telltale signs behind her. But, as she did so, she heard a voice speaking down the hall, dimly — a voice that chilled her blood.

A door opened, and the voice of Don Felipe rang fairly in her ears!

CHAPTER 24

Mrs. Mackay, sick at heart, clenched both her hands and strove to think; but she knew that when the tall and slender young Mexican stood before her she would be white as death, with her guilt in her face.

But then the door closed and the voice of Don Felipe sounded in the hall — and the smaller voice of Mary answered gaily in the distance, like the far-off tinkle of a bell.

That instant she made again for the window and scrambled through it, harum-scarum, and, landing on the gravel of the path outside, she bolted for the gate of the garden.

Arrived at it, she paused one instant to gather her wits and re-take her breath. Then she passed through and swept her glance over the larger patio; but nothing stirred in it saving the shower of the fountain, and the swinging tendrils of the climbing vines, with their delicate shadows beneath them.

So she made her way safely to the house, and up the stairs to her room, with no eye to mark her torn dress. Afterwards, she could explain it to her maid as a riding accident.

When she was safe again in her own sanctum, she slipped into a chair and, bowing her head in both hands, she went over the details of every move she had made while she was in the room of the Mexican. So far as she remembered, she had not made a single false motion, and unless the hard tiles of the floor betrayed the imprint of her feet, she felt that nothing earthly could detect her presence in that chamber. Then, being assured of this, she permitted herself to draw breath, changed for luncheon, and, after a preliminary interview with herself in the mirror, she went calmly down the stairs.

It was a gay luncheon, largely because Mary babbled like a brook, and was full of everything her eye had touched on or her ear had heard during her ride of the morning. For it seemed to be a new and transfigured world to the girl, and all that she had noticed today was noticed, as it were, for the first time.

They had claret, cool from the cellar; claret which the colonel had laid in at countless expense and installed deeper, it seemed, than prohibition could delve, and every time the glass of Mary went to her lips, her eyes sought Don Felipe, and always she received, for an answer, that faint and gentle smile.

Mrs. Mackay looked down to the table once or twice, and had to steady herself by touching the side of her chair with her moist finger-tips.

But somehow she got through the ordeal, and afterwards, when she was alone with the colonel, he wreathed the room with his cigar smoke and smiled at her through the circlings of the drifts.

"Ideally mated," said the colonel. "By heaven, it was a sort of preternatural foresight that came to me when I first met with Don Felipe! Instinct, Lydia. I'll think the better of instinct and myself as long as I live!"

"Like Falstaff," murmured Mrs. Mackay, but her voice was not heard. There were things which the colonel hardly could pay attention to, and the voice of his wife was among the first of them.

They were near enough to the land of mañana for siestas to be observed religiously, and so when the Casa Mackay was falling into its midday slumber, Don Felipe retired to his room and, picking up his book on the way, he stretched himself on his bed to read more of the vagaries and the whims and the bloodthirsty madnesses of the citizens of Ghent.

But no sooner had he started to read than he bounded from the bed and whirled about on Pedro.

The latter, though he had a room assigned to him, preferred, commonly, to spend all his spare time in the chamber of his master. He would have slept across the door of Don Felipe's apartment at night, had not the latter strictly forbidden it. Now he sat cross-legged on a strip of matting near the door which led to the garden. In his hand was a very long-stemmed pipe with a great bowl packed to the brim with fuming tobacco, which he would consume to the last morsel before he had his brief siesta. And every mouthful of the smoke would be drawn deeply into his lungs before it was exhaled, the smoke being made to sweep towards the floor and then, slowly, upwards towards the ceiling. After which, he remained for a moment with his head bent back, as though scanning some starry destiny outlined on the plaster above his head. After that, came the next long inhalation, and the same gradual movement repeated.

Don Felipe, starting upright in this

fashion, pointed an accusing finger at his servant.

"Pedro!"

The Indian laid the pipe on the floor and folded his arms.

"Señor?" he said.

"You have picked up this book!"

"I, señor?"

"Yes! Don't lie to me about it!"

"I, señor, never say the thing that is not so!"

"The book has been moved," said Don Felipe. "It was not at this page when I laid it down!"

The Indian nodded, and then, rising, he picked up his pipe and glided on noiseless, bare feet into the second and largest closet, beckoning to his master to follow.

When they were within, Pedro pointed to the knot on one of the large packs.

"Untie this, señor!"

Felipe Consalvo obeyed, not pausing to ask questions, for he knew his man of old, and Pedro's love of approaching matters obliquely. Direct statements were as poison to the Indian's way of thought.

"And now this," said Pedro, as the first knot was untied.

Don Felipe did as he was told.

"Was there a difference, señor?"

"Why," said Don Felipe, "the first one was tight, and the second was easier. What of that?"

"In all my life," said the Indian, "I never have tied knots in two ways. The tight knot is mine; the second I did not tie."

Don Felipe paused to stare, at this revelation.

"Then who in the name of the devil did tie it?" he asked.

"This one," said Pedro, and he led the way, quietly, out of the closet and to the window of the room.

There, adhering to the rough plaster of which the sill was formed, was a slender filament of wool.

Don Felipe loosened it and raised it, so that the light shone through it, transparent green.

"One of the mozas," said Don Felipe slowly. "She's been curious and opened our packs. And by heaven, Pedro, she's seen what's in them — or rather, what isn't in them!"

Pedro had returned to his pipe and smoked it as calmly as before.

"We've been discovered," went on his master with a low and rapid voice. "They've snatched the mask halfway off our faces. Was it a moza? Can we find out who it was? And then, how much money will it take to keep her silent?"

"Money will not keep her silent," said Pedro quietly.

"No?"

"It will not, señor."

"Then what will?"

Pedro tilted his head again to blow an inhalation at the ceiling, and as the smoke flattened, with curling edges, against the plaster, he gradually drew his forefinger across his enormous throat.

"Ah," said Don Felipe. "You know the woman then, Pedro?"

The Indian nodded.

At this, his master sat down on the floor, cross-legged likewise.

"Pedro," said he, "from the day when you saved me from the bear, I've known that you're tangled up with my life and my fate. I have known it as truly, Pedro, as though I heard it in the voice of the Thunder Bird!"

Pedro glanced, startled, over his shoulder. And then, mixing his creeds at random, he made the rapid sign of the cross.

"I have known," said Don Felipe, "that why I sleep soundly at night is because there is a lion near me. And the reason that

I can walk without looking over my shoulder is because there is a mountain lion walking at my back. Do you hear me, Pedro?"

The Indian, lifting his brows, closed his eyes, and drew in deeply from the pipe. But by a certain tenseness around his mouth, Don Felipe knew that the man was pleased to the very cockles of his hard and brutal heart.

"And now, Pedro," he continued, "you have found out the thing which means the most to me, just now, for you have found out the woman who has invaded this room and spied on us. Tell me — is she someone apt to tell the colonel what she has seen?"

The Indian nodded.

"I thought as much," said Don Felipe. "Well, if she has reported it already — he'll make a joke of it, perhaps. Call it vanity, eh? I wonder if she's told him?"

He asked his own silent judgment, rather than the Indian. But Pedro shook his head.

"She has not told," said he.

"You know a great deal," said Don Felipe. "You've talked to her, then, since she was in here?"

"No."

"Come!" said Don Felipe. "I don't believe that you have the least idea who she is. You're making a great smoke out of a small fire, Pedro."

"I? No, it is not so. But the señora wore a green cloth this morning."

Don Felipe leaped from the floor.

"Oh, marvelous gods!" said he. "It is she again! Pedro, Pedro, I am blind. I see nothing except with your eyes!"

Those eyes, at the moment, glowed with a profound satisfaction, and Pedro had to look hastily down to the floor to conceal his proud emotion.

His master stood by the garden window.

"Through this," he said, "climbing like a tomboy, and then stealing into this room, and then to the closet — and then actually daring to open the pack — and closing it again with the same knot — and listening for my footstep all the time — God, God! Since such a glorious creature was made, why was she not made of my own age? I knew she was an eagle, Pedro. Now you have shown me that she is a snake as well; she is complete!"

CHAPTER 25

Mrs. Mackay, with eyes half closed in thought, enumerated to herself the testimony which she had gathered, and though it was of the various kinds, still she was not satisfied. In the first place, this was a young Mexican adventurer, and his alien race and his condition were both qualities against him. In the second place, he was a person of consummate poise and an actor of the rarest ability, and, having these talents, he could, if he wished, excel as a deceiver. In the third place, she was convinced that such deception was in his mind, partly because of what the sheriff had told her concerning the shooting of the gunman, and partly because of her own discovery concerning the empty pack. Moreover, there was the affair of the rescue of Tag, when this pretender to a feminine cowardice had played the part of a hero, and played it with such a really nonchalant grace that Mrs. Mackay had not the slightest doubt that he had revealed his actual nature on that occasion.

Yet, when she added up these matters,

she saw that there was practically nothing — unless it were the affair of the stuffed pack — which would have appeared as evidence in the eyes of a jury of twelve good men and true, for instance.

When Mrs. Mackay had come to this conclusion, she did not fail to admit to herself that, really, what she had most against this young man was the strong action of instinct in her. And though she was willing to allow that instinct is a blind and often a foolish judge, yet she could not help trusting in the voice that accused Don Felipe of being, not a black villain, not a murderer or a low scoundrel, but simply a predatory creature who threatened to take from her, by wile, that possession which was of all the world the dearest thing to her.

So she pondered this matter, and instead of throwing up her hands in despair, she looked out on the thing as a general looks out on a field of battle, seeing his troops driven back in all directions, his last reserves vainly thrown in to stem the rout, and nothing remaining to him except the sheer power of his mind to conceive some counterstroke.

So Mrs. Mackay looked down upon the human snarl which lay in her path, and strove out of her own intelligence to find some way of solving her problem.

The sheriff — if he had been near — might have rendered her vastly vital help. But the sheriff was gone. Or, had she had the time and the courage, perhaps a further examination of all that was in the chamber of Don Felipe might have revealed to her as much as she needed to know. Or if she could find, in the world, one person who ever had known of Consalvo before. Or, indeed, if she could achieve what seemed impossible and draw from Pedro, the great sullen Indian, what he knew about his master.

Now that Pedro was in her thoughts again, she recalled that morning excursion and the intentness of purpose with which the Indian had struck across country, and yet had returned so promptly to the house, as if he had performed a set errand. What could the errand be which had sent him hunting so resolutely across the countryside? Or was it, indeed, to get in touch with certain confederates who might be held in the background by Don Felipe, ready to second him in some sort of a coup?

The thought made her tremble.

And yet, before the afternoon was old,

she was in the saddle again and away up the valley.

She went straight to the ravine, and rode up it until she had gained the commanding point where she had sat her horse that morning. From this vantage place she scanned once again the brush through which she had seen Pedro working, and so well had the picture been printed in her thoughts that she could pick out once again the exact course he had followed. It led straight from the direction of the house, and it pointed merely at the blank wall of the ravine-side. Yet, beyond a doubt, the trail of Pedro had led higher up the narrow gorge, winding close under the cliff.

She prepared to ride straight down the precipitous slope into the hollow when she remembered that if her fear, however far-fetched, should prove to have some substance, and if confederates of the Mexican were actually in hiding near by, then the noise of her horse through the thicket would be as ample as the sounding of trumpets to announce her approach.

And God alone could tell what might come of that!

Yet, if she abandoned her horse and trusted herself to her own feet — what then, if they were to come upon her?

She paused a few moments, trembling violently, in brief spasms, but once she had set before herself a great goal, she could not hold back from it.

She tethered her horse in a dense grove that stood up like wind-blown hair on the top of the ridge, and when she was certain that he could be seen from no side by any passer-by, she ventured down into the ravine and had come almost to the bottom of the slope when her foot dislodged a hundred pound stone.

She caught at it as it began to roll, but it slipped easily from her grip and, gaining headway, it bounded crashing through the brush below.

Loud, breaking echoes roared up and down the ravine. It seemed to Mrs. Mackay, as she stood transfixed, that heavy artillery was booming and that the reverberations never would die away. But at length silence closed like a wave about her, and all the valley lay waiting at her feet.

She turned to climb towards the height above her; at once fear rushed out behind her from the brush and she sank against the slope, half fainting.

Yet, when she faced the shrubbery once more, nothing stirred, nothing lived beneath her eye except the wind, softly pushing the tops of the bushes this way and that.

By degrees her courage and steadiness returned. And with that, she stood up, resolutely faced the valley, and walked down to the bottom level.

She had not failed, when she was above, to mark the place on the wall towards which the course of Pedro had seemed to be set, but, now that she was below, all was so different that she could not be sure of the spot with any certainty. However, she started on again, and winding as close to the wall as the heaps of rocks permitted, she came at last opposite her chosen goal.

There was a sheer face of solid rock before her, and nothing that could indicate the slightest possible place of concealment. For a moment her relief was greater than her disappointment, for she could tell herself, now, that she had been true to her purpose and made an honest and courageous effort.

Then, as she rallied from her first shock, she could not help smiling at the foolishly romantic fear which she had had.

And suppose that there were scoundrels concealed in this ravine, what could she gain by coming upon them, and how could she hope to observe them without being in turn observed? At that very moment, she saw, in a patch of damp red clay just before her, the print of a huge naked foot — and all her blood curdled at once.

She tried to reason herself out of her fear, because already she had known that Pedro had come this way; and yet the mark of him on the ground seemed to bring back his gigantic ghost to stare sombrely at her.

Twice she turned back to fly, and twice she checked herself with a mighty effort. The third time, she faced forward and went slowly, almost feeling her way, down the edge of the wall.

For another hundred yards or more she went, and she was about to turn back definitely — for there was no further sign of Pedro's footing — when the ravine at that side yielded back in a sharp angle, and, as she turned it, she saw before her a narrow and pitch-black opening in the rock.

It was both high enough and wide enough to admit a man easily!

This time, be sure, the heart of Mrs. Mackay failed her entirely, and all that kept her from rushing headlong back down the ravine was the terrible and nightmare weakness of her knees, which sagged helplessly; and there was a rush of giddiness, so that she feared for one frightful moment that she would faint.

For so it is often with highly imaginative people, and dangers which they have foreseen are doubly awful when they are realized.

So, for long and deadly moments she remained there, drawing her breath with difficulty and fighting off the blackness which surged in waves across her mind. Then, at last, her mind cleared, and she turned stealthily to make her escape.

Behold! The mouth of the cavern had become like a vast dark eye staring forth behind her and pouring out danger. In spite of herself, she could not help hurrying a little, and at the first hasty step, a small dead branch crackled underfoot — a report like the noise of a gun in the ear of poor Lydia Mackay.

Then, as fear halted her and made her twist around, both hands clenched, a crown was placed on the horror, for out of the narrow and black entrance of the cave came the low whinny of a horse!

Mrs. Mackay caught up a stone and gripped it until it cut her hands, with a sort of vague and hysterical impulse towards self-defense.

The neigh of the horse ceased; the hollow echoes rolled the last tones towards her, and she was about to shrink back around the edge of the cliff corner and then flee with all her might when she heard the voice of a man, calling loudly from the same quarter: "Who's there?"

And again: "Who's there?", more loudly.

At that, she began to run in fact and with all her might, but instead of retreating she pressed straight forward, for in that calling voice she had recognized without fail the drawling and distinctly nasal tones of Sheriff Rankin!

CHAPTER 26

Surely in all the music of the fabled spheres there never was a sound more welcome than the slow tones of the sheriff, and Mrs. Mackay, running headlong, like a girl to meet a lover, passed the dark mouth and stood in the throat of the cave.

It was not black at all, but suffused with a mild and pleasant twilight, and it was of ample dimensions, so that at one side stable room was preserved for the sheriff's favorite mustang which he had been riding on that unlucky morning.

As for the sheriff, he stood up, but he could not advance very easily, for his hands were fastened together and wrapped with strips of leather, and his feet were both hobbled and tied to a heavy boulder which he could not possibly drag after him.

When he saw Mrs. Mackay, the sheriff turned a bright, bright crimson.

"Well, ma'am," said he, "you can see how I been investigating Mr. Consalvo, can't you?"

She said not a word, but got out a little

knife which she always carried with her when she was riding, for with it she could cut any blossoming twigs or little branches that caught her eye.

Now, with that knife, she freed the sheriff in half a moment. He did not pause, then, to make any explanations, but hastily he saddled his mustang, and then, from the wall, he took down a pair of big Colts which seemed far too long and massive to be balanced by his slender wrists.

So, armed again and ready, he led his horse to the mouth of the cave. Only when he had the blue sky above him and freedom before his eyes did the sheriff pause and draw a deep breath.

"Maybe," said the sheriff, "it's the turn of the tide. I dunno. I ain't a prophet. But maybe, Señor Consalvo, I'm gunna be able to make you sweat blood from now on!"

"I don't understand a bit of it," said Mrs. Mackay. "Oh, I can understand that Consalvo might have met you — but you're living, Mr. Rankin!"

"I don't understand it neither," replied the sheriff. "Nobody, for that matter, could understand anything about him except that he shoots straight and tells lies."

"Will you tell me what happened? And is

there danger that they'll be back here — soon?"

"They won't," said the sheriff. "Pedro comes here once a day, late in the morning. What happened, I'll tell you. When I started for town, Consalvo come sashaying after me. When he came up, he started his usual chatter and foolishness. I tried to get the drop on him right there, but he made a fool of me," remarked the sheriff slowly. "And he shot the gun out of my hand."

He touched his forehead, decorated as it was with a black patch surrounded with a wide purple stain.

"But he let you live!" said Mrs. Mackay, apparently overwhelmed by that fact.

"He did," admitted the sheriff. "He let me live, although he knew it was dangerous. I told him that somebody might pass and if they did I sure would be turned loose to plague him. What would he answer?"

"That he was willing to take a gambling chance," said she, "rather than have a murder on his hands."

The sheriff whistled.

"It looks to me," said he, "as though you knew him pretty fair!"

"Of course I do," said she. "I've had to live with him all this time, the scoundrel."

"We'll just be drifting," remarked the sheriff. "You never can quite tell about him. He might of started trailing you, after you left the house today —"

She started, but then confidently she shook her head.

"He never could trace me," she said. "I followed a course that led over too many rocks where even horseshoes wouldn't leave a mark."

The sheriff was not convinced, for, he said, it was foolish to judge young Mr. Consalvo according to other men. "Where they leave off," he said, "he begins. How do things rest at the ranch?"

"Consalvo is engaged to my daughter," said she, and paused.

The sheriff blinked at her, and then he nodded.

"You couldn't do a thing?"

"I persuaded my husband to agree to the marriage. Everything is happy! Consalvo suspects me, I think, but he doesn't know that I've simply been fighting for time. But if he really feels that he's in danger, he'll whisk Mary away before we have time to draw breath!"

The sheriff nodded again.

"But now," said Mrs. Mackay, "it's too late for him! We'll go straight to the ranch and arrest him — an assault on an officer of the law is enough to put him in prison, I suppose?"

"And who'll put him there?" asked the sheriff calmly. "Me? I've tried him before, and he's too much for me." He made the admission without apparent shame. "Or am I to get together some of your cowpunchers and tackle him with them? Before I could get them together, he'd have the alarm and be off like a bird. No, that idea wouldn't work."

They fell silent, each turning over many thoughts and finding none that would exactly serve.

"I'm going back to the town," said the sheriff at length. "There I'll run through my papers and discover what I can. And there ain't one chance in ten that I'll miss finding out something about this man. After that, I'll pick up a few good fighting men and come back. You return to the ranch. You've just been for an outing, Mrs. Mackay. That's all! And be as kind to Consalvo as you can. Sometime between dark and morning, I'll come back to the house, and the first room that we go to will be Consalvo's. How does that sound to you?"

"I don't think that I could face him

again," said she. "He reads faces as other people read the pages of a book. How could I look into those cunning eyes again, sheriff, without letting him see that something has happened?"

"Try it," advised Rankin. "You take a high-strung sort of a person like yourself, and you always got a lot more strength than you imagine, when the pinch comes. Besides, what is there better to do?"

She pondered only a moment, and then she agreed.

But she said with a certain solemnity before they parted: "I'm going back to keep up the fight single-handed for a time, Mr. Rankin. For though there are so many men on the place, there's no one that I can confide in. There's not one! I'll go there and do what I can, and wait for you, and pray for you!"

The sheriff moistened his dry lips.

Then: "Tell me one thing," she asked. "I can understand why he would have left you alive, but why should he have left your horse with you? That was simple insanity on his part, wasn't it?"

"Insanity? Nope," answered the sheriff. "Softness. When you get a gent as hard as him, he's sure to have soft places. Most of us are just flesh. But when you find a fellow that's chiefly steel, there's always sure to be some unarmored places no tougher than dough. He was leading the pony away to shoot it, when old Midge threw his head around and whinnied for me.

"Mind you, now, there ain't any fondness between Midge and me. He tries to kick my head off when I catch him for saddling, and he unlimbers himself by trying to buck me off first and eat me afterwards. But just then, Midge he took it into his head to whinny, and the Mexican, he stopped like somebody turned to stone.

"He hung onto the reins for a minute and kicked at a stone with the toe of his boot. Pretty soon he says: 'This nag loves you, Rankin, I see?'

"I said nothing. I didn't want to lie, even to Consalvo. I didn't have to. His imagination had got to running away with him. Pretty soon he leads Midge back to me.

" 'I'm taking a wild and a long chance,' says he, 'in leaving you alive, Rankin. And it makes it worse when I leave the horse with you. To keep two in hiding is a hundred times harder than to keep one. And yonder there's a gulch where the body of that pony could rot away to bones, and nobody but the buzzards ever be any wiser.

But — by heaven, I haven't it in my heart. Here's your horse, Rankin. I'll leave him with you!'

"And so he went away, and ever since, when the Indian brought out chuck for me, he had to pack along oats for the horse. He hated that job, did Pedro. And he cussed the horse and he cussed me extra hard, each time. If it had been Pedro that had the handling of the job, me and Midge would have died a long time since. But it was the fault of Consalvo. You see, ma'am, every great crook has his weak sides. Even Napoleon did, they say!"

He mounted Midge, and that faithful horse, as the sheriff had prophesied, began to buck furiously, full of the energy which his long rest had piled up in his body. For five minutes the sheriff was hard put to it to stay in the saddle, but long experience had taught him just what to expect from the deviltry of Midge, and so he kept his seat until the flurry was over. Midge, then, broke into a headlong gallop. A twitch on the reins headed him straight across the hills towards the town, and, turning in the saddle, he took off his hat and waved it towards Mrs. Mackay.

Instantly she turned and hurried back towards the place where she had left her own horse on the ridge, for she feared to be left behind where the silence of that narrow gulch once again might sweep over her.

Up the steep wall she climbed — a far different task from the mere descent — and so she gained the top at last and went gasping for breath towards the dense little grove which rose before it. Into the center of it she passed and there halted with a shock of ice striking through brain and body. For her horse was not there!

CHAPTER 27

The disappearance of the horse lifted the whole matter out of the sphere of reality and made it as dreadful as some horror from a fairy tale. She looked wildly around her at the tall, rough trunks of the trees, and at the great wrists of the roots which projected, here and there, from the ground; and in that terrible moment she regarded the brilliant streak of a blue jay that flew rapidly across an opening in the tree tops. They were birds of ill omen, she had heard since she came West!

She was afraid to leave the group of trees for fear lest the man who had removed her horse would now be able to see her fleeing across the open; she was afraid to remain in the shelter of the boughs in the greater fear lest he should return and find her there.

And she thought, first of all, of climbing high into one of the trees and hiding herself there, as well as she could. But a second thought told her that the foliage was too thin and open. There would be little chance of protection, here, from such a keen eye as that of Don Felipe!

When she had made that point in her mind, she went cautiously forward towards the edge of the tree-circle, and there she hung in doubt for a moment. If she ventured forward, some watcher instantly might see her. Then what was her hope of escape?

Now the sun was dropping rapidly in the West, and, every little knoll lay with its long, thickening shadow beside it. If she could gain a slight hollow not far before her, into that she could drop, and lying flat, raise her head to survey the dangers that might lie around her.

She had taken a step out into the open when she saw a head and shoulders loom on the verge of the ridge, where it showed in bold outline against the sky; and Mrs. Mackay leaped back to shelter, biting her lips to restrain the outcry of terror.

It was the giant Indian, Pedro, coming at a swift pace, leaning forward as though to diminish his bulk in case some eye were spying upon it. He swayed a little from side to side with the strength of his running, and his face seemed to Mrs. Mackay more terrible than anything she ever had seen in her life, for there was the intelligence of a man, and the ferocity of a brute in it.

Straight toward her he came, and she knew that flight never could keep her from him. She thought first of screaming; but then she realized that Rankin was far, far away, now, and driving towards the town with all the strength of his mustang's gallop.

So she took out again the little knife which, already, had done one great task that day, and she held it in a firm hand. She was amazed at herself, for, though she was frightened more than ever she had been frightened before, her mind remained cold and steady; and through the drift of greenery before her she watched the Indian approach.

Then, as he drew closer, the ghost of a hope came to her that, after all, he had not marked her, for his course did not point so accurately at the spot where she was standing.

A moment more, and he had entered the circle of the trees. There was no crashing of the underbrush; there was no thudding of feet and no crackling of dead pine needles, but like a shadow he went past her not three yards away.

She was safe for that instant, then, beyond the best of her dreams; and she slipped out and began to run as softly and swiftly as she could.

If ever God brought her safely through this terror, never would high heels appear on her shoes thereafter!

The direction she chose was the one from which she had seen Pedro approach, for in that way she hoped to come upon her horse and safe means of flight.

Glance behind her she dared not, for though she felt that she had run as swiftly and as softly as a shadow, still the ear of the Indian might have heard! But when she came to the very verge of the high ground, a cold fear gripped the small of her back and made her jerk her head about.

There was Pedro! And if he had run swiftly before, he came at her now like a thunderbolt, and she could see the gleaming whites of his eyes as he rolled them in his fury and in his effort.

Mrs. Mackay screamed and flung herself down the slope before her, gained the brush, and, venturing another glance behind, saw Pedro towering like a giant into the heart of the sky. Once more her throat went numb with her shriek, and facing forward, she fled with a blind speed.

Ah, no, there was one sight which could bring back sense to her sight, and that was the form of her horse, the reins thrown over his head, and now looking up cheerfully, ears pricked, to watch her race, still gathering in his last bite of grass. One of Pedro's mules stood near by, saddled and bridled, and so she knew how he had been able to follow so swiftly after her.

Towards her horse she flung herself, grasped the pommel, and flung herself upwards and to the side until she found herself in the saddle. There was no need to speak to her mount or touch him with a whip. This mode of approach might have alarmed him had he been a lion, and now he was flying before she was well seated in the saddle.

Behind her was the dark form of Pedro, springing closer. She dared not glance at it, but leaned forward to escape the reaching hand; while Pedro's mule, equally alarmed, darted away with a squeal and a whinny, stepped on his reins, broke them short, and then kept on like a wild, mad thing.

Up the ravine she sped like an arrow; when she looked back once more, there was no sign of Pedro. Then she remembered that during all this adventure the Indian had not uttered a sound, and for some reason that thought made her sick with more mortal dread than ever.

However, she managed to check her horse, and gathered the reins over his head. Then she went on steadily, riding neither hard nor fast, but with her mind working hard.

For she realized now that the die had been cast and this trouble was taken out of her guidance almost entirely.

Pedro would catch his mule, no doubt, and then go to the cave to make sure that his prisoner was well. When he found the sheriff gone, he would come like a homing pigeon for his master. And then?

She caught her breath and set her teeth.

Whatever Don Felipe did, at that moment, he would do quickly; and she had no doubt that, in some manner, he would be able to turn Mary around his finger.

There was only one slender hope, and that was that Pedro would be so delayed in the catching of his mule that before he reached the house the sheriff would have come and settled everything with one grasp of the iron hand of the law.

So she thought, and hurried her horse homewards. There was no need to speed the sheriff on his way. Already, beyond a doubt, he was feverishly turning his records to find the notice that he wanted of a handsome young Mexican who spoke little

English, who rode a splendid horse, and who was cleverness incarnate.

If that record proved to be at hand, then the case was made out letter perfect, and the end of Don Felipe's career in the house of the Mackays had drawn to a close.

So the house loomed before her, at last; she drew closer, eyeing all its details; and took heed, as she swept nearer, that her impetuous husband already had put a gang to work trenching foundations for the new bunk house, which was to rise so splendidly as to be worthy of a nobler name. Little mark had she made upon the big place since her first coming. All was the work of the colonel, and she was sure of only one thing — that Mary was hers, first of all, and that this one treasure now was imperiled.

She gave her horse to a half-breed stable-boy and then walked lightly to the big house.

For she had no sense of fatigue. She felt, instead, an exhaustless strength to do the work which lay before her.

The instant that she entered the patio, she encountered Don Felipe, strolling idly here and there — a blue and a red flower in his hand, and his eye wandering to find an appropriate third.

A little bouquet for Mary, no doubt!

He bowed low to Mrs. Mackay. He would assist her into the house. He would carry the hat which she was swinging in her hand. He would carry her riding whip.

No, she wanted no help.

So he was left behind in the patio, but she was conscious, as she entered the house, that his last gaze had been fixed most intently on her or on the ground just behind her.

She, in the shadow of the hall, looked downwards and saw that both her heels were deeply stained by the red clay into which she had stepped in the ravine.

It caused her an instant's shock. But, after all, there must be hundreds of places where there was red clay. Certainly even the brilliant brain of Don Felipe would not be able to deduce anything damaging from that!

Yet she was more subdued and more desperate, as she went up to her room.

The colonel saw her passing his study, where the door was open. She had a trapped sensation when she heard him sing out:

"Lydia! Oh, Lydia! Come in here a moment, will you, my dear?"

She stood helplessly before him.

"I've a grander idea than ever. Look here — you see it? A fine sweep of lawn all across the front of the patio, with two splendidly curving paths for the men to ride in and out by. I'll transplant a couple of strong young trees. Make that lawn look a century older inside of two years. By gad, Lydia, it will round off the whole place. What do you think?"

She smiled. It was all he wished. And so she was allowed to go free to her own chamber.

CHAPTER 28

When the sheriff reached the town, he went straight to his office. Half a dozen times he was hailed from the edges of the street, and he waved his hand idly in returning the greetings. But his heart was before him in the midst of the records of his office.

When he got to the little veranda in front of his office, he found there four men seated on two chairs and two boxes, tilted back against the wall. One was his old deputy and caretaker; the remaining three were strangers. Of these one stepped forward to him.

"You're Sheriff Rankin?"

"I am."

"Name is Morgan. Can I have five minutes of your time, sheriff?"

"Morgan," said the sheriff, "I'd like fine to sit and have a talk with you, but I'm mighty busy."

He stepped on to the door, but there his shoulder was tapped.

"So am I," said Morgan. "Mighty busy, I mean!"

The sheriff passed off this interruption with a smile and went on into his room.

There, in an instant, he had his files open and was spreading them on the desk when there was an abrupt, loud knock at his door and another of the three strangers entered.

"Afternoon, Rankin," said he. "My name is Lucas. Can I talk to you a minute?"

"Lucas," said the sheriff, "I'd enjoy to talk to you, but I got a mighty important job on my hands, just now. Can't see you now."

He advanced on Lucas, and the latter retreated through the door, protesting: "My business is tolerable important."

"Mine is life and death," said the sheriff.

And he closed and locked the door.

He was irritated by these two interruptions, for, at a time when he had to count seconds, it seemed as though there were a conspiracy to steal his time.

He heard the voice of his deputy calling through the door: "Mrs. Mackay, she come asking for you the other day, sheriff."

"Damn it," snapped the sheriff, "keep still, will you? And never mind Mrs. Mackay."

He began to delve into his files.

They were neatly and alphabetically arranged with the pictures and the records and the detailed descriptions of hundreds and hundreds of criminals of all sorts, not only those who actually had appeared in his own or adjacent territory, but also of others who were of what might be called the migratory type of criminal — yeggs and pushers of the queer and others who were apt to wander here and there across the country.

The sheriff began at "A," and halfway through that letter he looked at his watch and groaned.

Even by this time, who could tell what was happening at the Mackay place?

He wished now, as he had wished before many times, that there had been some efficient way of filing his material other than alphabetically. Often he had wished that it could be arranged by the class of crook — yeggs, gunmen, gamblers, sneak thieves, confidence men, and so forth — and again he had vowed that some day he would undertake the arrangement according to age — men between fifteen and twenty, twenty and twenty-five, and so forth; or, today, if he could have made two or three broad divisions, of blond and dark fellows, and young and old, then he might have made better progress; but, as it was, he was like a hunter for information with the whole of a vast library before him and only an hour at his disposal.

When he had come to this conclusion, and that only patience would help him, he set his teeth and settled grimly to his task. He decided that he would do what he could, and, if he failed to find any clue within a few hours, then he would simply gather some helpers and ride straight out to the ranch of the Mackays.

So time began to pass, swiftly, with a terrible smoothness, slipping away from beneath his fingers, so to speak.

Suddenly someone cleared his throat at the open window, and the sheriff glanced sidewise, scowling, a packet of papers in either hand.

It was the third of the strangers.

"Excuse me, sheriff," said he, "my name is Lodge!"

"It ain't," snapped the sheriff, and, dropping one sheaf of papers, he pointed with a stiff arm at the other. "It ain't Lodge. It's Truman — Mr. Bert Truman, what d'you want with me here?"

The beetling brows of Mr. Bert Truman gathered together. But then he made himself smile.

"You know about me, old timer?" he

said, shrugging his heavy shoulders.

"I know you're a gunman, Truman, and that you cracked the safe of the First National at Lorington, and — I could tell you a lot more about yourself, but I ain't got the time."

"I've done my stretch and taken my medicine," said Truman. "Nobody has got anything on me now!"

"All right," remarked the sheriff angrily. "Maybe you're all right now, but you won't be for long if you keep right on bothering me. Get out, Truman, and leave me alone!"

He turned back to his work.

He had only reached "D"!

Then he was aware that a shadow still hung in the window. He set his teeth, glanced sidewise, and there was Truman still.

"Now what in hell —" began the sheriff.

"Speakin' of life and death," said Truman, "I would like to say —"

"Will you get out of that window?" roared the sheriff, "or do I have to slam it in your flat face?"

Mr. Truman blinked a little, and his black eyes glittered.

"Speakin' of life and death," he said, "I would like to tell you that you would be doin' me a good turn if you could tell me where there's a black-haired, blue-eyed skunk in this part of the world that I'm lookin' for!"

"Shut up!" bellowed the sheriff, and half rose from his chair.

Truman slunk from sight, and the sheriff returned to his task.

Nervous perspiration was beginning to stand out on his forehead, now, and his breath came and went rapidly, as though he were straining forward in a race. A race it was, and against him was the splendid and ruthless talent of the young Mexican. Then, in the middle of the "F's," he was aware once more of a shadow hanging in the window and regarding him.

He turned; and there, hardly credible to his rage, was Mr. Lucas, sun-withered, blond, with a smile upon his lips that was really no smile at all.

"Sheriff Rankin," said he, "I dunno what you're doing, but I got an idea that the three of us have got something just as important on our hands. We're looking for a gent who —"

"By the loving God!" shouted the sheriff, "I'm gunna shoot up the whole gang of you!"

And he snatched up his revolver.

Mr. Lucas glided from the window, and

the sheriff sat down again.

His nerves were jumping, however. Outside his office windows the shadows of the trees along the street were swarming, and the light was diminishing apace. It seemed to the sheriff as if he had entered in a race against nature and its shadows themselves. And they were winning!

For, not long after dark, when the Mackay household met at the supper table, matters would be drawing to a crisis. Then the Mexican and Mrs. Mackay would sit close to each other, and, if there were a great secret in her eyes, what could keep that serene youth from guessing at its nature?

It seemed to the sheriff that he could hear the rather loud voice of the colonel aimlessly dominating all the conversation, all the thoughts of others except his delicate and indomitable wife, and the Mexican.

And then — no, it was a thing to be imagined but never to be realized — another shadow hung in his window. He turned his head by inches away from the "L's" which he was wading through at that moment. He saw that evening was upon him, and that was one reason that his eyes were beginning to ache, but he also saw that in the window were the head and the shoulders of Mr. Morgan.

"Sheriff," began Morgan.

"Out!" yelled the sheriff, and swung up his gun.

Morgan flinched, but then he grasped the ledge of the window with both hands and steadied himself in that position.

"Sheriff," said he, "sure as hell the gent that we want is in your county, and if you can steer us to him, it'd be a grand saving to us and to the law, too. Because if we want him, so do you. You got to!"

"Why, you fool —" began the sheriff.

"There's ten sheriffs that want him!" pleaded Morgan. "For God's sake give us a steer, will you?"

The sheriff wiped the perspiration of rage from his brow.

And the other seemed to take that gesture as one of resignation for he began to pour out the words rapidly.

"Black hair and blue eyes," said he, "and young and damn good-looking. Almost like a pretty woman, he is. Only he ain't. Skinny looking, pretty near; only he's stronger than a mule — rides a horse —"

"My God, that's queer," said the sheriff, wild with sarcasm. "Actually rides a horse, does he? That ought to locate him for you!"

"Rides the grandest looking horse you ever saw — not too big — but it can run all day like a bullet flyin'."

"Damn the horse — damn him — damn you!" said the sheriff inclusively.

But Morgan persisted desperately: "And he's got a big hulk of an Indian along with him —"

The sheriff heard, and he rose slowly and stiffly from his chair, a man transfixed.

CHAPTER 29

To the sheriff it was as with some hardy mariner who, having set his course by a known star and for a known desert island, comes instead upon an uncharted land of beauty and delight.

He could merely murmur: "Come in. All the three of you come in!"

Hastily he unlocked the door, and the three men trooped in, relief and excitement in their faces.

They stood against the wall, their hats in their hands, for the sheriff was a known man, and all stood in awe of him and of his reputation. Yet it seemed to Rankin that never in his life had he faced three grimmer specimens of humanity. Eyed like hawks, with mighty shoulders, gaunt of belly and hip, they had all the air of warriors, and warriors he guessed them to be.

"You know a gent," said the sheriff, "with a big hulk of an Indian, do you, tacking along with him?"

"We do," they said in chorus.

"You, Morgan; what might this gent, this Indian, be like?"

"If you was to take a heavyweight pug," said Morgan, "and then dip him in copper-colored paint, he'd do pretty well for a twin to this here Indian, if he'd had his nose bashed in."

It was a rough but most ready description of Pedro, and the sheriff could not help smiling with joy.

"You got something against this bird that has the Indian, Morgan?" he asked.

"Against him?" said Morgan. "Aw, nothing much, except that I had a five thousand stake, and I was all set pretty to quit the rough stuff and go straight the rest of me days. And then I sit in at a poker game and this gent takes a chair at the same table with me. And we clean out the rest of the three —"

His eyes gleamed faintly, as he recollected.

"And then," said he, "we had a little quiet game of Black Jack —"

"I hear that you're an expert, sort of, at that game?" said the sheriff.

"I am, am I?" said the other. And he began to stare at Rankin: "Say, Rankin, d'you know everything about *everybody?*"

"Not about the gent that has the Indian," smiled the sheriff. "But I expect to find out something about him now! Go on. What happened then?"

"I *am* pretty good," agreed Morgan. "And I can handle the cards. I ain't a fool! Well, I played with him, and I got two thousand cold off him. After that, I pushed the betting up pretty high, because I wanted to clean out the sucker as fast as possible — but by God, the luck seemed to turn. And, all on one deal of his, I was cleaned out to the last penny. Suddenly I seen that I was playin' against a master crook, and I reached for my gun!"

"It's all right," said the sheriff, nodding and sighing. "Where did the bullet hit you?"

Morgan opened eyes which had been half shut in his effort of memory.

"It was no bullet at all that hit me," he answered. "It was a bunch of fives that he hung on the point of me jaw. Who would of thought it? And he looked like a girl, pretty near, and yet I felt as though I'd been clubbed with a joint of lead pipe. There's still an ache in me jaw when I bite into something hard. And by God, I hope that the ache never leaves me, till I meet up with him again and finish the fight that he started then!"

The sheriff paused, before he continued his inquiry, considering Mr. Morgan and his bitter complaint.

"Well, Lucas, what you got against him?" he continued.

"I was up in Butte," said Lucas tersely, "when I run into this bird with the Indian. There was a little job on hand." Here he looked the sheriff defiantly straight in the eye.

"What was it, Lucas?" asked the sheriff. "What you say to me here is as if you said it to a dead man. And if the man you're after is the man that I want, I'll be your friend for life if you can help me to get him!"

"Well," said Lucas, "I dunno that I mind telling you, then. The job was the cracking of a little safe. While some of us was planning the job and the getaway, we seen this pair floating around the town pretty gay. But we thought nothing about them. We done our job, and a good clean one it was, and we come away with twenty-five thou between the four of us. But as we was getting started, this gent stands up before us out of the darkness with a pair of gats. Two of the boys he got through the legs, or somewheres. I seen it was no use, because when I went for my gat it stuck in my coat lining and jerked out of my hand. So I held up my hands and let him go through me. Every cent of that coin he got away with, sheriff, and then the two that he had dropped was grabbed by the cops and soaked, God knows how many years for each of them, and both of them pals of mine. Would that make you take a skunk's trail, I ask you?"

"It would," agreed the sheriff rather slowly. "There's two of you that have lost money to this here pirate. And what about you, my son?"

The third member of the party said in a slow, rather hoarse voice: "I was fixed pretty in Chihuahua. I had everything all laid out for the marrying of a swell little Mex girl, y'understand. Her old man had so damn much coin that he didn't know what to do with his income. I figgered that I could of helped him a good deal. So I started working on the girl, and she was pretty reasonable. She hadn't happened to see many of my kind, and everything was about set, including the marriage date. And then this damned baby-eyed wolf came in between the pair of us. It took him five minutes to make that girl pretty dizzy. After that, she couldn't see me inside of ten miles for a limit. My game was spoiled.

I'd wasted six months going straight, and I had to pack up. But I swore that when I packed I'd never stop traveling until I lined up this —"

He relapsed into a terrible strain of profanity which lasted for some minutes, and finally he ceased, fairly frothing at the lips.

To this the sheriff had listened with the utmost attention.

"And what did he get out of the girl?" he asked.

"She was his quick ticket into her old man's casa," said the other. "And what he done to her old man was plenty. He got thousands out of him, and then he blew the camp. But what good did that do me? The girl went to grieving for him, and afterwards to damning him and all other men, including me. That was the point!"

"Well," said the sheriff, "no matter how, you've all been done by him. How long have you been on his trail?"

"The shortest time is Lucas," said Morgan, "and he's been hanging on for pretty near six months."

"And you all want him dead?"

"Dead as hell would about suit us."

"Well, then, I would say that I have your man located —"

"Ah," cried Lucas, "if you mean that, sheriff —"

"Except," said the sheriff, "that his hair is yaller like a kid's, and not black at all!"

There was general consternation at this announcement.

"But," went on the sheriff, "he fits in with everything else. He's kind of soft and sappy looking. He's fine looking, pretty near like a girl. He looks weak and he's as strong as a mule. He can handle a gun like tamed chain lightning —"

"Ay," said Lucas with a bitter emphasis.

"And he's afraid of nothing on God's green earth!"

"That's him," they chorused.

"Besides, he has along with him an Indian that's a ringer for the one that you talk about."

"It's him!" they cried in one voice.

"Now," said the sheriff, "I figure that God has sent you to me, the three of you. I'll tell you, boys, that this man has made a worse and more shameful fool of me than he has of any of the three of you. And if there's a chance to make his arrest, now I can do it for something more than the trick that he played on me!"

"Were you waiting for causes for an arrest, sheriff?" asked Morgan, amazed, "and yet he'd done a trick on you?"

"He could have killed me," admitted the sheriff frankly. "He could have finished me off, and he didn't. But after that, how could I arrest him for a thing that he might have fixed quiet and safe for himself by putting a bullet through my head?"

The three stared at the sheriff and then at one another, as though this were a type of conscience such as they could not quite comprehend.

"The point is," said the sheriff, "that now I know enough to arrest him and put him where he'll keep; and while he's in keeping, if I don't find enough more evidence against him to keep three men in prison for a lifetime, then he's not what I take him to be. As for the hair — that's the sticking point! He wouldn't be the first man in the world to put on a wig. Boys, I got to make extra sure. We've got to get to the place where he is, and then one of the three of you has got to have a look at him and tell me if that's the man that you mean. And if it is, we'll have out four guns and try to argue the point with him — because mind you, it'll mean fighting. Y'understand all that?"

There was no answer, except a murmur of savage agreement from Morgan, and Lucas was heard whispering softly to himself:

"I'm gunna bash a couple of bullets through the fine looking mug of him! I'll fix him so's he'll bust no more hearts, livin' or dead, and hell take what's left of him!"

"It will," agreed Morgan instantly.

"Have you three good horses?" asked the sheriff.

"Three of the best that ever stepped, and all of 'em near busting for the lack of work, they been waiting here and eating grain so long, while we hoped for you to come back, Rankin!"

"We're off, then," said the sheriff.

He added, as he stood by the office door: "God be good to the souls of some of us, but I figure that more than one man is gunna die tonight, boys!"

"Whist!" said Morgan. "Leave the under-taker to be the mourner, will you?"

CHAPTER 30

The colonel had labored all the day with the most exemplary patience, and the result was that at the dinner table he was able to produce a finished water color of the proposed building.

It was placed at one side of the table where all could view it while they ate. Mary would pay it hardly the slightest attention, for in these days she had eyes for only one object in all this world; and that was for the glory and the beauty and the splendor of that man of men, Don Felipe. Mrs. Mackay said that she hoped the cowpunchers would be happy there, but Don Felipe was so cordial that his words covered any silences which must, otherwise, have arisen.

It reminded him, he said, of some of the old castles which the conquistadores had built on the summits and defensible ridges here and there, in the early days of the glory of his family. It was a good deal smaller in scale, of course, and in place of the sky-reaching telescope of Mr. Mackay there had been earth-scouring cannon gaping downwards.

The colonel was delighted.

"Knew," said he, "that there must be an archetype of this thing. It came out of my mind so easily, and full-grown, so to speak! By heaven, Lydia, did you hear that? Mexico is full of just such things. Now, I've never seen Mexico. How could the lucky resemblance have been hit off? It goes to show you, my dear, that there's something in telepathy! What?"

"No doubt," said Mrs. Mackay gently, "but then, you see, if telepathy is mental, and the old houses of the Spanish conquerors in Mexico have no minds — and I suppose that they really haven't —"

"Don't say another word!" exclaimed the colonel. "By heaven, Lydia, I really am surprised. Even from you, this surprises me! But I tell you, Felipe, that women are the practical creatures! A piece of stone is a piece of stone, to them. To a man — it may be a bright picture of the creation of the universe — ha! — the throwing off of worlds, the cooling of suns, the rising of mountains and the deepening of the great sea!"

"A very eloquent picture, sir," said Felipe.

The colonel leaned back in his chair a little, and placing both hands upon the edge of the table, he looked upwards. The ceiling seemed much too low for his thoughts.

"I have times like this, great feelings, outrushings of the spirit, Felipe," said he. "And I thank God that I shall have you here to listen to me. There are silences, Felipe, which are not the mere lack of words. There are silences, my boy, which may be filled with noise, and yet they are emptier than the vast deserts!"

"A magnificent metaphor, sir," said Señor Consalvo nodding so that it was almost a bow. "I wonder, sir, if there may not have been as much poet as military man in your mind?"

"Ha!" exclaimed the colonel. "Do you think so? Well, I've had that said to me before, and perhaps there's something in it. Too bad, Felipe, that in one life a man of some little largeness of mind cannot express and exhaust all of his possibilities! Sometimes I feel, my boy, as though there were untapped oceans of emotion and thought dammed up in me and exerting pressure, now and again, to burst forth. Ah, well! We all are exiled, I suppose. We all have our boundaries limited. We see what once seemed wide empires beginning to shrink as we grow older, my dear lad! And so, at the last, we seem confined to our St. Helenas!"

"That is very eloquently put," said Don Felipe, "but, after all, this rancheria of yours is a canvas where you can paint on a large scale. It seems to me, sir, that here you can adequately express yourself. Because here you can express the ultimate thing!"

"And what, Felipe, do you take that to be?" asked the colonel, a little anxiously.

"The fine art of living, sir!"

"Ha!" cried the colonel. "You touch a match to all my trains of thought! Magnificently said, Felipe! Every day I feel the greater nearness of you — a kindred spirit, masked, a little, behind a foreign language! But if I could learn to speak Spanish as you do — or if you could master the English idiom — then, sir, we'd have a feast of the mind! Yes, the art of living! After all, as you suggest, that's the ultimate thing. All science, all art, simply the overflow, the expression of the surplus energy. But first there must be the surplus. How accumulated? By the understanding of the art of living! The thing grows upon me! And out of Casa Mackay to make a school for living, a sort of pattern of broad and beautiful existence — ! Ha?"

"The very thing, sir!"

"How wonderful of you, Felipe," burst out Mary, her soul in her great eyes, "to have thought of it all!"

The colonel, parting his lips on another sentence — was arrested by this statement, and glared heavily upon his daughter.

But Don Felipe murmured in the quietest of reproofs: "I merely hinted at a picture that I couldn't fill out. It was your father who expressed the whole idea!"

"You see, my boy," said the colonel, stirring in his chair with a recaptured pleasure, "she's young *and* a woman!"

And he made a gesture to indicate the limitless universes which lay quite outside the reach of Mary. She, however, seemed to hear neither her father, nor the reproof of her lover, but she continued to shine upon Felipe Consalvo, gathering the glory of him deeper into her heart of hearts.

"I see the future," said the colonel, "expanding before me. The barriers are being cast down. The complete expression is possible here. Mountains — but not near enough to crowd the sky. Vastness overhead. Vastness underfoot. Regions for the eye to roam in. The spirit expanding. The soul growing. I swear to you, Felipe, that the construction of an earthly paradise is possible here!"

"For you, sir, I have no doubt," said he.

"It is not the work of one lifetime," said the colonel generously. "I shall block out the work and in part complete it. Then, having studied my work, with your infinite tact and good taste, you will carry on the business. Refine and polish what I have left rather crude, perhaps — in short, Felipe, I feel that I can welcome you not only into my life today, but into my life tomorrow! We can make of it a single long existence, perhaps to be passed on, again, to the children which you and Mary leave —"

"Oh," said Mary, "what a splendid thought, father!"

The colonel shrugged off this compliment, as not at all balancing that recent lack of comprehension.

He returned to the contemplation of the water color, and with Don Felipe for an audience, he sketched in on the margin a few notes for amplification and for change of detail. He grew more and more mellow with the thought. And when Tag got out from beneath the chair of his mistress and came to the Mexican, Don Felipe pushed back his chair and took the terrier on his knees.

"Regard the house, Tag," said he. "If it had not been for you, perhaps that plan never would have been drawn. Some way, sir, I think that Tag should be remembered in the house!"

"Ha!" cried the colonel, the idea striking him instantly into a heat. "Of course he must! But how? Well, there's the name. Tag's Rest. I think we've about settled on that for the name of the house, Felipe. What do you say?"

"Restful," said the Mexican. "But hardly dignified enough for such a beautiful — bunk house!"

The colonel glanced suddenly askance, biting his lip in suspicion, but the face of Don Felipe was blank with childlike innocence and naïveté.

"Or," said the colonel, recovering his enthusiasm quickly, "we could attack the problem from a different angle. Suppose — suppose — let me see! Ah, yes. Suppose that we erect a little fountain in the patio. Must be a fountain there, eh? Well, a dog in marble — bronze would be better."

"Much nearer to Tag's actual color," said Don Felipe.

"Certainly it is! Bronze it shall be. A dog, let us say, pictured on the roof of a burning house, eh?"

"How clever!" said Mrs. Mackay. "Unless the flames should prove a difficulty to the artist!"

"Nonsense!" said the colonel. "Modern art laughs at such a difficulty as that! And the fountain spray rising, let us say, from the mouth of Tag as he looks upwards, and showering down —"

"On the flames?" said Mrs. Mackay, while Don Felipe suddenly had to look down at the table.

"Ha?" cried the colonel. "There's no sympathy in you, Lydia. You crush the inspiration out of a man! By heavens, Felipe, doesn't she, though?"

Don Felipe was forced to gather his brows, as in thought.

"It would be a most original idea for a fountain," said he, looking up at the last.

"But I tell you there's something wrong," said Mary, breaking in with strength. "If Tag's to be remembered, what about Felipe? That's what I'd like to know! For there wouldn't be any Tag at all if it weren't for Felipe! Would there, Tag darling?"

Tag wagged his tail violently, and then attempted to kiss the nose of Felipe and barely failed. Since the fire, Tag had become a great person in the house. Even the colonel took notice of him.

"If you chatter like this," said the colonel sternly, "you really need another year at school, Mary, to calm you and sober you. Not really mature enough for matrimony, I'd say. The idea grows on me, by Jove! Back to school with you for another year, Mary."

"I wouldn't go!" gasped Mary, turning pale.

"What do you say, Lydia?" asked the colonel. "A good thought, eh?"

Mrs. Mackay looked up.

But her glance encountered not the eyes of the colonel but went straight across the table where Don Felipe sat and watched her; and there was a cold, keen gleam in his eyes. A year of waiting? As well ask Consalvo to wait an eternity! And she knew that the proposal would drive him into desperation — then farewell Consalvo, and Mary with him! How well he would become the part of the young Lochinvar!

"I really don't think," said Mrs. Mackay gently, "that we should interfere with their plans too much!"

And she saw a sudden softening of the eyes of Don Felipe, and a gradually growing wonder in them.

CHAPTER 31

Go back, now, to the huge Indian, at that time when Pedro was racing in pursuit of Mrs. Mackay on this same surcharged day. He saw the horse flick her out of his reach and, giving vent to all his savagery, he reached for a revolver from his belt and would have fired if it had not been that he remembered, at that moment, certain injunctions of his master who had told him repeatedly that never must he use firearms except by express command. And much as Pedro dreaded this strange white woman, much more he dreaded his master, and he dared not to fire the bullet even in his master's service.

If he could not reach her with a bullet, then he would at least get on the mule, and if he pursued on that animal, the fear of his coming might drive Mrs. Mackay to ride frantically. By speed the mule never could overtake the horse, but the horse, hotly pressed by its rider, might make some false step that would put the game at once in his hands by leaving Mrs. Mackay helpless on the ground.

So he swerved and started after the mule.

Of the three which bore the bulky packs of his master, this was the chosen one, whether for height, power, or speed of foot. Catlike among mountain rocks, and able to maintain a trot endlessly across the desert, it was more than a fair match for most mustangs as a saddle animal. And had the chase been long this day, Pedro would not have doubted to wear down Mrs. Mackay and her thoroughbred. To this chosen one of the three, Pedro had given unremitting attention, stealing grain for it, seeing that it was not overburdened by the pack, and spending much of his time with it whenever he had spare moments from the care of his master's clothes, and from the errands which were committed to him. However, never did creature repay kindness more cruelly, for the mule now stood quietly until the big Indian was close — then it lashed out furiously.

One heel quite missed the mark and shot over the broad shoulder of the Indian, but the other struck him fairly between the eyes, and he went down in a blanket of thickest darkness.

Out of the dark he opened his eyes when the twilight was gathering, and, as he raised himself on shaking hands, he saw the mule standing close by, with ears pricked, as though admiring his heel-craft and its result.

Pedro forced himself upon his knees. He was hideously weak; clotted blood had formed all over his face and run down across his breast and shoulders until air and sun had stopped its flow; and moreover, a dreadful pain smote him with every pulse of his heart between the eyes and shot back across the crown of his head.

A sick feebleness enveloped Pedro and made him sink down again, panting, and grasping the earth with both hands.

"I die," said Pedro to the senseless ground. "I die!"

And then he saw his mighty hands, though a film seemed to hang between them and his vision. And as he looked at them it appeared to him that death was still far from him. To die by the kick of a mule!

So he mastered himself and got to his knees, and then, staggering, to his feet. But they gave way beneath him, and he crumpled up on all fours, and hung swaying, feeling that if ever he fell prostrate again he never could rise a second time, for his arms were as water, bending under his weight, and his legs shook.

There was such a thirst burning him as he never had known before on the longest desert march, but into his semi-delirium ran the cool trickling of water near by. Blinded, he fumbled towards it, dragging his great body, and when he came to it, he plunged in his face and drank, and paused, and drank again. Then he washed the blood from his face as well as he could, and the touch of the water seemed to take away a small portion of that world of anguish.

However, the wound began to bleed again after it had been washed clean, and so he cut long strips from his shirt and bound them about his forehead. The pressure caused him the most exquisite agony, but he knew that the small trickle of blood was draining the last strength from his heart.

And, in the meantime, the mule, like a tamed dog, stood beside him, and drank of the same stream, and turned its head to look at its master, and then stood patiently, switching its tail at the flies.

A sort of kindness swelled up in the heart of Pedro, at that.

"Felice!" said he.

And the mule turned her head and sniffed at his face.

"Felice," said the Indian, "you have killed me, but take me back to my master to die and to warn him of the white witch. Felice, if you love me, stand still — be patient!"

And Felice stood like an image of iron, while Pedro pushed himself slowly up to his knees and grasped the stirrup leather.

Beyond that point, however, he could not raise himself, and when he strove, though Felice still did not move, shudders of weakness passed through all his great body, and the muscles twitched but did not respond.

Then a great brightness streamed down the ravine, and Pedro thought that he was dying, and that this was the brightness of the happy hunting grounds opening to receive him. But when he faced a little towards it, he saw that what he had taken to be twilight was no more than the gathering of the western horizon mists across the sun. Now those mists were brushed away, and he found himself looking into the fierce red face of the God of his fathers, and taking the last of his heat.

Pedro dared not relax his grip on the stirrup leather, but, clinging to it with one hand to keep from falling, he stretched forth the other towards the west and prayed aloud: "Father-sun, I am about to go into darkness, like you. You will come again in the morning and Pedro will not see you. He is sleepy and wishes to rest forever, but he has one thing to do before he dies. He has a father on earth as you are his father in the sky, so give him strength to go to that father and speak a warning. Give me strength, and remember the rifle that I sacrificed to you by hanging it in the manzanita bush outside of Tlacopan. Remember also the bearskin that I gave you to keep you warm in the under-water world. All the inside of it was painted by a wise man. Give me strength, father!"

He closed his eyes a little and waited, and it seemed to Pedro that strength began to flow into his limbs, and behold, he could draw himself erect, and grasp the pommel of the saddle.

Thrice he essayed, and three times all the blood in his body seemed to gather and burst in a wave of blinding anguish upon his brain, but at last he swayed himself up the side of the patient Felice. He lay across the saddle for a long moment, gasping, then he struggled his right leg across and lurched forward, exhausted, his arms falling about her neck.

But Felice was true to her trust, and

went softly and easily forward, never stumbling, picking her way with a tender care, and now and again turning her head to look with wonder at this lurching, helpless, shaken humanity that once had been her iron-handed master.

Then the brain of Pedro cleared a little and some strength came back to him, so that he thought of fixing himself in the saddle, and he tied his belt to the pommel and he tied his wrists to the pommel also. After that, no matter if he fainted, for the mule would doubtless take him truly back along the home-trail.

This ride began in the red glory of the sunset, and it endured into the night. But it seemed so long to Pedro that sometimes, rousing from a lapse of consciousness, he felt that he had been going forward through the blackness for infinite ages.

But always Felice held steadily forward, nodding wisely to herself.

As he lay along her body, he saw her long ears bobbing among the stars.

"The other warriors shall have great horses and flying stallions in the hunting grounds," said he to her, "but I shall have Felice!"

At that, she pricked both her ears, and he took it as an answer and as a sign.

Sometimes it seemed to Pedro that the stars swam under his feet, and then he was sure that he was riding through the black sea of the stars, and drawing close, no doubt, to the gates of the other life, where his pain would be lifted from him, taken like a burden from his shoulders.

But then he felt his cold flesh, and he knew that he still was riding on this mortal earth.

So he strained his eyes forward, and the lights which seemed to swim all around him steadied and grew fewer and farther away, until at length he saw that he was coming upon the house of Mackay!

The sense of familiarity swept warmly and sweetly upon him and gave him more strength, so that he was able to push himself erect in the saddle.

"It is the will of my sky-father," said Pedro to his heart, "that I should live and give the warning. Now nothing can prevent me!"

Felice, in the meantime, went steadily on towards the stable, and stood at last before the closed door.

"José!" called Pedro.

A faint whisper was all that answered his will. Sweat began to stand on his forehead, when he thought that he might lie here on the mule and die, and his master have no word from him because his voice had been stolen.

"José!" he called, and this time the strength of his fear entered his throat and the call rang far away.

The door was pushed back with a rattle, and not José but another stableboy stood before him. The difference was not known to the Indian, however, and he said: "Is my master still here?"

"Padre de Dios!" gasped the boy. "It is Pedro! You are hurt!"

"Fool!" said the Indian. "Go to the house; speak to Maria; tell her to go to my master and whisper to him that he is wanted in the stable. Wait for him and bring him to me. But if you mention my name to Maria or say one other word to her, I shall tear out your heart and feed it to a bird!"

The boy ran like mad for the house, terrified; and, as Pedro fainted again and fell heavily forward, Felice went softly into the barn, found her stall, and began to nose comfortably in the hay.

CHAPTER 32

All was apparently quietly cheerful at Mackay House, that evening. The colonel, wrapped in speculations, continually pulled out a pocket sketchbook and jotted down notes or made little drawings, even of such details as windows and windowpots, for he intended, as he said, to make every room have a few notes of color, and nothing is so excellent, for that purpose, as the natural color of flowers, producing a touch of spring, said the colonel, even in the bleak midst of winter. Spring, he declared, must be made to triumph and winter to fall down in his valley; so he would plant here and there on the hills patches of winter-blooming flowers —

"How dreadful if the cows should eat them!" sighed Lydia Mackay. But her husband waved this doleful suggestion to the side.

In the meantime, Don Felipe found an opportunity to sit down beside his future mother-in-law and he held her in serious conversation.

"You never have told us much family history," said she.

"Oh," said he, "the Consalvos are like a hundred other Mexican families. First fighting under Cortez, then getting great principalities and huge land-grants; and after that spending and living like kings for centuries, actually, until the revolutions wrecked them!"

"How sad!" she murmured.

"But just, too," he remarked.

"Do you mean that?"

"Seriously, yes. We had become wasters. We made nothing. We did nothing but ride. We kept up a great front even when our purses were getting thin. I feel the same instinct in me. Why should I go about all gilded with silver and what not? Because of the old shameful impulse, you know — trying to sustain and make a grand impression. When I am with a clear-seeing person like you, I see the mistake and can laugh at it!"

She pondered a little over this speech, remembering so well the stuffed pack in his room, and suddenly she felt that perhaps this young man was not so bad as he had seemed to be. At least, his pretense might be chiefly the effect of heredity, just as he had explained it. There were other matters, of course, which were more seriously against him; there was the sham which he had played so long, and the tiger claws under the velvet touch. The sheriff could testify to that. Nevertheless, her attitude, she found, was changing a good deal. And, when she looked at this youth from certain aspects she felt that he hardly could be improved upon as material. He was intelligent, gentle, brave. But the handling of the material had been wrong. The army had been organized, and then used merely for the plunder of the world!

How much of that was his fault and how much the fault of the environment in which he grew up, she could not tell. But, at least, this evening's confession made her feel much more kindly towards him.

Yet even that feeling of kindliness she was rather afraid of, guessing that he might have chosen purposely to disarm her on this occasion; and as for the real Consalvo, that was a self she never had had a full glimpse of.

He left her shortly afterwards; the house moza, Maria, had signalled from the doorway, and Don Felipe went to her.

"There is something in the stable," said the girl. "You should go there, señor!"

He went without asking for another

word of explanation, and outside the house a terrified stableboy met him.

"Pedro has come in. I think he's drunk. He's lying on the back of his mule. He won't get off. He groans, señor, and sure he is drunk. He speaks terribly! He is going to tear my heart out. Prevent him, kind señor. Be to me like a good father and prevent him from tearing out my heart!"

Consalvo began to run, and so, the boy panting beside him, he came to the barn.

"Pedro!" he called as they entered the dark.

Out of the warmth of that blackness there came, for answer, only the sound of many noses shuffling in hay, and the powerful noise of huge grinders at work.

"Pedro!" called Don Felipe again, and this time there was a faint but ready answer: "Ay, señor!"

Something in that voice told Felipe Consalvo a great deal more than a long message. He slipped a coin into the hand of the stableboy and said to him: "Run along. There is no need for you now. You have done well, and Pedro shall not touch you with the tip of his finger!"

The boy hurried away, glad enough to be gone, and Consalvo stepped down to the stall of Felice. There he struck a match, and, stepping to the head of the mule, he was able to look into the face of the Indian.

What he saw made the match fall from his hand.

Out of the darkness a hoarse, feeble voice said to him: "Father, I die. The white witch has done this. She found the cave and set the sheriff free. I tried to catch her, but she got to her horse and rode away. She made Felice kick me, Felice who loves me. Beware — go quickly — Dios! Dios! Dios! — Now I die —"

There was a faint groan and a sound of the heavy body slumping to the side, and Don Felipe knew that the man had given his last strength to this work.

For his part, he turned and ran to the door of the barn, but there conscience overtook him, and he turned and leaped back to the side of his servant. A few touches of his knife, and the whole vast bulk of Pedro descended into his arms, hanging there limp, head and legs and arms trailing down; yet Consalvo carried that burden lightly down the length of the barn and, at the farther end, laid the body on the fresh and clean straw of an unoccupied stall.

He lighted a lantern which he took from the rear wall, and hung it from a harness peg near by. Now he could examine Pedro with care and in as much detail as time allowed; but time, he knew, was pressing short and hard upon him. He could understand, now, the little touch of nervous surety, so to speak, which he had perceived in the attitude of Mrs. Mackay this evening.

He could understand, also, the kindness with which she had smiled upon him; for she was to keep him in play until the sheriff and his armed men could sweep out from the town and bag this great fish!

Time, time! How much could be accomplished in a few seconds! But first there was Pedro!

Kneeling beside the Indian, he listened to the feeble and uncertain flutter of the heart; there was no perceptible pulse in the wrist, even to the delicate touch of the Mexican. He put his hand on the forehead of Pedro, beside the dreadful wound. The flesh was cold, damp, and clammy, as though death already had invaded that body by some degrees and was kept away only by the failing labor of the heart.

Don Felipe remained upon his knees, with the thick of the darkness gathering closer and closer around his soul.

Then he stood up and hurried to the little circle of huts behind the barn. The white men, cow-punchers and the rest, lived apart; but the workers of the soil and the shepherds and random workers of all kinds were Mexicans of the peon class, and these were housed all together in a little whitewashed village of their own liking, each house with a tiny patch of land attached to it. Don Felipe ran straight down the back row of these houses, vaulted a wall, dropped softly into a backyard, and so gained the rear door of the hut.

It was open, and he stepped into the interior. There was one room. The rearward portion served for cooking. The forward was the bedchamber, and here six people were ranged along the wall. He made out the huddle of their forms, and then touched on the shoulder the one that lay nearest to the door. At once a tall form rose before him. Consalvo took him by the arm and led him into the open air.

"What have I done!" whispered the frightened Mexican. "Where do you take me, señor?"

"Do you know who I am?"

"Dios! It is Señor Consalvo!"

"Listen to me, Miguel. You are a man to

be trusted. Listen to me closely. In this hand of yours I close some pieces of money. They are gold pieces, Miguel. They make you a rich man. With that money you could buy five horses."

"The señor is an angel and God has sent him to me!"

"You do not know what I wish of you."

"If it is to go into hell-fire and come back to you carrying the flames in my hand, I shall do it. I shall go and laugh at the danger. Señor — I am rich! You have made me rich. Rosa shall wear a golden bracelet —"

"Go into the stable," said Consalvo, "and on the eastern side, near this end, there is a vacant stall. There lies my servant, Pedro. He has been hurt by the kick of a mule. He is, perhaps, dying. Well, do your best. You are paid beforehand. I know that you understand sickness; that is why I came to you. But if you make Pedro well, Miguel, for every gold piece now in your hand, I shall give you ten or twenty! Do you hear?"

"I shall save him," said Miguel in a voice that trembled with fervor. "I shall save him if he already is clasping the hand of death. I should raise him from the grave for such a reward, señor!"

"Hereafter, you will hear strange things about me. It does not matter. My promise to you is a sacred thing. Do you believe it?"

"Señor, I do not think except as you bid me to think! Only tell me one thing — do you see in the black of the night that you were able to find me in my house?"

"Adios!" said Felipe Consalvo. "Remember!"

And he disappeared into the dark, hurrying back towards Casa Mackay; his mind flew before him to the great chance he was about to take; and yet one portion of his thoughts lingered behind, and he smiled. A little touch of such mystery would do him no harm with Miguel. No, it might hold the fellow more strongly than all the gold. And yet how simple it had been to guess that the place of the young master of the hut would be nearest to the door!

CHAPTER 33

At the patio gate of the great house, in spite of the narrow limit of his time, Don Felipe paused and stepped back a little until he could see all the line of lights that glimmered along the great front of the building.

There had been a time when he had hoped peacefully to inherit this grand property, and still he felt that the thing had slipped from his grasp by inches only. Now it was lost to him, and he stood here in most terrible peril, for he knew well that the one sensible thing for him to do was to mount Conquistador and fly!

Somewhere on the road which tossed up and down along the hills and then leveled across the plain, Rankin was coming with many men; and the fact that he came so late meant, simply, that he was coming with a great power; it would be with a hundred hands that he would hunt Consalvo on this night!

And yet, though Don Felipe looked into his heart, he found little actual fear or regret there; instead, all nerves were drawn taut, his pulse leaped with expectation, and his whole soul stirred like that of a runner on the mark.

He paused as he entered; Maria was waiting at the door.

"Maria, you are a brave girl and a good girl. This is a little present for you!"

"Señor, a thousand prayers —"

"Pretty Maria would pray me out of Purgatory! Now go quietly to José, the stable-boy. Give him this, from me, without fail."

"May fire strike me if I keep it from him!"

"Tell him to saddle Conquistador and the red bay mare of the señorita. Do you hear?"

"Ah, señor, tonight?"

"Maria, you are a brave and a good girl, but tonight you must not think. Do you understand?"

"Señor! My heart stops!"

"Make it beat again. Do as I tell you. You see that I trust you! When you have given the message to José, go up to the señorita's room and there, perhaps, she may need you. Do you hear?"

"I hear you, señor! Ah, my heart! It is killing me!"

Consalvo leaned closer to her and laid one finger on her hand.

"If you fail me, Maria — !"

He felt her tremble and heard her gasp; then he turned on his heel and went with a light step into the room where Mary and Mrs. Mackay were murmuring in a corner and where the colonel, in another, had fallen asleep over the profundity of one of his thoughts.

"I must get him to bed," said Lydia Mackay. "The poor dear will nod his head off in another moment," and she went to her husband.

Don Felipe paused by the girl.

"I am going to my room," said he. "In ten minutes I shall be at your window."

Who has seen a thoroughbred in the pasture suddenly lift its head and look up the wind towards some mystery beyond the horizon? So the girl looked up, turning her head slowly, and met the eye of her lover.

"Good-night!" said Consalvo.

"Going to bed so soon?" asked Mrs. Mackay, as her husband rose with a prodigious yawn. "So soon, Felipe?"

"Yes, at once."

"You look as though you could begin a day rather than end one!"

"I am a lucky man, señora. I lie in my bed; I turn on sleep as from a tap; suddenly I am gone!"

And he laughed pleasantly.

"Then you have no nerves," said Lydia Mackay. "You clever fellow!"

"But after one falls asleep," said he, "who knows what dreams may come?"

"It's simply the beginning of another bright day for you, I suppose," smiled she. "You'll never have trouble with your digestion, Felipe! Good-night, then!"

But, as she went upstairs, carrying her husband's notebook as she walked beside him, her mind was moving very fast indeed. And when she left the colonel, she stood for a moment outside his door, her hand upon the knob, and looked eagerly up and down the hall.

When, when would the sheriff come?

She went to her room, turned on the light, opened the door of her dressing room; then she stepped back into the hall, and in the black shadow of a corner she waited.

From that position she could command a clear view of the door of her daughter, and on this night it was that view which she wished to keep clearly before her. Mary had entered. Mary must not leave.

And so Consalvo might scheme and plan as he chose! She drew a great breath. As to what was about to happen, she dared not envisage it; she made the near future a complete blank and let her mind rest on the actual present only.

However, it was not by so matter-of-fact an approach as the stairs and the halls that Don Felipe intended to see his lady. Had there been nothing but the great stalk of the climbing vine that climbed the side of the house, he would have mounted to her window with ease, but there were other aids, and a child could have managed, with no difficulty, to clamber up the ledges of brick and so gain the balcony of Mary's room.

Don Felipe went up to the halfway point, and there he paused, listening intently, for he thought that he heard the pounding of many hoofs blow clearly to his ears by a turn of the night wind. Eyes closed, all faculties lost in one, he waited, but the sound was not repeated, and he felt that he might have mistaken for it the hurried fluttering of his own excited heart.

So he went on to the balcony, and, at his tap, the window yawned, and there was Mary before him.

He took both her hands.

"Mary," said he, "in two minutes I must be on the back of Conquistador. I can't tell you why. Afterwards, they'll tell you plenty of reasons, but still they won't know. I'm going to ride Conquistador and put a hundred miles between me and this house. I had to see you alone, tell you this, say good-bye, and tell you that all the promises you've made to me you're free from, if you wish to be!"

She, struck half a dozen times in that one rapid speech, confused and staggered, clung closer to his hand.

"You're afraid, Felipe!" said she. "What has frightened you? I don't care what it is — my father — I can protect you, Felipe!"

He answered her: "I have such enemies, Mary, that they ride day and night to find me. They have hunted me from my home. They have followed me north across the Rio Grande. And they have come south for me. I am hunted, Mary, and I shall have to ride and live like a brigand!"

"No!" said the girl. "Do you hear me, Felipe? We are not like Mexico. There's a strong law here — it will keep you as safe —"

"Dearest, their guns would fire at me even through the bars of a prison window. I have had a message. In this house of yours the danger begins."

"It can't!"

"Tomorrow you'll learn the truth. Only

cling to this, Mary. Whatever they say of me and whatever they know of me, they know only a part. I'm not what I seem!"

"I've always guessed that," said the girl. "But if you go, Felipe — I'll ask no questions!"

"No, for they'll be closing on the house!"

"God help us! Felipe!"

"My dear!"

"If you go, you'll come again?"

"They will have you fenced around, Mary. They'll take you away."

"I wouldn't go!"

"They would find a way to make you. But no matter where you may go, I'll try to find my way to you —"

"Felipe!"

"Every moment is my life, Mary!"

"Wait for me here one instant. I'll be ready, then. If you have to ride, I'll ride with you. But I'd rather be in a grave than stay in this house after you're gone."

"Mary, to go with me, sleep on the ground, live in the wilderness —"

"I can be like a man. Felipe, wait for me!"

She closed the window on the reply he tried to make, and Consalvo turned and faced the stars, and the black heads of the trees, and waited, singing so softly that only his own ear could hear; and once he snapped his supple fingers without noise. How simple it had been!

But all the time he listened; he bowed his head and bent all his strength on that great effort. Yet not a sound came to him except, from time to time, the soft whisper of the night wind in the climbing vine which showered its tendrils around him. The sweetness rose gently from the garden. He looked up, and Vega and Altair burned brightly overhead, and, far north, Cassiopeia's Chair was tilted on the horizon. And if he could have changed this moment for one of utter peace and certainty of lifelong repose, he felt that he would not have accepted the alteration.

All was as he would have had it be!

The window opened softly, and the girl stepped out beside him in riding clothes, a little parcel in her hand, the broad brim of her hat keeping her face in utter darkness.

But he could hear her rapid breathing.

"Mary, I'm a scoundrel and a thief to let you come!"

"If you went alone, I'd try to follow. Oh, if I have made you wait too long!"

CHAPTER 34

Then they heard, at the door of the girl's room, a gentle tapping. They held their breath.

The tapping was repeated, and then, barely audible, the voice of Mrs. Mackay: "Mary, it is I! Let me in, dear!"

Consalvo whispered: "Did you lock the door?"

She shook her head in the darkness, and at the same time there was the click as the door swung open, and — "Mary! Where are you, child!"

They heard a hurrying footstep, a gasp, and then the long and sharp note of a woman's scream with such an agony in it that the girl drooped against her lover.

"Go back!" whispered Consalvo.

"Never," said the girl, and swiftly she began to climb down.

He was on the ground beside her; already in the house voices were rousing everywhere, and then that terrible cry of grief and terror from the room above them. The window was flung open: "Mary!"

cried Lydia Mackay into the great black heart of the night.

But Mary and Consalvo already were half way to the stables, and beside a wide-spreading tree near the big building they saw the dim silhouette of two horses, and could make out the outline of the saddles on their backs.

"Conquistador!" said Felipe. "I know him even in the dark of the night. And that is your mare, my dear."

"Felipe, you knew that I'd come!"

"I dreamed and I prayed it; I didn't know. How could I know that you loved me as I love you, Mary? Listen! The house is up! God forgive me for the pain I bring to your mother!"

They reached the horses.

"Give me the reins, José," said Consalvo, hurrying up, and then he paused abruptly, for it seemed to him that José had grown wonderfully since he last laid eyes upon him. And at the same moment, two suddenly unhooded lanterns flared in the very eyes of Consalvo, and voices burst on him; they shouted at one instant:

"Gregg, let me see you stick up your hands or I'll blow you to hell, you rat!" "It's me; Lucas! I'm here for you, Tomason!" "Kilpatrick, stand fast — don't budge; I got you covered!"

Three voices challenging in one instant — and then a slender form leaped in front of Consalvo — Mary! — and her voice crying: "Felipe — quickly!"

He bounded back into the black shelter of a bush; even with the girl before them, sheltering his retreat, they fired. Three guns flashed and boomed in the night, and Consalvo, a weapon in either hand, now, saw four men rush past the girl.

He could have killed them, he told himself, with the greatest ease, as they rushed down the little slope, outlined against the stars, and driving their bullets before them. But instead, he sent two shots humming past their ears.

That was enough. They split to either side to dive for cover, but before they gained it, Consalvo was back in the shadow of a group of poplars, whistling a sharp call. Ten men could not have held Conquistador after he had heard that familiar signal. Even in the dimness of the starlight his body seemed a flash as he bolted for his master. Consalvo clung to him as he darted past, and in another moment the long sway of that gallop had carried horse and man over the hilltop.

Sheriff Rankin did not even attempt pursuit, and he called back the cursing, raving trio as they made for their mounts.

He himself had reached the head of the girl's horse barely in time to prevent her from mounting. By one wrist he held her now, gently but securely. "Let me go, Mr. Rankin," she was whispering. "Let me go, or I'll die of the shame of it. And I'll find him again anyway! Let me go for God's sake —"

"Steady, steady, my dear!" said he to her.

Then, to his men: "Back up, Lucas. Morgan, get off of your horse, will you? Are you gunna catch Conquistador with those played out nags? You might as well try to catch thunder, or a doggone sight better!"

He added: "Go ahead and meet those folks that are spilling out from the house and tell them that it's all right — Consalvo's gone, but he's not gone far."

Then he took Mary by a little circuit through the dark, and so into the front of the house.

The colonel had gone raging into the night, bellowing orders that nullified each other as fast as he could shout. But Mrs. Mackay waited by the door, like a general of reserve; so that she was the first one who had sight of the girl.

What she wanted to do was to take that barely reclaimed truant in her arms and weep over her, but when she saw the great, tragic eyes of the girl and the stubbornly defiant manner in which she carried her head aloft, she changed her mind.

"I wish that you were young enough to be spanked, Mary," said she. "But I see that you're not."

"There's been a plot and trap!" said Mary hotly. "He knew it — he knew that it was arranged from inside my own home! He knew it! Oh, mother, if you have anything to do with it, I'll never forgive you — never!"

"Come upstairs with me," said Mrs. Mackay. "I want to talk to you, Mary. Sheriff Rankin — God bless you!"

"Bless yourself, ma'am," said the dry sheriff. "What I've done is to let the bird slip through my fingers. And — I'm going to be pretty surprised at you, Mrs. Mackay, if I see you cry like just ordinary folks."

She managed to laugh faintly; and then she went up the stairs with Mary, a very sullen Mary, who threw herself into a chair in her room and rested her chin on a clenched fist.

"Will you talk to me, Mary?" said Lydia Mackay.

She stood before her daughter, and clasped her hands together, as though partly in fear and partly in entreaty.

"I'll say one thing," said Mary fiercely. "I wasn't being kidnapped, if that's what you're all so excited about. And I'll say another thing. I'm going to find Felipe! I'm going to find him and — marry him — and be his wife forever — and — I — I hate everybody! It was a low, cowardly, cruel trap!"

Lydia Mackay said instantly: "It was, Mary. So many men against one! But we didn't dare try to do a thing against Felipe except with numbers, you see!"

"You're scoffing at him," said Mary savagely, "because he isn't — because he's not so very — brave — with weapons, I suppose?"

"Mary, dear, will you listen?"

"I won't! I don't want to! You can't persuade me. I know that you've tried to break my heart. But — I'll find him still. I will! I will!"

"And I'll help you," said Lydia Mackay suddenly.

"You?" cried the girl, suddenly bewildered, and so taken out of her burst of rage.

"I'll help you, dear. Only, I want you to know what we know. Afterwards, you can make up your mind. And if you decide for him, I'll help you all that I can!"

Mary was struck dumb; with parted lips she listened, while Mrs. Mackay said: "Sheriff Rankin could have attempted to make the arrest today, but he frankly was afraid to attack Felipe single-handed."

"Heavens!" cried Mary. "What do you mean?"

"Did you see the sheriff's forehead?"

"Yes — a hideous bruise. What of it?"

"He had a little disagreement with Felipe just the other day, Mary. And Felipe shot him off his horse, you know."

Mary gasped.

"The bullet would have killed Mr. Rankin," went on the mother calmly, "but it happened to strike his revolver on the way to his head. That was what saved him."

"Felipe did that!"

"It seems that Felipe was fond of pretending, Mary. Perhaps he liked to surprise people by showing them his real self in the end, just when they didn't expect it, you know!"

"Felipe — but he wouldn't lie," said the girl. "I don't know how it's happened. There was a mistake somewhere —"

"And Budge Lakin," said Mrs. Mackay

— "the doctor says that Budge is sure to recover, now — but Budge, you know, really didn't shoot himself. It was Felipe who shot him, Mary."

The pale lips of Mary moved, but they made no sound.

"And the sheriff says," said Mrs. Mackay, "that of all the professional gunmen he's ever encountered, Felipe is by far the most dangerous. But suppose that we let the sheriff tell you all about that, Mary?"

"I don't want to hear it!" said Mary, more sullenly than ever. "What chance did you give Felipe to explain?"

"You know it's hard to do," said the mother. "I mean, it's terribly hard to ask a man to explain things he says that he didn't and couldn't do! And we always were afraid, you see, that if Felipe suspected anything, he'd persuade you to go away with him."

"But there!" cried the girl. "You see how completely you're wrong. He didn't persuade me. He just begged me not to go. He *begged* me. But I went in spite of him, and he kept asking me to turn back! You see you don't know *anything* about Felipe!"

"He's a wonderful and complicated young man," said the mother simply. "He's far too hard for me to understand. I only know that I'm dreadfully afraid of him, and so is the sheriff! But as for persuasion — why, that's the way with Felipe. He lets other people convince themselves. You know, it's a good way, at times. And the point is — we were afraid that he'd take you away — and he almost did!"

"I think I'd better be alone," said Mary stiffly.

"Just as you please," said her mother. "But wouldn't it be fairer if we all sat down around a table and tried to thrash this thing out, Mary? We'll tell you everything that we've found out. You can blame us for our methods, but perhaps you'll blame Felipe a little, too. Won't it be better to talk the whole matter over — man to man, you know?"

"At least," said Mary, "I'm not a bit afraid!" And she stood up, straight and tall.

CHAPTER 35

The colonel, bewildered, was talking himself out of a fog. First he rushed here and there, shouting orders at the barn, and at the bunk house, and, having arrayed his fighting cowpunchers, had them wait while he returned to the house to get his new rifle.

There he encountered the sheriff, his wife, and his daughter, all in the library, having, so to speak, midnight tea.

"A pretty piece of work!" he boomed at Mary. "Good God, Rankin, are you here? Are you here, man, with such work to do?"

"What work?" said the sheriff.

"What work?" thundered the colonel. "When a scoundrel has dared to attempt to tear from my home the — Why, man, what do you mean by asking what work?"

"As for our friend, Consalvo," said the sheriff, gently stroking the great bruise upon his forehead, "he'll find his way through the hills interrupted, I think. I've sent out warnings by telegraph, and even if he takes off his blond wig —"

"His blond wig!" cried Mary.

"His hair is black," said the quiet sheriff.

"I knew there was something wrong about his looks," declared the colonel. "I knew it, by heaven, and that was why I always had a sort of distrust for him."

"It's not fair to say so!" cried Mary. "What have you been saying to him this very day?"

"The persuasions and the nagging of women," said the colonel, inviting the sheriff into his confidence with a wave of his hand, "would change the mind of any man. Even Samson couldn't hold out against them!"

He liked the comparison and squared his shoulders, lowering powerfully upon his family.

"From the first," said the colonel, "I guessed that he wasn't a fellow to be trusted. Amusing, yes. But that was the end — and —"

"I'm going to leave the room," said Mary, standing up. "I've never heard of such, of such —"

She paused to find a word blasting enough, but she found none, and so ran out from the room, and they heard her sobbing on the way upstairs.

The colonel, greatly disturbed, ran after her to the door and there hung, swinging back and forth, first towards his wife, and then as though about to pursue his daughter to her room.

"She's in a fearful state, Lydia," said the colonel. "She may do something desperate!"

"I think she'll simply cry," said Mrs. Mackay. "Women generally just do that, you know."

"She's my daughter," announced the colonel, "and therefore she's capable of action — think of tonight! To run away! Elope! My daughter — a damned rascal of a Mexican! Heavens, sheriff, if this comes to be known!"

"I'm afraid that it can't help but be known," said the sheriff.

"You don't mean it! Then I'll have Consalvo torn to pieces by wild horses!"

"If that's his real name," suggested Rankin.

"What? Has he — isn't he really a Consalvo?"

"He's carried a good many aliases," said Rankin. "He's been Consalvo, Gregg, Tomason, etc. It would take a pretty clever detective to guess which is the real one. His names are like his languages. He forgets them when he pleases."

"Ah!" gasped the colonel. "You mean

314

that he speaks English?"

"Like a college professor," said the sheriff. "He speaks it fine as silk. French, too, and Spanish, and German, and all so nacheral that he could pass himself off for being any one of 'em. Same way with his profession. He can crack a safe or he can stack a pack of cards just as easy. He's one of these all around handy men, and ready for any sort of a job that might come his way. Sort of a roustabout in crime, you see!"

"We'll have the scoundrel in prison for the rest of his career," said the colonel. "You don't think that he can get away?"

"I don't think that he can," said the sheriff. "Those mountains are as full of posses, by this time, as a pine cone is full of nuts. If Consalvo expected them, he might slip through. But he won't expect 'em. I waited to come out here until I'd posted my friends in every mountain town. They're out with everybody that's big enough to pack a gun. Consalvo won't get through!"

"I hope he does!" said Mrs. Mackay, closing her eyes fervently. "I hope that he wins through them!"

"Lydia!" cried the colonel, aghast.

"Not because of what he is," said she,

"but because of what he might have been!"

"Stuff!" said the colonel. "A precious lot you know about character! Leave such affairs to the sheriff — and to me!"

Mrs. Mackay made no reply, but since Tag had bounced into the room, she leaned and patted the head of that sage creature.

The next morning there was excitement of another kind in the house. A long delayed telegram arrived at the house announcing that the governor, if possible, would be the guest of the colonel and was coming on at once to talk over certain projects.

The "certain projects" were perfectly definite in the mind of the colonel. They had to do with the matter of water rights which, if the colonel could acquire them, would enable him to dam the river as it flowed through his valley, and use the water to irrigate a vast deal of unproductive ground, besides furnishing him with electric power, as he was fond of putting it, "sufficient to run a freight train to New York and back."

It was because of this that the colonel had chosen to back young Mr. Tarbell for the governorship, and in certain circles it was hinted that without the tide of the colonel's money, Mr. Tarbell never would have been washed into office, even by the narrowest of margins. He was now touring the state to examine the "highways and waterways," and in due time he had approached the Mackay estate. All must be done as a matter of form, and the state then would sell the wanted rights to the colonel and his heirs and assigns forever.

It was the matter which lay closest to the Mackay heart, but at this particular moment he would gladly have postponed the visit. It was much too late, and a fat young governor lurched down from his saddle in front of the patio gate precisely at midmorning of the next day.

His suite was small, but the colonel was wild of eye as he received them. Upstairs his daughter lay murmuring and moaning in her bed, crimson with fever; in the guest wing Budge Lakin still needed a nurse; and in the domestic quarters the giant Indian, Pedro, hovered feebly between life and death, with Miguel, eager of eye, above him, and striving to bring back that wandering bark to the safe shore.

When he was alone with the governor: "I am in my house like a general on a stricken field, Tarbell," said the colonel, "or like a lone survivor after a tornado has passed.

The scoundrel Gregg, or Tomason, or Kilpatrick, or Consalvo, or whatever his name may be —"

"I heard the news when I was already half way to your house," said Mr. Tarbell, removing his cigar and summoning an expression of pain and sympathy. "I came on to see what a friend could do for you, Colonel Mackay!"

"Put a ten thousand dollar reward on his head, alive or dead!" said the colonel.

The eye of the governor wandered a little.

"It could be done — perhaps," said he.

"It must be done," said the colonel. "A scoundrel, an absolute villain, sir! Without sense of gratitude or decency. But we'll catch him. Rankin has spread a dozen nets for him. Every mountain pass is blocked. Rankin himself and all my men are riding up the valley to block this end and his retreat. By heavens, Tarbell, it will be a happy moment for me when I look at him behind the bars! Born and matured for the prison cell and the hangman's rope, sir!"

The governor made mental note; he could use that handsome phrase.

Then the telephone clamored. The colonel rushed to it and presently was heard shouting denunciations across the wire. He came back in a passion of excitement.

The militia should be called out and a state of war declared throughout the range. The sheriff should be removed from office and a new one appointed. Federal troops — a twenty thousand dollar reward for the apprehension, alive or dead — such phrases burst from the trembling lips of the colonel.

For, after all, Consalvo had burst through!

In Leverage Gulch five good men and true from the hardy town of Buffalo Head had rushed the fugitive, gun in hand.

Now two of the five were down, badly wounded, a horse was killed, and through the gap raced Conquistador almost faster than bullets could fly in pursuit.

Then he was sighted by a flying party of scouts near a bend of Little Giant Creek; they thought that they had tagged him with their bullets, but they could not be sure; and again Conquistador had floated away beyond their ken.

Consalvo was through, and the vast wilderness of the higher mountains had received him.

The colonel could hardly believe the sad news.

"But after all," said the governor, "it

seems to me that you ought to be congratulated, colonel. You've managed this affair so cleverly that Consalvo hasn't touched a hair of your head or a dollar of your money. What more could a man ask, my dear fellow?"

The colonel blinked.

But then suddenly he saw that he could accept this favorable interpretation.

"Generalship, Tarbell! But, like Nelson, I consider a battle lost if a single enemy escapes from me that could have been captured. By heaven, man, I'm going to go on this trail myself, and I'll show these Westerners what can be done!"

CHAPTER 36

So the colonel prepared for his expedition.

He took six expert riflemen with him. He took a cook, a cook's helper, and three roustabouts.

"The fighting corps must have their hands free!" said he.

"Only," said the governor, "you have to remember that they slow up the pace of the whole body to the pace of their pack mules — and you have Conquistador to catch up with!"

"Strategy," said the colonel, "a little strategy will overcome all that!"

And he prepared to leave.

He went to his daughter's room and leaned above her. The fever was still burning in her. She opened her eyes wide and stared upwards, out of her trance.

"Felipe!" she cried, and threw up both her slender arms.

The colonel retired to the wall and leaned there, a very sick man, until his wife came to him and touched his arm.

"You'd better go away," she whispered.

"Every shock — you know —"

"Lydia!" breathed the colonel.

"Yes?"

"We're not going to lose her?"

Lydia Mackay grew white, but she answered steadily: "Not a bit of it! She's too strong and sensible a girl. It's more the blow to her pride, I think. She feels that she's been made a fool of. And perhaps — it's a little more than that! You'd best go!"

"I'm going to find him," said the colonel, his voice trembling, "and I'll lay him in a mountain grave! I swear that!"

He went back to the governor, who was to remain on the place ostensibly to carry on his survey of the water supply in that valley and what could be done with it of most advantage to the state.

"I'm taking the field," said the colonel. "I leave you here to guard the base of supplies. Good-bye, Tarbell. Give me luck, and keep all safe here. A week, and I'll be back. Tush! These fellows won't be able to stand against real tactics!"

So he departed, and Mrs. Mackay, pushing back the curtain of her daughter's bedroom, peeped out and saw him go, and then smiled a little, a sad, faint smile.

She was growing worn from constant attendance at her daughter's bed, but still her nerve held up, and she showed no sign of surrender. She could have had a dozen nurses to assist her, but she felt that she must be alone with her girl.

Twice a day she looked in on Budge Lakin, who was beginning to be able to enjoy a cigarette and who always greeted her with a subdued: "Doin' fine, ma'am, thank you a lot!"

How different from the fire-eating Budge of not so many days ago!

But everyone in the house was subdued in the same manner. The house was changed. It was as though lightning had flashed in their very eyes, and left them partially blinded.

She herself felt that difference.

She went twice each day, also, to the room in which the big Indian lay. He still was close, terribly close, to death. And all that sustained him was the miraculous patience and care of Miguel.

"Do you love this man, Miguel?" said she one day. "You take such very good care of him!"

The Mexican answered mildly: "He is of my people, señora!"

But she knew that that was not the correct answer; there was no little mystery behind that strange devotion, but what was important was that poor Pedro was kept alive — even though he would have to pass into a prison cell when he regained all his strength!

She pitied him doubly because she had known him so wildly formidable, as on that day when he had pursued her in the hills, more like a beast than like a man. Now his great arms and hands were like an infant's, remaining helplessly where they were placed. His cheeks sank in; his eye had fallen into a well of shadows.

In those days of delirium, only two speeches were upon his lips, reiterated ten thousand times. For, starting out of deep slumber, he would cry with a sudden sharpness: "My father, does he live?"

The hand of Miguel ever was ready to touch reassuringly the shoulder of the giant and say: "All is well with him, Pedro! Have no fear. All is well with him. He lives, he lives, he lives!"

Then the great Indian would sigh and perhaps sleep again.

These were moments when his strength was reviving, but when his power ebbed again, waking in the same manner he would moan: "Father is dead and calls me. My father is dead, Miguel!"

Then the answer was the same: "Your father lives. Have no fear, for all is well with him. He lives, he lives, he lives!"

Having heard those speeches reiterated many times, Lydia Mackay asked at length: "Is it not strange, Miguel, that he should love his father so dearly?"

"He speaks," said Miguel, "of the great Señor Consalvo, his master." He corrected himself instantly and added: "For he does not know, as we know, that his master is a great villain!"

Mrs. Mackay appeared to accept the emendation, but nevertheless she knew perfectly that the first words had expressed the heart of Miguel. To him, Don Felipe was a great man and always would be one no matter what the hand or the bullets of the law might accomplish against the fugitive.

So she went back to her daughter, on this day, in a strangely thoughtful mood; and, as she went, she encountered Maria at the door of the bedroom. And Maria put something cautiously behind her back as she bowed and smiled to her mistress.

"Were you going into the señorita's room?" asked Mrs. Mackay.

"To say a small prayer beside her bed, señora," said the moza.

"That is a kind thought," said the lady, "but give me what you have in your right hand, Maria, and I'll take it to your young mistress."

Maria turned the palest yellow-green.

But terror so numbed her mind that she could think of nothing to do except to hold forth her trembling hand, and from it Mrs. Mackay took a letter.

Maria fell suddenly upon her knees, slumping down inert, and with praying hands she moaned: "Burn it, señora, but do not read it! He will hear that you have received it, and then he will send and have me strangled in the night!"

"Who is he?" asked Lydia Mackay.

"The señor! Señor Consalvo!"

It struck Mrs. Mackay sharply, hearing two people almost in one moment refer to the youth in such tones of awe.

"Is he so great," said she, "that you still serve him while you work for me?"

"Dear señora," sobbed the girl, beginning to wring her hands, "I work for you not for wages but because I love you, and the señorita, and the señor who is so grand. I love you and I would die for you, but when the great señor sends me commands, who am I to disobey him?"

Mrs. Mackay frowned thoughtfully. She

might discharge this poor girl; but, after all, Maria was a perfect servant, and though she might have been a tool in the hand of Consalvo before, she was less apt to be again.

Besides, Mrs. Mackay was consumed with an overwhelming curiosity. It seemed to her that she never had known more than a single phase of Consalvo's nature. Now, in his absence, she was learning more and more.

"I must read this letter," said she, "but I can promise you that what is in it I'll not speak about to anyone. So Don Felipe never will know."

"Ah, señora, do not do it, do not say it," cried Maria. "He will know. The devils who serve him will tell him. Dios, Dios, Dios — I am lost!"

She stumbled to her feet and ran weeping down the hall, and Mrs. Mackay, a sadly puzzled woman, stared after her. She had been a very good and kind mistress to this girl, and she felt that Maria loved her, but she knew that never could she draw from the Mexican girl that perfect devotion which springs from both love and dread. Consalvo was a master of that art, and Mrs. Mackay both envied and wondered at him.

Truly it was very strange; and, no matter how long the youth was away, the very shadow of his presence still hung over the house.

So Mrs. Mackay looked at the envelope and in the beautifully flowing hand of Consalvo she saw written:

"For Miss Mary Mackay."

That alone would be a shock to Mary — that quiet and calm admission that Don Felipe understood English, after all. She gripped it to tear it open, and then remorse and a touch of conscience prevented her.

She entered her daughter's room softly. The head of Mary was turned, and the fever-dimmed eyes watched her dully.

"You have been a long time away," said Mary in complaint. "I thought — I thought — I dreamed —"

Her eyes closed. Mrs. Mackay thought that she slept, but presently the eyes snapped wide open, glaring bright, the film vanished from them.

"Felipe! They have murdered him!" said Mary.

And the reassuring recitation of Miguel came instinctively to the lips of Mrs. Mackay as she murmured: "Have no fear, dear. He is alive and well. He has escaped.

He is well. He lives, he lives, he lives!"

An enchanted smile, still half incredulous, stirred on the lips of Mary Mackay and made her, for the moment, wonderfully beautiful.

The next instant she was asleep, and her mother sat with a frown beside her.

Until, at last, she looked upward for help — it was her first sign of weakness!

CHAPTER 37

It was not long afterwards that she went to her own room and there she opened the letter resolutely.

It read:

"Dear Mary,

"Whatever they have told you probably is right about me. Except that I am not a murderer. I've never killed an honest man, Mary. That's my one small boast. Think of me however you please, but not as a blood-stained slaughterer."

Mrs. Mackay looked up from the letter with a sudden gasp. It was as if, indeed, that muted prayer of a few moments before had been answered as soon as this.

But from Don Felipe a confession! And yet there it lay before her in his own fair hand, clearly and precisely written, and addressed directly to her daughter. She wished heartily, now, that she had allowed the letter to be delivered to Mary, for it ought to work at once the cure for which the mother hoped so fervently.

She opened the folded paper and read again:

"I ought to make a list, of course, of all my crimes, now that I'm confessing. But that list will be supplied by others, and I have no doubt that it will be long enough.

"Your wise mother saw through me, and she kept me from my greatest crime of all. She knew that I was an adventurer, giving that word its worst of meanings, and from the first it was a duel against her. She won; I bow to her.

"I am not a Consalvo, Mary.

"Once I met a young rascal who carried that old and honorable name. He was about all that a man should not be — a sneak and a traitor, to sum up. We fell in with one another, but we fell out again in a few days. And it occurred to me that I might carry his name, in this affair, partly because I was at least as worthy of wearing it as he, and partly because he would never challenge my right to use it.

"My real name is of no matter, because in a few days I'll be no more than a foolish dream, to you.

"I'm not ridiculous enough to ask you to forgive me, and I'll plead no excuses. I've merely written to confess, because I owe you a confession, and to say good-bye.

"FELIPE."

She read and re-read that letter several times, and when at last she re-folded and placed it in the envelope, she was more puzzled than ever, because, after all, if she herself had dictated the thing, it could not have been more nearly what she would have asked for.

There was no brutality in it, but the light matter-of-factness should do the business with Mary thoroughly, once for all. It pre-supposed a startling element of honesty in Felipe that he should have written at all, unless it were to send in a romantic epistle denouncing his enemies and swearing eternal love. But here was the letter in her hand, and surely some kind deity had placed it there!

That very afternoon Mary wakened and sat up in bed.

The fever-red was gone, leaving her a little pale; her eye was clear once more.

"How long has this been going on?" she said briskly.

"A day or two," said the mother.

"But just exactly?"

"Three days, Mary."

Mary sat with her chin on her fist.

"I've been a fool; I hate to think that I could have been such a fool!" said she. "Such a weak, flabby baby. I'm ashamed of myself, mother!"

Mrs. Mackay merely smiled. One could not be too comforting and reassuring with Mary, for the girl was above too much sentimentality.

She did not even advise a slow convalescence, but let her daughter go out alone for a walk; and that same evening for a canter. And that night, Mary sat at the table, and held her head high, and talked cheerfully to the governor, though now and again a little wandering of her eye told that she was putting a vast strain upon herself.

She slept, then, until the following noon, and came out once more as fresh, as cheerful, as gay as ever; but her mother was not deceived, and, watching in the unguarded moments, she saw the high head droop and the mouth fall.

Now, she decided, was the time to let the letter strike a blow for the good cause; so she carried it to the girl and said simply: "I got this from Maria. I shouldn't have opened it, but I was dreadfully worried about you, Mary. You may judge me just as harshly as you wish."

Then she hurried away and left Mary to the letter and solitude.

What she hoped for was a flare of rebellious anger from the girl. Or if that were not possible, then a flood of tears from a wounded heart and wounded pride. But instead, Mary came directly to her.

"You're going to reproach me," said Mrs. Mackay, "and you have a perfect right to, dear."

"Reproach you? Of course not!" said Mary. "If I were a mother, I should have done the very same thing. But I wanted to talk to you about the letter. I wanted to ask what you think of it, honestly?"

It was the very last question which that wise woman wished to hear asked, or wished to answer.

"You'd better make your own conclusions," she suggested.

"A few days ago," said Mary bravely, "I would have done just that, but now I realize that I'm not so wise or half so strong as I thought. And now my head is all muddled and spins around. Of course he's what one would call a rascal, mother."

Mrs. Mackay said nothing.

"And it's quite base to — to hunt down a foolish — girl — for the sake of her inheritance, isn't it?"

Mrs. Mackay merely waited.

"Won't you help me a little?" said Mary.

"I want to, dear. I want to, dreadfully. But it hurts me to say the words."

"It hurts me," said Mary, as bravely as before, "but I need to be hurt, I suppose. And after all the bad things are said — about criminals, I mean, fighting-men, and all that —"

"Yes, dear?"

"He didn't cringe," said Mary.

"No, he didn't."

"He didn't yammer, if there's such a word."

"No, he didn't."

"And you know, mother, I thought that there was something clean-bred about that letter. In the first place, why should he have bothered to write at all?"

"I thought of that," agreed Mrs. Mackay, though she would have liked to say something else.

"It seems to me," continued the girl, in the same thoughtful way, "that Felipe" — here she had to pause a moment, but then she managed to go right on — "that Felipe was rather decent and brave to write as he did. It's the sort of a letter that would do me good if I were an idiot. I mean, mother, the sort of a brainless creature that has heartbreak, you know!"

She smiled, but only a little, and she was very white.

Mrs. Mackay took the bull by the horns, deliberately.

"What a silly thing it would be to try to make him out a complete villain," she said, "when, of course, he isn't one at all! He's a hero, as Tag knows! And that's a virtue. I do think that the writing of that letter was rather brave, too."

"Because he didn't sob about things, you know," suggested the girl.

"Exactly."

"And he made it so brisk — and sort of open-air, mother."

"Yes, he did."

"Well," said Mary — and then she made a long pause — "I think I'll go for a bit of a walk," said she.

She said it as steadily as she could, but in spite of herself, her voice wobbled a little.

Off she went, and presently, from the window, Mrs. Mackay saw her girl stepping lightly up the ridge. Tag went racing after, but when he arrived, his young mistress stopped short; then she waved him violently away, and Tag shrank back towards the house, turning again and again to cast a heartbroken glance after this strange human.

But Mrs. Mackay, her heart in her throat, and aching dreadfully, understood, and she covered her face with her hands. She got out her needlepoint, which was to her a sort of Rock of Gibraltar, from which she could defy the world invincibly; but today it failed her wretchedly and left her with idle hands and eyes that stared helplessly out the window.

All her sense of triumph had been stripped away from her and she began to feel that, after all, there might be tragedy in this. For she could conceive of Mary growing older, smiling by a process of mechanics but never from the soul, and so withering in this strange and cruel world.

Death, after all, would be better, and simply a memory of Mary as she had been and of what they had hoped for her. A sense of awe began to grow in Mrs. Mackay, also, for though she knew that her daughter was a strong and brave and healthy-minded girl, she had not dreamed that the scale was quite so grand, or the soul so deep; so that Mrs. Mackay felt herself shrinking, in comparison. And at last she folded her hands together and sat like an old woman in the sun, her eyes closed against the light, and trying with all her might not to think.

She had almost reached that ideal Nirvana when she heard the piano begin downstairs, tinkling gaily.

She sprang up, at that, and she cried out — as though the girl could hear — "Mary! Mary! Don't do that!"

The piano swept on with a jolly rhythm, and Lydia Mackay dropped into her chair and began to cry like a very small girl.

CHAPTER 38

With Colonel Mackay, among his chosen marksmen, was old Zeke. He talked little, he listened well, and therefore he was made the commander's confidant, for the colonel had been so long in the bosom of a family that he had formed the habit of thinking aloud, and without an auditor his brain was apt to grow stale. With Zeke, therefore, as an audience, the colonel developed his theme.

"First what we know!" The colonel was wasting no words, and even left out a verb or two. It made him feel more official. It was like a curt bulletin. It seemed to cut closer to the point. "Consalvo — that name for the lack of a better — a rogue confessed and proved, clever, unscrupulous, a deadly fighter, full of wiles. His enemies determined, difficult, wild. The trails unnamed and innumerable. The countryside population apt to sympathize with a refugee who can pay for what he needs. You agree?"

"You lay the situation down like a map," said Zeke, and resumed his work of worrying a large chunk from his plug of chewing tobacco.

"Very good!" said the colonel, clearing his throat and frowning profoundly. "Now, what we don't know. The will of the criminal. What he wants. What he'll try to do. Upper passes thronging with possemen. Whole country raised against him. Where will he go?"

"Higher up to the tall timber," ventured Zeke. And then he added, "But maybe I'm wrong."

"The ordinary viewpoint, perfectly expressed," said the colonel generously, but he added crisply: "Undoubtedly wrong! Consalvo will work by opposites. The rest hunt him in the highlands. I'll watch the lower passes. He's coming back to the desert to disappear into it. By what road? Some dark and obscure cañon that works its way down to the low level. Agreed?"

"I dunno," said the sage Zeke. "Hunting for a needle in the dark ain't easy."

"No," admitted the colonel. "Not easy but necessary. Watch the results! Rankin is a fine man, intelligent, brave. Good in tactics. But strategy is a different matter! Now, Zeke, you know the country. Pick out some cañon like the one I speak of!"

Zeke spent an hour chewing thoughtfully

and scratching on the ground.

"Lauderdale Creek ought to about fit in," said he. "It's so doggone mean and crooked that even a snake would hate to wriggle in it."

"The very thing!" said the colonel. "Consalvo is as good as in our pockets!"

So they headed for Lauderdale Creek, and for two days they marched hard, with the colonel riding proudly at the head of his little column. Then they reached the gorge, and it was all that Zeke had promised. Brush-choked, rock-walled, twisting nervously here and there, it dodged among the mountains and at last led out to the desert where its stream meandered for a few miles, and then sank from sight in a dismal lake.

Five miles from the mouth the colonel pitched camp. All was arranged with the greatest precaution. An outpost was placed up-stream, consisting of two men. The cooking was done across the ridge and the food carried down to the camp, so that no warning smoke might appear; and at night there was no fire permitted. Not even a cigarette could be lighted. There was grumbling, at this, but the colonel resolutely led the way in all of these privations, ate the cold food with a gusto, and pretended that smoking was a most unnecessary luxury. Besides, every man was drawing down five dollars a day, and that served to stop all murmurs. In addition, all reward money was to be divided in the posse; the colonel would have none of it.

So they kept strict guard for three days in this gloomy ravine, and nothing happened more than falling of leaves. Every day the sun, reflected from the polished rocks, made the place an oven, and at night no wind could dip down between the lofty walls. They smothered in excessive heat, and waited with a growing sense of failure.

Even the colonel, indeed, began to grow a little restless, but, as he said to Zeke, good strategy could not fail, and his plan, he declared, was faultless.

Nevertheless, on a morning, he could not help wandering alone up the valley — a liberty he would not permit another man to take — because, he said, he thought that he might find a more commanding point higher up the creek.

It was not eight o'clock when he started, but already the heat had commenced, and for ten hours it would grow worse and worse. The colonel could not help sighing. He was losing weight; beneath his chin the flesh hung in a thin fold; and his whole heart yearned to be away from this scene. So far as he could tell, the capture of Don Felipe might have been effected whole days before this, and he would return from the wilderness with all the satisfaction of a perfectly sound strategic campaign, but the certainty that many unsympathetic people would call him a fool!

It made the colonel sweat far more than the hot closeness of the air, this thought; but, as he went on, he kept his eyes narrowed, and approached every covert with consummate caution until, a mile or more beyond his patient outpost, he came to a spring that burst up from the surface of a rock and sparkled in the shadow.

He touched the water; it was ice-cold. So he kneeled beside it and washed his face and hands. Then he drank with deliberation and care; there is nothing so foolish, on a march, as to gulp cold water to excess!

After that, he stood up and began to dry his face and hands with a neckerchief, which he wore as a concession to the customs of the country — when in Rome, you know, do as the Romans! And then it seemed to the colonel that something was a little odd in the outline of a neighboring bush. It looked, in fact, rather like the silhouette of a man — yes, a man with a rifle across his knees.

The colonel rubbed his eyes and looked again.

Just above him, not ten yards away, Don Felipe sat on a brow of rock smoking a cigarette and holding his rifle carelessly across his knees; and behind him was the glorious head of Conquistador.

In that dreadful moment, the eye of the colonel noticed many small things, such as the fact that Don Felipe seemed not at all overwarm; and that, from the length of his cigarette, it must have been lighted only the instant before. Had the colonel respected himself a whit less, he would have suspected that this showed an entire contempt of him in the mind of this young warrior.

Thirdly, he noticed that the hair of Don Felipe was a glossy black, unstained by dust!

"Good morning," said Don Felipe. "Coming up these cañons always is hot work. For my part, I prefer to do it by night. You'd better follow my example, Colonel Mackay!"

His tone was so gentle, so respectful, that for a moment the colonel almost forgot —

And then he began to wonder how any

creature, man or beast, possibly could venture through this tortuous ravine in the dark, over these boulders, through this dense thicket; yet suddenly he knew that Don Felipe could do it; yes, and on the back of Conquistador!

He delved into his mind for an answer; but all that he brought up was strangely innocuous: "Yes," said he. "It's hot!"

He was ashamed of such a remark. He hoped it would not appear in any book of memoirs. What he wanted to say was something like: "Gentleman, fire first. We never do!" But his mind had gone blank, it seemed. The rifle had a strange effect, for it bore quartering upon him.

He had a vague feeling that he ought, if a hero, to reach for his holstered revolver, but he also knew that, if he did so, this accurate young man would unfailingly shoot him through the head. And what, after all, is the use of heroism unless it inspires others? The colonel was not leading a column. That is to say, he had no audience.

Since he abandoned all thought of firearms, he threw more dignity and meaning into his voice.

"By heavens, young man," said he at last, "so I meet you again — and in this manner!"

"Extraordinary, isn't it?" said Don Felipe. "But in this odd part of the world, odd things will happen!"

"I smile at the sheriff and his men," said the colonel. "By heaven, I smile at them and their boasted knowledge of the men and ways of their district!"

"Do you?" asked Don Felipe, blowing out a cloud of thin blue smoke. "But why? I always thought Rankin a charming fellow!"

The colonel stared a little.

"Charming?" said he.

"Naïve, gentle, honest, and kind," said Consalvo. "Don't you agree?"

"A brave man," said the colonel, "but without strategy. It is I, Consalvo, who alone could find you!"

"In a way," said Consalvo, "you're right. Although perhaps it's better to say that the needle finds the magnet rather than that the magnet finds the needle."

"I don't understand you," said the colonel gravely. "What do you mean, Consalvo?"

"I mean that I've been wearing out Conquistador for days and days trying to locate you. I worked the upper mountains at first. It never occurred to me that I would find you down here. But patience and Conquistador will take a man a long way, won't they?"

And he smiled, a beautiful, slow smile.

"You?" cried the colonel. "You have been hunting for me, Consalvo?"

"Because," said the other, "I have come to a great resolution. I intend to go straight, as the saying is. And who could help me in the right direction more than the famous Colonel Mackay? No, there's no one else to take your place in my esteem, sir!"

CHAPTER 39

At this, the mind of the colonel began to spin a little. He drew a great breath.

"Young man," said he, "is it possible that you are attempting to jest with me? No," he answered himself, "that is not possible! Not possible! It never has been done before!"

"Jest?" said Don Felipe. "Good heavens, I never would dream of trying to do that! Won't you sit down, sir? Here is a comfortable rock beside me."

The lip of Mr. Mackay fairly curled.

"No!" he said sternly. "Young man, I shall not sit down!"

"In that case," said Don Felipe, with a faint sigh, "of course —"

And he rose, almost wearily, and leaned upon his gun. The hands of the colonel twitched. If he could get his revolver out of its holster and fire —

He bit his lip and checked himself, for rumor called this youth a magician with weapons and the colonel had an accurate picture of his own Colt half drawn when a gun would explode from the hand of this adventurous gentleman. He restrained his first impulse. In fact, he considered it a tactical blunder!

"A cigarette, then?" suggested Don Felipe with another courteous smile.

"No, sir!" snapped the colonel. But then, watching the smoke curling from the lips of Felipe, he added brusquely: "I prefer to smoke my own!"

And, with precise motions, he drew out his cigarette case, snapped it open, selected a smoke, and snapped the case shut. But — he found that he had no match.

"May I offer a light?" said the gentle voice of Consalvo.

"Ha!" cried the colonel. "What, sir? — In fact — if you please!"

The match was almost reverently held. The colonel could not help noticing the reverence; his nerves were a little smoothed by this deference, and still more by the first smoke in several days.

He began to feel that, after all, there were decent qualities in this young man.

"But as for the matter in which I came to beg your assistance," began Don Felipe —

The colonel cut him short with: "Ridiculous and impossible! You are not mad, Consalvo?"

"All of us," said Consalvo, "who differ a shade from the average man are a little mad, I suppose. No doubt it would be policy for me now, for instance, to raise this gun and fire — I shudder even to say it, sir! But in that manner my way would be open, except for your friends down the cañon, and I believe that they might be avoided. However, being a little mad, as you suggest, it seems to me that it would be better to ask you to assist me, out of your great kindness, which I have experienced before!"

The colonel found nothing to say; he found it necessary to wipe his brow and wait, breathing rather hard.

"In fact," said Felipe, "when I speak of reform, I'll tell you what first brought the idea into my mind. It was that you, sir, with your broad experience of men, your wisdom and insight, felt that there were possibilities in me. Even possibilities that might make me worthy of your friendship! I began, from that moment, to take a higher view of myself!"

The colonel looked into the large and serious eyes of the young man; then he exploded: "And taking that higher view, sir, you deliberately attempted —"

"Ah," said Don Felipe, "it is not easy to

turn over the page before it is read to the bottom! My evil nature took command. I fell!"

Suddenly he added in a changed voice: "God forgive me for it!"

The colonel was a little touched.

"I think," said he, "that you feel some remorse! My daughter lies ill — very ill, Consalvo!"

To this the youth returned no answer, but such an odd tremor appeared in him that the cigarette fell from his loosened fingers.

He said at length: "It occurred to me that we might be mutually useful to one another, Colonel Mackay."

"Mutually?" said the colonel stiffly.

"You wonder, of course," said Don Felipe, "how I could be of use to you. But let me describe a picture that I have in my mind's eye. Consalvo riding his horse, his hands tied behind his back, the reins of his Conquistador in the hand of the colonel, and so led down the main street of the town — you understand me, sir? It would be the sort of a picture that would remain in the minds of people for a long time. It would discourage crime, I make bold to say. And what, sir, could be more appropriate than for Colonel Mackay — already the father of his county — to appear in the central rôle, leading the captive?"

The colonel was astounded; but all at once his heart began to beat wildly. . . . He, too, saw the picture with a wonderful clearness. And now, when he looked at the youth, the eye of Consalvo seemed more grave and earnest than ever before.

"By heavens, Consalvo," said he, "do you mean to say that you have determined to give yourself up to the law?"

"I have," said the youth simply, "but with a little reservation. I give myself into your hands, sir, feeling that, having seen something in me once, you may be interested in me again! You would not, I am sure, leave me to rot in a common jail!"

"Felipe," said the colonel, "I am the first to admit — I was the first to observe — that you possess many remarkably fine qualities. A certain sympathy and understanding of superior ideas — ha? Well, I shall not expand. You have been a frightful disappointment to me, Felipe. And if you surrendered yourself into my hands, of course I should use my influence — not inconsiderable in these courts — to secure the shortest possible sentence for you!"

"I knew," said Felipe gratefully, "that you would answer me out of the kindness of your heart. For I have a vast trust in your judgment, sir! It might even be that you could use your influence with the governor. He has the power of pardon, I believe?"

"Ha?" gasped the colonel. "Young man, do you expect, after your criminal career, to be washed clean and —"

He stammered and stopped.

"I should submit to punishment," said the youth with a grave air, "and certainly I should go to prison willingly for the sake of the many evil things that I have done. But on the other hand, on the few occasions when I've attempted to repent, I've always found that prison food is extremely disagreeable. And a smell of cookery usually is through the entire building. A man of your sensitive refinement will understand, sir, what another would consider mere nonsense, perhaps! But having submitted to the law — with the certainty of a pardon in prospect, sir — and having been brought to the jail under your auspices — I hope you follow me, Colonel Mackay!"

The colonel writhed. No matter how the thing were put, it seemed that this youth surrendered only to be set free. And then there was that tempting, that wondrously tempting picture of himself leading the famous desperado helpless through the streets of the town, and delivering him up at the jail door!

He drew a great breath.

"If the governor, however, should refuse?" he suggested.

"I do not think," said the gentle Consalvo, "that jails are made to hold me when I wish to leave them. And if I were not free within three days, I certainly should call on you to learn why there was such a long delay!"

At this, the colonel winced a little; and yet the thing certainly was not spoken as a threat.

"Suddenly I see the truth!" said the colonel. "It needed this affair to put you in the proper train of thought. But," he added as an afterthought, "the — ah — relation between you and my daughter —"

"I am not worthy to mention her name," said Consalvo in the faintest of voices. "As for that, I'll give you my promise to leave this country forever, if you wish!"

"Your word?" echoed the colonel.

At this, the head of Consalvo was raised a little.

"My word, sir, in which you will trust as I trust in yours!"

"It grows frightfully complicated," murmured the colonel, with a shake of his massive head.

"It is in your hands," said he. "In three days I can ride out of your sight, sir, and you never will hear of me again!"

"If I can deliver a pardon to Felipe Consalvo?"

"It must be in my real name," said the other.

He paused and appeared to make a great effort.

"You may tell the governor," said he, "that my name is William Kilpatrick O'Shane."

"O'Shane!" cried the colonel. "You're an Irishman, Felipe!"

"I was born in New Jersey, sir."

"New Jersey or Limerick. It doesn't matter. An Irishman is sure to raise the devil on land or sea, if he has a proper chance to use a free hand. Why, Felipe — William, I mean — it alters my entire impression of you! I think, William, that we may as well shake hands on this bargain!"

And O'Shane — Consalvo, willingly enough, took the hand of Colonel Mackay in his soft and yielding grip.

They sat down side by side near the bubble of the spring; Conquistador, as though realizing that a crisis had been passed, stole from the covert where he had remained hardly half-hidden, and he stole up behind his master.

"We must settle the details," said the colonel. "My strategy, after all, was right. The tactical details turned out, perhaps, not exactly as I expected. But the final result is what tells. However, my dear fellow, you and I must arrange every particular. We must get into the town — and I think we won't bother my good lads down the cañon. I'll send word to them later. There's no need of a cavalcade. I'll just bring you in alone."

"And the governor, sir?"

The colonel set his jaw.

"If the governor can't take my word that you're worthy of an honorable gentleman's opportunity in life — I'll break his political career into twenty thousand pieces — and he knows what I can do!"

CHAPTER 40

There was no time to work the thing up, but the colonel did what he could. He stopped at a ranch on the way to town, and the astonished rancher — having furnished the drink of water which ostensibly was the cause of the halt, — of course telephoned the great news ahead and the approximate time of arrival.

The colonel did not hurry from that point to the finish. The longer he waited, the larger the crowd which would have a chance to assemble; and the colonel firmly believed that the multitude should have their amusements. As for Don Felipe — for the name of O'Shane did not come easily on the lips of the colonel — he had no objection, and he merely chuckled when, full two miles from the village, a cloud of horsemen swept towards them and whirled around them with shouts.

The host was recruited, immediately afterwards, by a throng of girls and boys riding broken down mustangs, mules, donkeys; and later on another crowd of pedestrians streamed out to meet the hero and his captive.

The colonel was modest. He sat erect in the saddle, and his rifle was balanced across the pommel, but he seemed to wave aside the congratulations with a cheerful nonchalance.

"You can see he's a soldier," people said. "Things like this — they ain't nothing to Colonel Mackay!"

The colonel, in fact, hardly saw their faces, for his gaze looked far off towards other and grander days. Money meant a great deal in the political game, of course, but this day would not fail to give him the sort of popularity which meant votes. He had an idea that Governor Tarbell would not succeed himself. For that matter, far off in Washington there was a need for politicians whose hands were clean, whose minds were cultured, who could look into the future and devise the best for their country. The senate?

Afterwards, one could not tell.

Indeed, this great land was constantly scanning the horizon to find a proper man to fill the chair of chief magistrate. And a proper amount of persuasion might induce the colonel to sacrifice his domestic peace and all the felicities of Mackay Valley and Mackay House!

So, his eyes upon the great future, the colonel advanced with wonderful modesty through the town. Beside him rode Don Felipe, erect also, seemingly regardless of the rope which bound his wrists together, and certainly unashamed of his captivity. And when a leering cow-puncher assailed him with: "It took only one man to get you, you damn greaser!" he replied merely with: "But that man was Colonel Mackay!"

It was deemed a sufficient answer. The colonel heard it, and grew a violent pink in his pleasure. He could feel his heart swelling and warming towards this boy. He looked down upon him, as it were, with a fatherly kindness and interest; he wished him well, and he felt the urgent honesty which would ring in his voice when he persuaded Governor Tarbell to grant the necessary pardon.

They reached the jail; the heavy door opened; the prisoner marched through; and then, as the colonel was leaving, he was restrained on the steps of the building by kindly forceful hands while a fat and perspiring blacksmith who served as stump speaker for the Democratic party of that district during election seasons, beat the air with heavy hands and delivered an impromptu oration. When he had to pause for words, cheers filled the intervals. The colonel, from time to time, struggled mildly to escape; and he heard himself pointed out to that throng of tossing, waving hats as an honor to the country, a true Westerner by adoption, a brave and honorable gentleman, one whose riches did not stand in the way of his integrity on the one hand or his public spirit on the other, a force from which much would be heard later on. Then there followed a quite imaginary but convincing picture of the manner in which the colonel had mastered the desperado in hand to hand battle. And the crowd, taking all this as gospel truth, yelled itself hoarse in approbation.

After that, the colonel, by a slightly more decisive effort, managed to free himself, and he was allowed to go simply because the blacksmith had reduced his throat to a stage of incoherent hoarseness.

And so he walked down the steps, with every sensation of a king walking down from a throne; he mounted his thoroughbred; and he journeyed out from the town not unattended, you may be sure, but surrounded by a coterie of screeching, whooping madmen.

They accompanied him to the very door of Mackay House, and then they circled away to the town again, making as much noise in their departure as in their coming.

The colonel, giving his reins to a stable-boy, confronted a situation of some gravity, and he was a sober man as he walked towards his home.

In the distance, it had seemed a simple affair to persuade Tarbell to do all that he desired of him; but now that he viewed the matter more nearly, he became a little dubious, for the governor was almost sure to point out that three days was an extremely slight space of time.

After that, he might take revenge upon the governor as he chose, but that would not remedy matters; indeed, he might not be alive to take his revenge, for, at the end of that time, Don Felipe had promised with much feeling that he would break jail and come to seek for an explanation, and if he came in that manner, the colonel was reasonably sure that he would feel the claws of that young tiger.

Soberly, therefore, he entered the house.

The men from town had not departed so suddenly that they had failed to give some story of the happenings to the people within. Tarbell and Lydia Mackay greeted the man of the house with wonder in their faces, and Mrs. Mackay, indeed, might have been described as a trifle incredulous.

Mary was in the background, with a frozen smile on her lips.

"You actually found him!" said Mrs. Mackay. "You actually brought him in to town, dear! How — wonderful!"

The colonel waved the speech away.

"These young rascals," he said, "have to be kept in order. They may race around and evade authority for a time, but after a while, they have to be put in their places. I'm tired, Lydia. I hope I haven't to change before dinner!"

Certainly he did not have to change.

They went in to dinner as soon as he had washed his hands, and they sat down at the table, full of questions.

With an aching heart, he gave up the spirited narrative of the talented blacksmith. These people knew both him and Felipe better. And besides, it hardly mattered what he said in his house. The blacksmith's version was that which would be bruited abroad through all the newspapers. This would make New York copy, too. Columns and columns of it.

In fact, he saw that he had become a

national hero and that his autograph now would be asked for.

No wonder that he had to bite his lip to keep from smiling. And the only point he wished to make to this intimate circle was to take from the eyes of his wife, forever, a certainly veiled light of mockery which, he thought, was never quite out of them so long as he was near her.

So he related how he had come upon Don Felipe at a spring in the cañon; how the capture had been very simple, and under his steady gun —

"But weren't you dreadfully frightened?" asked Mrs. Mackay.

"Let me have some wine," said the colonel. "No, my dear, I never felt more at ease in my life. We all are actors, you know," he continued with delightful grace, "and we have to find our proper stages. Ahem! This meat is underdone, Lydia."

Mrs. Mackay leaned a little forward and searched his face earnestly.

Then she settled back and merely murmured: "What an extraordinary person you are, my dear!"

But, in that moment, the colonel saw that a vast and total disbelief possessed her. It angered him; it angered him vastly more than if he had been telling them the truth. Also, it made him more than a trifle uneasy, and he turned his stricter attention to the governor, barely hearing the whisper of Mary: "Mother — what will they do — to him?"

"He really is a fine fellow in a thousand ways," said the colonel.

"Especially with a gun," grinned Tarbell, his fat face wreathing.

"He was tired of playing wild man," said the colonel. "He told me that the time had come when he wanted to go straight."

"After you'd captured him?"

"Well — of course."

"Natural thing for the scoundrel to say! I don't understand your sympathy for him, colonel!"

The colonel, alarmed, began to expatiate at length upon the virtues of this scape-grace. He was not a Mexican, in the first place. His real name was William O'Shane. Well-bred, good family. But full of Irish. One knows what the Irish are! Terrible — but delightful people. Sometimes rascals; but often heroes!

The governor was not impressed:

"The better the family, the worse he is."

And the colonel was silenced. He began to grow cold at heart.

After dinner he saw his girl go slowly up

364

the stairs as though she had turned suddenly very tired; then he went out in the garden with Tarbell and put the question bluntly to him simply because he could not endure the suspense.

"In fact, Tarbell, no young fellow ever has made such a good impression on me. I tell you, he means it. He'll go straight. And as a great favor to me — I really want you to give him a pardon!"

Tarbell chuckled.

"I mean it," said the colonel, his panic growing greater every instant. "I really mean it, old fellow! You've got to listen favorably to me."

At this the governor replied with a sudden tartness: "I hope you don't, colonel. I trust that you're only joking. I'm your friend; I have a good many reasons for wanting to please you; but also I'm the chief magistrate of this state and I have taken an oath to my people. I tell you, colonel, that ten men, all Colonel Mackays, could stand beside you and ask the same request, and I'd tell them that my conscience wouldn't let me. I hate to say this. But it's as final as though it were written on a rock and thrown down from heaven!"

CHAPTER 41

Showers of honeysuckle overhung the front of the sheriff's office, and though it was clouded here and there with dusty spider webs, still on the whole it was a shower of brightness. The sheriff, when he called out, saw the door swing open, and then Lydia Mackay framed in this drooping green.

"Ah," said he, "I was expecting you! I knew you'd be in soon after!"

She lingered there in the doorway, as though she hated to leave the fresh air and the sun to enter that place of dingy papers, heaped, and swirling pools of cigarette smoke, and butts stuck on the window sill, on the edge of the spur-scarred desk, or scattered on the floor.

But she came in at last.

"Soon after what?" she asked. "It was such a soft and pleasant day that I had to get into the saddle, and then I had to come this way, by instinct, you know. I couldn't leave you here to gloom in the dark, dear Mr. Rankin!"

The sheriff placed a chair for her and

then he stood above her with his hands on his hips.

"You knew where she'd go, no doubt," said he.

"Where she? Where Mary?" cried the mother.

The sheriff shook his head.

"All right, then. You didn't know. You just guessed. It was just guessing that fetched you here ten minutes after she left!"

Mrs. Mackay had dropped all pretense at equipoise, now. She clasped her hands and cried to him: "*What* did she want?"

"Would you guess?" asked the sheriff darkly.

The lady winced, and then she motioned with her hand.

"It was that," agreed Rankin. "She wanted a permit to see Consalvo — I mean, O'Shane!"

"What did you do?"

"Nothing till I'd heard from you. I just put her off till tomorrow."

Mrs. Mackay sighed.

"She don't look very well," continued the sheriff. "I would of thought by the look of her that she'd ought to be in bed at home. I asked her was she very fit, and she said that she was fine. I hope —"

He failed to finish this speech. Mrs. Mackay opened her half-closed eyes and said frankly: "I don't know what to do. Do you?"

"I don't," said the sheriff.

"What do you think of him since you've had a chance to talk to him in the prison?"

"I don't know what to think."

"But you must think something!"

"A man has to be examined before he's put in a jail cell," said the sheriff.

"I know that."

"He knew it, too, and when he was coming in, he got the colonel to take out his wallet, take a little envelope from the wallet, and tear the envelope up."

"Why did he do that?"

"I don't know. I been thinking and thinking about it. And I don't know."

"Colonel Mackay," said his wife, "is now working very hard to persuade the governor to pardon this man for all his crimes!"

At this, the sheriff started violently.

"Ah, ah, ah!" said he. "Is that the dodge, after all? Is that it? I thought it, but I didn't dare to guess out loud! That explains, does it?"

"I suppose it does," said Mrs. Mackay gloomily.

What it explained they did not develop,

but they stared at one another with the deepest and quietest understanding.

"A fair exchange," said the sheriff with a sort of sneer, "is no robbery, and something gained on both sides. Well — I suppose that the governor has got to grant the pardon?"

"He won't," said Mrs. Mackay. "He seems an extraordinarily bold and determined man about what he thinks is right and what he thinks is wrong."

She went on: "My husband grows more and more worried. Today he's almost desperate. He had a dreadful scene with the governor. I think the governor, in fact, is about to leave. And my husband — I believe that he's coming in later to talk to you about the security of the jail!"

The sheriff rubbed his small, hard knuckles across his chin.

"That's it! That's it!" said he, and he looked very much like a fox on the trail of interesting information.

"And is the jail secure, Mr. Rankin?"

"You mean against Consalvo — O'Shane, I mean?"

"I suppose that's what my husband means."

"Well, ma'am," remarked the sheriff, "I got irons on his feet and irons on his hands, and he's in the strongest cell that I got, and there's four guards to it that relieve the watch in couples, all day and all night. I dunno how better I can have him watched. Those guards all are armed with sawed-off shotguns. If he made a stir to get away, they got enough powder and lead to blow him through the side of the jail, I'd say."

"And still?" murmured Mrs. Mackay. "You see, my husband really is *frightfully* nervous! He doesn't eat and he doesn't sleep, and I've heard him shout at the governor: 'It has to be by tonight!' "

After this, Rankin manufactured a cigarette. He seemed totally lost in the delicate labor, and he held it up and sighted along the perfect cylinder, with a dreadful anxiety lest it should be in the slightest degree out of true. Mrs. Mackay had locked her hands together, and there was not the slightest trace of the delicate and yielding woman about her now. She looked, indeed, like a bit of pale iron.

"The point is," said the sheriff gently, after a long wait, "that handcuffs can't be made that can't be shed. A gent may fold his hands in and make them smaller than the shackles and the irons have to slip off. Or else, he'll get a sliver of steel no bigger than a bit of a moonbeam, so to speak, and with that he'll pick the locks of his irons, and then he may pick the locks of his cell."

"But the four shotguns that are watching him?"

"The best of men will sleep," said the sheriff, "or at least they'll doze. And for a cat like Consalvo —"

"His name is O'Shane, I believe," said Mrs. Mackay with a needless rigor.

"O'Shane, ma'am, would pull out the beard of a lion, hair by hair, a hair every time he winked his eyes; and the lion would never know that his beard was disappearin' off his chin!"

Mrs. Mackay did not smile.

She said with a sudden tremor: "Then this terrible creature is to be allowed to escape and rush over the country and murder Colonel Mackay first of all and then —"

"He'll never escape," said the sheriff, "if I can help it. But I've already had to admit that he's a better man than I am!"

"If I were you," said she, "I'd see the iron welded into his very flesh!"

"Ma'am," said the sheriff, "if you was me, you'd remember every minute that the only reason you was alive was because

O'Shane saw fit not to kill you — and in a fair fight!"

She could not sit still, but repeatedly she drew through her hands the long, nervous lash of her riding whip. And now she stood up, very much shaken.

"I'm almost beaten, Sheriff Rankin," she admitted in a sudden burst.

"This would beat almost anything," said the sheriff. "I'm terrible sorry that I wasn't able to shoot him down that day, and since I couldn't do that, I suppose that there's nothing left to try!"

"You know what it means?" she asked him.

"I guess I do. *If* he breaks jail and gets away, he'll do one of two things. Either he'll kill Colonel Mackay, or else he'll run away with Colonel Mackay's daughter!"

By a certain darkening and brightening of the eye of the lady, one might have guessed which of these two possibilities seemed to her the more dreadful.

"I think you've put the matter clearly enough," said she. "Now — may *I* have a permit to see your prisoner?"

"You?" cried the sheriff.

"Yes."

"I —" He hesitated. "Well, if you think it's best."

"I have to see him. I have to see him alone, Mr. Rankin!"

The sheriff again began to rub his chin, and she waited anxiously.

"I'm not in the least afraid," she said cheerfully.

Mr. Rankin answered with a sort of quiet growl: "That's not straight. You'd rather walk into a lion's den — when they was more than half-starved. Oh, I know you, ma'am! But — I suppose that you have a right to do what you want to do."

They left the office together and stood in the sun, as though they enjoyed its fierce brightness.

"If the governor pardons him and he promises to stay away — do you think that he'll keep that promise?"

"He won't," said the sheriff instantly.

"He's really a low and black scoundrel, then, without honor?"

"I dunno," said the sheriff, "that you can say that any man in love really has got much honor!"

"In love!" murmured she. "In love, Sheriff Rankin!"

"I was telling you about the envelope that the colonel tore up. When I heard about it, I looked in the wastepaper basket over in the jail office. I got to rummage around in odd corners pretty often, you see. And I fished out the four quarters and put them together dead easy! Why, ma'am, here's what was in that envelope that he was carrying around next to his heart, and which he specially wanted nobody to see! It was the picture of a lady, ma'am, and, though you mayn't think it good reasoning, I take it to be the picture of the lady he loves."

He held it out on the palm of his hand, and, though the face was greatly marred by the four great tears which crossed it, yet these had been smoothed down with paste, and it was perfectly easy for Mrs. Mackay to recognize the features of Mary.

"And he wouldn't have her, you see," said the sheriff, "thumbed by a lot of jailors, and such. I say, ma'am, that it means something, and I see by your sick look that you think so, too!"

CHAPTER 42

It was a very hot afternoon. Not all the trees around Mackay House, not even its thick walls and its shaded windows could shut out the heat. In twilight they sat, the governor and his host; and Mrs. Mackay, in the brightest corner near the window, did needle-point. Nothing was very clearly to be seen except her white hands at ceaseless work.

The colonel and the governor pretended to be talking about water. But there was no doubt of the subject which lay deepest in their minds. The colonel at length brought it out sharply, without prelude:

"In short, Tarbell, you have the opportunity of delivering the world from a dangerous man and making of him a good citizen!"

"Prison bars," said the governor in quiet answer, "will deliver the world from that danger; and we'll simply have to get on with one less 'valuable' citizen — in case he ever could have been made into one."

"Don't put him in the past tense," said the colonel with a touch of greater emotion. "The fact is, Tarbell, that this fellow can make himself, apparently, ubiquitous. He can be where he wishes to be, and to slip out of a prison is no harder for him than for a fish to slip through water."

"Now that we have a grip on him for an instant, pardon him before he can get away!" said the governor. And he laughed, though with a perfect good humor, for he felt that the colonel, whom he did not wish to alienate, was reducing the whole question to an absurdity.

"What my husband fears —" began the gentle voice of Mrs. Mackay, when her husband turned upon her and cried furiously: "Lydia!"

"My dear?" said she.

"I don't need an interpreter! I — really, Lydia, you must step out of the room with me for a moment. Excuse us, governor!"

The governor was pink with shame. It was not in this fashion that he expected to hear a lady addressed, and his jaw muscles began to work a little. So, rising from his chair, he looked at the floor until the pair left.

Outside, where a blast of heat and light poured into the hallway, the colonel paused, sweating not from warmth but from passion of the soul.

"By the eternal heavens!" said he. "I never have heard any remark so ill-timed, so desperately useless and ridiculous! Lydia, the time has come when you must begin to put a guard upon your tongue."

She looked sadly up to him, but this glance had no effect, and he raged on: "Unless, as it seems, you prefer to trust to your own powers of persuasion!"

And she replied: "Perhaps I'd better, dear."

"What?" said the colonel, turning his other ear.

"Perhaps it would be better on this occasion," said Lydia.

Her stronger half retired a pace; in his eye was that expression of fear which comes when we face a thought of the other world. He stared at Lydia Mackay as though she were a chill and fleshless ghost.

"You see," said Lydia, "you don't seem to be getting on with the governor, and so perhaps I'd better try my hand."

"By heaven!" cried the colonel. "Do I hear? Do I understand?"

"I wasn't about to say, in the other room," said gentle Lydia, "that you are afraid of William O'Shane —"

"I trust not," he said bitterly. "I trust that you were not about to accuse me of being afraid of any man. And on the heels of my capture of the desperado, I beg to presume, my dear Lydia — I really beg to presume that such a thought would be a trifle too absurd — ha?"

He was silent, biting his lips to keep back a still more stinging speech; and Mrs. Mackay, folding her slender hands together, seemed to be looking up to him in admiration of his adamantine strength.

Then she said: "Of course I understand, dear, that having made your arrangement with Mr. O'Shane, you want to keep up to the letter of your understanding, and —"

"What?" gasped the colonel.

And then he seemed to unfurl, for his chest sank, and the cheerful pink left his face, and his back drooped, and his shoulders fell, and his clothes were loose and shapeless garments upon him as he lowered himself into a chair.

"I'm so sorry," said his better half, "that I've had to touch on this subject. No one else suspected; and I had only a suspicion that —"

"A false suspicion!" cried the colonel. "Do you dream that I would compromise myself to actually bargain with a —"

She raised her hand. The colonel ceased speaking, his white lips parted and frozen.

"But now, of course," said she, "I'm certain. You've agreed that if he would surrender to you, you would arrange his pardon with the governor. Is that correct?"

Colonel Mackay reached for his handkerchief and drew it from his pocket in order to wipe away the beads of sweat which bejeweled his forehead.

"And in this arrangement," continued his wife slowly, "I want to know if you thought of Mary?"

"Mary was my first and only thought," said the colonel hoarsely. "I — she — he, I mean, agreed to leave this part of the world, never to return!"

"And Mary?" said the wife. "Did you make her agree to live, find happiness, heal her heart, and be gay again? Did you consult Mary?"

Her husband could not speak.

"You did not consult me," said Mrs. Mackay. "Of course, I don't expect you to consult me about most matters, because your great masculine brain handles things so much better than I do! But Mary is my daughter, you know. I mean, dear, that I have a little interest, a sort of minor claim in her. And I'm so extremely old-fashioned about my girl, dear! I could have told you that her heart is breaking!"

"In this day and age —" began the colonel, but his voice supported his thought so feebly that he did not attempt to finish his sentence, and the soft voice of his wife went on: "It's such a hot afternoon, and you've been overworking, lately. Don't you think that you'd better go up to your room and rest until dinner time? I'll go back and talk to Governor Tarbell!"

He raised himself with a trembling hand upon the back of his chair, hung there for a moment trying to meet her eyes, and then he turned and went feebly down the hall.

She did not watch him out of sight, but resting a hand against the wall, for a single moment she stood with closed eyes, as though gathering her strength.

After that she went straight back to the governor.

"My husband thinks that I should put the matter to you, Mr. Tarbell, because he's felt a sense of delicacy about bringing forward an important side of the question —"

The governor bowed her into a chair and sat down close to her. He was one who knew men — and women. He was vastly interested.

"Do tell me the other side," said he.

"It's simply that my daughter loves this

man," said Lydia Mackay.

"Then won't the prison bars do a great deal towards remedying the trouble by keeping her from making a foolish alliance, perhaps?"

"I'm only a woman," admitted Mrs. Mackay, "but I don't think that prison bars will hold Don Fel— William O'Shane, I mean to say!"

The governor made a little gesture, as though to say, in short, that he was willing to trust to the honesty of stone and steel to perform that task. Then she added: "You haven't seen enough of Mary to know her, but she's an old-fashioned girl. I think that her heart is broken; I am sure of it!"

All at once the governor stopped arguing, as one who confronts an old idea upon a new plane and cannot handle it easily. He looked down to the floor; he looked up to his hostess. He recognized, also, the difference between an argument and an appeal, and into his mind slipped the bright picture of Mary as he had seen her at the table — and the memory, also, of those pauses in her talk when a shadow dropped suddenly across her face and her eyes became blank.

He said at last: "I've been held up in this matter of the pardon partly by my sense of justice; but after all, justice to your girl is more important than justice to him. Tell me frankly: Do you think he could settle down and become a law-abiding man, as the colonel feels he will?"

"I think," she said thoughtfully and honestly, "that there may be one chance in four — or less than that!"

The governor stirred in his chair.

"A dangerously narrow percentage — for your daughter's happiness to be built upon," he suggested.

"Oh, very narrow," said she.

"And she's young. Time is a healer, as the book says. I don't mean to say that you haven't thought of all that."

"Thank you," said Mrs. Mackay. "But you know women are apt to be much like one another — beneath the skin, I mean. And men are very much the same. But now and again you'll find some one who stands aside and is apart from the rest. I don't think that she ever could forget Mr. O'Shane."

"Are you fairly sure of that? For there's the crucial point, isn't it?"

At this she said: "If I were Mary, I never should forget him!"

The governor opened his eyes very wide. He stood up and he bowed to her.

"My secretary knows all about the forms of these things," said he. "I'll have him come up to my room, and between us we'll soon have the matter worked out in detail. I think inside of half an hour we'll be able to put the pardon of O'Shane in your hands, Mrs. Mackay. And I don't doubt that you have fast riders who'll get it to the town jail at once! Will they take along a message that I'd like to see Mr. O'Shane at his earliest convenience?"

And he was out of the room before she even could attempt to thank him.

Then she went to her daughter's chamber.

When she opened the door it was quite dark; she could not make out the form or the face of her girl on the bed; but a delicate scent hung in the air and touched Lydia Mackay like the hand of a ghost.

CHAPTER 43

"My dignity!" said the colonel. "My dignity — my God! You have compromised it forever! To take into my house as a son-in-law an outlawed renegade, already driven by his crimes from civilized society, and to welcome him as —"

Mrs. Mackay raised her hand and bent her head; the colonel listened likewise, and gradually he could hear in the distance a sound more delightfully musical than the bubbling of a fountain in the midst of a desert. It was Mary, laughing and playing in the garden with Tag.

He seemed to find it hard to go on, after this; so she left him.

Maria met her in the hall, wild with excitement and with undisguised joy.

"He has come! He has come, señora! The great señor has come again! Señor Consalvo!"

"Where is he?" asked Mrs. Mackay, growing very weak.

"He has gone first of all to the hut of Miguel where Pedro is lying. You see what a good man he is, señora! You see what a great heart of gold! But this you know, for everyone understands that you have won his pardon from the governor! And the governor shall have many votes for this. I, Maria, would scratch out the eyes of a peon who dared to vote for any other man!"

She added: "The governor has gone to meet him, señora!"

That worried Mrs. Mackay.

She hardly could restrain herself as she walked up and down in the patio, for she had felt that telltale interview with Tarbell properly should take place when she was there to guide and guard the conversation.

But now it was beyond her guidance, and she began to feel that the engine of mercy which she had started working might drive heedlessly ahead and carry her whithersoever it willed; she was helpless before it! It gave her a dizzy sensation as though she were tied to the tail of an avalanche.

At length her impatience grew so great that she started to leave the patio garden, but as she came into the gateway, she had sight of Don Felipe and the governor walking down the hill. The arm of the governor was linked in the arm of the young man; and Mr. Tarbell talked with many gestures. Even at that distance he seemed to be overflowing with happiness.

So that Mrs. Mackay, amazed, shrank back a little.

"Perhaps I have done right," said she aloud. "Perhaps I have managed to do right!"

She looked about her and had no answer except from the heads of the flowers, stirring in the wind.

The two were nearer, and suddenly a third had stepped into the charming frame which the arched entrance made for the picture. And it was Mary — behold, shamelessly in the arms of her lover! And being kissed by him in the broad and brilliant eye of the day!

They came on once more, the governor between them, an arm of each through his, so that he seemed like the happy father of two grown children.

Their merry voices chimed and showered music in the distance —

And then a fourth — yes, Colonel Mackay himself, splendidly erect — hearty — holding forth both hands!

At that the courage and the self-possession of Mrs. Mackay melted utterly away. She turned and fled from the garden and up to her room, and there she cowered into a chair and caught up her needle-point.

She could not even see the pattern, but crushed it in her hands, and closed her eyes, and lay back, trembling.

So hours passed, or long eternities such as those in which souls are formed and born again, or die.

Or was it only minutes before a light step sounded in the hall and a hand tapped at her door?

Twice she made a strong effort before she was able to speak. Then Don Felipe stood before her.

Yet he obviously was not Felipe Consalvo now, for the change from the blond hair to the black somehow gave him more reality in his new rôle than ever he had had in the old. She stood up, because she felt that, standing, she better would be able to withstand the triumph and the mockery of this bold and bad young man.

William O'Shane fell upon his knee before her and kissed her hand.

Still upon one knee he looked up to her, and all at once it was as easy for Lydia Mackay to look down into his blue eyes as though they had been the eyes of a child of her own bearing.

"All-good, all-wise!" said he. "How have you dared to know me and trust me so far?"

"Trust you?" said she. "I — I came to feel that you had to be good, my dear. Otherwise, God wouldn't have put so much in your hands!"

Let us draw together all the final facts so that the picture may be complete.

Budge Lakin went back to sober work as a cow-puncher and never again drew gun.

Pedro recovered and continued the faithful shadow of his master whose changing of names was to him no more than the changing of shadows before the eternal face of the sun.

Sheriff Rankin, declaring that he had grown old, turned his hand to ranching, and found cattle hardly more tractable than criminals.

The colonel flourished amazingly. On the strength of his capture of the great Consalvo, he went to the legislature and made many resounding speeches. He even was nominated for governor, but something stood between him and the ultimate triumph. However, he felt that he was a force in the government.

At Mackay House, however, his manner

had altered; and at table he hardly could retell an anecdote without turning to his wife for confirmation. And the result was that he felt himself more and more at ease when he was far from his hearth.

As for William O'Shane, there were certain anxious hours, guessed at by Mrs. Mackay, but known only to himself, until the birth of a child.

Lydia Mackay brought it to him.

"Here," said she, "is The O'Shane."

"God make me worthy to be his father!" said he, and she knew that her work was done.